Capturing Paris

Capturing Paris

KATHARINE DAVIS

ST. MARTIN'S GRIFFIN

NEW YORK

www.stmartins.com

Library of Congress Cataloging-in-Publication Data

Davis, Katharine.
    Capturing Paris : a novel / by Katharine Davis.—1st ed.
        p. cm.
    ISBN-10: 0-312-34098-2 (pbk.)
    ISBN-13: 978-0-312-34098-8
    1. Women poets—Fiction. 2. Americans—France—Paris—Fiction.
3. Spouses—Fiction. 4. Triangles (Interpersonal relations)—Fiction.
5. Paris (France)—Fiction. I. Title

PS3604.A5557C37 2006
813'.6—dc22   2006040804

D 10 9 8 7 6 5 4

For RPD

Acknowledgments

Thank you to all my friends and family for their love and support. A special thank-you to Terry Carstensen, who insisted that I needed my own laptop and encouraged me from the beginning, and to my dear friend Anne Edwards for her careful reading with a poet's eye. I am grateful to Jane Drewry for her good advice when I decided to become a writer. Thanks also to Lisa Tucker, Gretchen Ramsay, and Kathy Richards, who read early drafts of the novel.

Many thanks to the fine teachers I've had, especially Sigrid Nunez, Roxana Robinson, Lee Smith, Richard Peabody, Mark Farrington, and Elly Williams. Their advice has been invaluable, and their writing is an inspiration.

I will be forever grateful to Meredith Blum, who directed me to my agent, Katherine Fausset, and to Katherine for her enthusiasm and excellent advice. Many thanks to Linda McFall, an excellent and insightful editor and fellow lover of Paris.

I wish to thank my parents, who gave me the wonderful years in Europe, especially Paris. Most of all my deepest thanks to my husband, Bob, and my children, Brooke and Andrew, for their unfailing love.

Capturing
Paris

ONE

La Crépuscule

Annie Reed walked along the rue de Rennes wondering if her husband still loved her. Paris was colder than usual that fall. She loved this time of day, *la crépuscule*, the nebulous period that floats between day and night. Her heels clicked as they struck the cold pavement. She wished that she had gone to the basement storage in her apartment building to take out her boots. The approach of winter had crept up on her. Gone were the golden dry October days, like those you saw in movies, where couples strolled along the Seine, pausing to look at old prints and books in open carts. The damp November air had already settled into her bones.

Dreary, dark, dusk—words she was trying to put into a poem on the seasonal shifts that changed the mood and tempo of the city. She admired the French poets who were able to capture the feel of the tight, cold air, the closing down and pulling in particular to this time of year. The French language had a musical quality, a natural lyricism, that belied the darker message within. Annie wanted to capture this feeling in English. She wished she could breathe in this poignant beauty and exhale the words and images onto the page. She could hear the words, like puzzle pieces floating in her head, but she struggled to find the flow, the thread that would order the images and bring them to life.

Why did she bother? She tried not to think of the envelope in her briefcase. Stopped at a red light, she drew her shoulders up and released them, trying to get rid of the tension in her neck. Her job at the Liberal Arts Abroad program had kept her cooped up in an overheated office all afternoon. She had published only a few poems in the last few years. She wanted her poetry to take precedence again, not easy after years of being busy with other things. Wesley certainly didn't seem to care. A thin sheet of ice had formed between them.

Annie arrived at the subway station and descended toward the rumbling trains. She pushed open the steel-and-glass door at the bottom of the steps, trying not to inhale the warm, dirty air rising from the tunnels below. Annie disliked crowds and walked toward the far end of the platform hoping to find a less busy spot to wait. She longed to be home; being with people all day tired her. The dark tunnels hummed with the possibility of approaching trains.

On the opposite platform Annie noticed an unusually tall young woman in a brilliant blue cape. She had to be foreign. When Annie moved to Paris over twenty years ago with Wesley and baby daughter Sophie in tow, she'd wanted to fit in, to look French. She loved the way French women dressed; understated, discreetly fashionable, they wore their clothes confidently, hinting at sexiness, suggesting the unexpected. Most of the women here on the subway platforms wore coats in subtle colors—brown, gray, or black—with perhaps a bright scarf arranged artfully at the neck. The first thing Annie had noticed when she moved from New York was the French addiction to scarves.

The woman across the platform looked like an exotic bird, unafraid to flaunt its colorful plumage. The theatrical-looking cape had a black velvet collar and could have been from a vintage clothing shop had it been more worn and faded. Her honey-colored hair fell heavily, just reaching her broad shoulders. She was more handsome than beautiful, with wide-set eyes and a full mouth. Annie thought of Baudelaire's words, "*Luxe, calme, et volupté.*" She knew she shouldn't stare, but her eyes kept going back to the woman. There was something disconnected about her. She looked calm, almost dreamy. While probably in her thirties, the age of a young mother, she didn't have the intense fixed look of a mother eager to get to the school or day care center to find her children.

Moments later a train pulled up to the opposite platform, stirring up the odor of wet clothing, tired bodies, and stale air. Passengers jostled their way into the full cars, and Annie lost sight of the woman. The train pulled out of the station, and she experienced a momentary feeling of loss when she looked back at the empty place where the woman had stood. Why had this woman caught her attention? Lately she found herself contemplating other women's lives. Studying the faces around her, particularly women close to her own age, Annie wondered if they too felt the ache of an empty nest, or faced unhappy husbands at the end of the day. Her own train arrived and screeched to a halt. The doors slid open. Annie clutched her briefcase and got ready to board the crowded car.

Darkness blanketed the city when Annie emerged at her Métro stop, Hôtel de Ville, in the Fourth Arrondissement. City of Lights, she thought, what a misnomer in November. A cold mist, not quite a drizzle, gave the streets an oily sheen. Drivers blew their horns impatiently in the heavy traffic. Annie looked at the closed shutters of the apartments above the street. She loved the sight of lamplight seeping out between the louvers. At the end of the afternoon, she relished going from room to room in her own apartment closing the outside shutters and drawing the curtains. The sense of warmth and enclosure of a home tucked in for the evening filled her with pleasure.

She used to love coming home and having an hour or two alone when she would putter, look at the mail that the concierge had slipped under the door, and start to put dinner together. She might take out her poems and revise work that she had started that morning. Late afternoon, with its dense quiet, was a productive time of day for her. Now Wesley would be there, awaiting her return.

The fierce noise of a motorbike revving its engine at the next corner jarred Annie back to the present. The rue des Archives teemed with small cars, motorbikes, and pedestrians carrying parcels from neighborhood food shops along with the necessary baguettes. She made a quick stop at the greengrocer to buy haricots verts. Heavy woven baskets overflowed with tender carrots and fat bundles of broccoli; robust purple cabbages glowed in the evening mist. She smelled chickens roasting on a spit in the butcher shop next door. She went in and selected one, which the butcher, a pasty-faced man with multiple chins, wrapped and added to her shopping bag.

Almost home. Annie imagined the exotic woman she'd seen in the subway entering a quiet, dark apartment, throwing the blue cape over the back of a chair, pouring a glass of wine and nibbling on a slice of pâté left over from the night before. She wouldn't have to face a disgruntled husband or worry about a daughter living on her own far from home. Annie arrived at the heavy wooden door of her own building, number 38, pressed the digits of her code, releasing the lock, and stepped into the quiet courtyard.

"You're late today," Wesley said. "Where've you been?"

Annie didn't answer. Asking about her whereabouts had become a habit since he'd started working at home. She'd been out all day, but he didn't come over and pull her into his arms for a kiss, not even a quick brushing of lips on her cheek.

"Did you hear from Hal today?" She pulled the chicken out of the bag, set it next to the stove, and turned on the tap. The water was slow to warm up, and she shuddered as the cool stream splashed over her hands. Her delicate wedding band glimmered through the water. She wished she were heating the kettle to make a solitary cup of tea. But it was time to start dinner.

"The phone hasn't rung all day," he said flatly.

"Well, it's early in Washington. He could still call tonight." Annie closed the curtains and turned on the kitchen-table lamp, casting a cozy glow on the yellow plaster walls and high ceiling. She'd painted the kitchen that golden color to remind her of Provence with its lavender-scented fields and sunny days. Her polished copper pots hung from a rack above the stove. She placed a colander into the sink and dumped the green beans into it.

"I've been waiting all afternoon." He picked up the mail from the kitchen counter and sat down at the table. "All we get are bills."

"Wesley, I'm sure that Hal will call."

"Well, I'm glad you're so sure. I wish I were." He thumbed through the stack of envelopes and said in a louder voice, "Annie, getting this business really is important."

"I know that. Just think positively."

"Think positively. Now, that's helpful."

Annie turned toward her husband. At fifty-one he still had boyish looks despite deep wrinkles in his face and the graying blond hair, which now fell across his forehead. His gold wire-rimmed glasses gave him the appearance of a kindly intellectual. He was as thin as he had been in college, but he moved with more purpose and economy of gesture. She thought he'd grown more handsome through the years, his regular features more interesting. It was as if the city itself, the Paris they both loved, had cast a glow on them that had woven them inextricably together. However, now their life seemed tinged in a different light, and Wesley's uncertainty was beginning to unravel both of them.

She leaned against the sink. Wesley's lips were set firmly in a straight, closed line. "If Hal can't offer you the project, something else will come along."

"I still can't believe the firm closed the office here," he said, leaning back, balancing on the back legs of his chair.

"It wasn't your fault. I just wish they'd given you more time to turn things around." They'd had this conversation before. The Paris office hadn't been generating enough business.

"Yeah, right. Time is money. That's the old saying. I keep thinking I should have gone back to New York."

"Let's not talk about it anymore. It doesn't do any good. Besides, if you went back, you'd really be starting over completely. You always said you wanted to practice on your own."

"Yeah, but it's harder than I thought. My clients seem to be evaporating."

"You're a great lawyer, sweetie. I'm sure you'll get other clients."

Wesley shook his head and lowered his chair. "When? They're not exactly lined up at the door. I'm amazed that you still believe in me."

Annie still remembered when Wesley, in the summer before his final year of law school, got the offer from Wilson & James. The name had sounded loyal and steadfast, suggesting a place with mahogany desks, Persian rugs, leather-bound books, a sea of dark suits, silk ties, and polished shoes. The firm stood for excellence and tradition. Annie and Wesley had spent their entire week's grocery money on champagne to celebrate the start of his career at the auspicious law firm.

"Of course I believe in you. I love you, for heaven's sake. Come on, let's have a nice evening. Are you hungry? I bought a roast chicken."

"So I see. It smells good." He gave her a weak smile and went back to the mail. "By the way, no e-mails from Sophie."

Wesley seemed to miss Sophie even more than she did. Sophie was so much like her father: industrious, diligent, taking pleasure in her work. As a small child in a French school, she had delighted in showing her father her *cahiers*, the thin blue notebooks of lined paper, filled with her small tidy script. Wesley coached her on her spelling words and praised her for her excellent memory. When she was twelve, Annie took her out of the French primary school and moved her to a big international school, hoping she would have a more creative experience. Instead, she took all the prizes in mathematics and went back to the United States for college, where she majored in economics. "Numbers are creative too, Mom. We don't all want to spend our time playing around with words."

"She'll probably call this weekend. Why don't you pour us some wine?"

Wesley went over to the tall pine cupboard on the far wall and got out two glasses. He pulled the cork out of a bottle of red wine that they had started the previous night. The purple liquid had trickled down the bottle, staining the label. He handed her a glass, sat down at the kitchen table, and opened the *Herald Tribune*.

The Reeds' kitchen, large for a Paris apartment, had been Annie's favorite room when they moved in during their first year in Paris. The table, covered in a faded pink provincial print, sat in front of the window overlooking the courtyard. When they had guests, they ate at an old French farm table at one end of the living room. Tonight Annie decided to use their good dishes, pottery plates from Quimper. They had purchased them when they rented a cottage in Brittany one August. She took a long sip of wine. The rich Burgundy tasted of warm, mellow afternoons far from rue des Archives. She thought of that little house in Brittany, with its thick stone walls, solid and unyielding to the relentless winds that battered that wild coastline even in summer. She pictured the three of them wearing sweaters and long pants as they hiked along the beach, Wesley's arm around her and Sophie chasing gulls, her laughter sailing off with the clouds. At night they would burrow under a fluffy eiderdown quilt, while Sophie slept on a tiny cot at the foot of the bed. Annie captured those idyllic days in the poems she wrote that summer, poems that contrasted the dramatic weather with the tender love inside the cottage.

> *Gray gulls diving through silver sky*
> *laugh in the wind and pierce the fat clouds as*
> *they soar toward heaven.*

She thought of that line whenever she saw seagulls flying above the Seine.

Now, the beans almost ready, she got the silverware from the drawer and set the table. "Two more weeks until Christmas break," she said. "Mary's giving me a lot to do at the office. I'll be glad for some time off."

Wesley poured more wine into his own glass and topped off Annie's.

"Would you mind carving the chicken?" Annie pushed a strand of hair behind her ear.

"Yeah, sure." Wesley pushed back his chair. It scraped loudly against the tile floor. Annie handed him a knife. The comforting smell of roast chicken cheered her. She thought of Sophie. As a little girl she called her favorite meal "white dinner": roast chicken, mashed potatoes, and applesauce. It had been quite a long time since the days of her picky eating, when Wesley would take forkfuls of food and make chugging noises like an approaching train. "Uh-oh, here comes the choo-choo. Where's the tunnel?" At the very last minute she would open her bow-tie lips and accept the next bite, her bright eyes riveted to her father's.

"This is a lousy knife," Wesley said. "Where's the sharpener?"

"I don't know. Do we still have one?"

"Never mind." He continued slicing, the meat falling easily from the bones. He served the chicken onto the plates. Annie drained the green beans and returned them to the pot with a lump of butter. She added salt and a grinding of pepper while the beans sizzled in the residual heat of the pan.

"Maybe this weekend you could help me bring up the rest of the winter clothes from the basement storage, I wished I'd had boots on today." She carried their plates to the table.

"Sure. I want to see what wine I've got stored down there too."

They sat down before their rapidly cooling chicken. "I got another rejection today," she said. The discouraging thin envelope was still in her briefcase.

"Which poems?"

"I sent the series I did on Paris churches. Remember the one on Saint-Eustache? I can't believe it. It's a really good poem. They didn't take any of them."

"Why don't you send them to the *Canterbury Review*? Didn't they publish one last year?"

"That was two years ago. Anyway, that magazine folded."

"Well, try somewhere else. At least you still have your job. Besides, you can't make money writing poetry."

"That's not the point. You know that." They finished the rest of their meal in silence. She could see the worry in the lines across his brow, and she didn't want to complain further about her own disappointment.

Annie got up and carried the dishes to the sink. She could feel Wesley watching her as she loaded the dishwasher. Her hair swung forward as she reached for a glass. She knew he liked her thick bangs and simple hair that she usually wore loose, falling a few inches below her chin. Wesley stroked her hair soon after they first met, before he'd even kissed her. "Fawn-colored silk," he'd called it. It was his first gesture of intimacy. Now, as if reading her mind, he walked over, put his hands around her waist, and kissed the exposed pale skin of her neck. She couldn't remember when he'd last hugged her, when they'd last made love. There had been a gradual decline after the firm closed Wesley's office in the spring. She hadn't worried about it during the first uneasy weeks, but now it hung like a veil between them. She hadn't realized how important their sexual life had been and how keenly the loss of it would affect her.

"I'm sorry. I don't mean to be such a crank. I'm sorry about your poems; I really am."

His tentative embrace caught her off guard. She put down the plate she had been rinsing and turned to face him. "Oh, Wes, I need you so. I miss you too, in every way." She reached up, putting her arms around him. She nestled her face into his neck and inhaled his familiar scent. He felt brittle, the muscles across his back tight and unyielding. "I hate to see you worrying so much about your work," she said, drawing him more tightly against her.

He pulled away, shaking his head. "Do you mind if I go back to the computer and finish a few things? I'll get the phone if it rings."

"No, go ahead." She made an effort to smile and turned back to the sink, her arms more empty than ever.

By eleven-thirty that night, the phone still had not rung. Wesley had spent most of the evening in his office. Annie had hoped he'd come join her in the living room and finally took refuge in bed, the big down comforter pulled up around her. She leafed through a book on Gustave Courbet. She had studied art history in college and, after reading a recent biography of the nineteenth-century painter, had started a series of poems inspired by his work. She studied the reproduction of *A Young Woman Reading*. Courbet had painted an ordinary-looking woman of no particular beauty, reading in a lush green forest. Her neck and arms are browned from the sun, but her round, plump shoulders, revealed where her summer frock has fallen away, are pale, the skin having never been exposed to sunlight. Annie wondered how she could capture in her poetry the solitude and sensuality of this woman lost in thought. She picked up her pen and began to write whatever words came into her head. Her eyes went back to the picture in her lap, the white shoulders against the deep green of the woods, a woman alone except for the artist, whose eyes had translated the moment with paint.

It was almost midnight when Wesley finally came to bed. "What do you think of this one?" She gestured to the page of her book, still resting in her lap.

"I'm not in the mood to look at art books."

Annie closed the book. "I'm sorry Hal didn't call."

"I'm sorry too, but that doesn't change anything."

She looked over at him. It was as if his good nature had faded like his cotton pajamas. "Maybe Hal thinks it's too late to call here," she said; "you know, the time difference."

"Annie, that's enough." He sat heavily on his side of the bed.

"Why don't you give him a call?"

"That makes me look desperate. I refuse to do that."

"Wesley . . ." She reached for him.

"Please, leave me alone. I don't want to talk about it anymore."

He lay down, drew the comforter up around his shoulders, and rolled over to face the wall. Annie put her book on the skirted table next to the bed, tossed the big extra pillow onto the floor, and turned out the light. She listened, waiting for his breathing to shift into the deep regulated rhythm that indicated sleep. She loved Wesley. She couldn't remember a time when she hadn't. Now, lying still in the darkness, she felt her worries intensify. What did she have to be afraid of?

Pulling her knees toward her in a protective curl, she forced such thoughts aside. She pictured Courbet's woman in the forest and wished for some of that bucolic peace. She remembered the woman in the subway. She could still see the blue cape and the handsome face. She had the same kind of natural beauty as the woman in the painting, the kind of beauty made to be touched. Annie wondered if she lay alone too, listening to the November night. The early-evening drizzle had turned to a hard rain that now beat steadily against the windowpanes.

TWO

Le Déjeuner

"*Bonjour, mes adorables,*" *Céleste gushed. She ushered Annie and Wesley* into the hall with its sparkling chandelier and picture-covered walls, a welcome relief from the dimly lit staircase up to their apartment. Céleste wore her usual tailored wool skirt, cashmere sweater, and silk scarf. She had worn the same classic but somewhat matronly outfits when Annie first knew her, and Annie could picture her twenty years from now looking exactly the same, only thicker around the middle, with deeper laugh lines and wrinkles. She gave them their customary kisses on both cheeks, emitting wafts of Shalimar and anointing Wesley's cold face with a touch of lipstick.

Georges, wearing gray flannel pants and a maroon cardigan covering a modest gentlemanly paunch, greeted his guests. His sand-colored hair was combed closely to his almost-bald head. He had a loose, easy laugh, and if he were heavier, he might be described as jolly. Céleste and Georges Vernier were the Reeds' oldest friends.

Wesley shook Georges's hand and with his other arm gave him a congenial squeeze, his expression brightening. "You're so great to have us," Wesley said. "You're our anchor in this sea of Paris."

Annie was surprised at Wesley's choice of words, almost like those of a French person speaking excellent English. She was relieved to see him smiling; she didn't want his bleak mood to spoil the Sunday luncheon. He'd barely spoken on their walk over, his mouth drawn in tightly like the winter day around them. He used to enjoy their walks, commenting on the architecture, noticing an unusual doorway or a finely crafted iron hinge, the kinds of details that made Paris unique. Now all he pointed out was the violent graffiti scarring the façades of buildings and walls or the way the French never cleaned up after their dogs.

"*Mais oui, mais oui*," Georges said, taking Annie in his bearlike embrace and offering the ritual kisses. "Here, let me take your coats. Later, we'll warm you up with a good red. My brother brought us a lovely case from Burgundy." Georges delighted in speaking English but never lost the guttural r that rolled out of the deeper regions of his throat.

"How is Antoine?" Annie asked.

"Never better. He and Monique are off to Morocco for the winter."

"Lucky man," Wesley said.

Annie thought longingly of hot sun, vivid blue skies, and soft, sandy beaches. Years ago, when Sophie was old enough to be left with a sitter, she and Wesley had taken a vacation there. During that blissful week Annie had rediscovered the passion for Wesley that had been buried under her round-the-clock preoccupations with motherhood. Now it seemed like a lifetime ago.

"Come in, come in," Georges said. "First some champagne." Then, lifting his eyebrows, "We have a new *anglaise* we want you to meet."

"Yes," Céleste explained, "Georges's cousin, the painter from Provence, introduced us. We met Daphne last weekend at an art *vernissage*, how do you say it"—she paused and searched for the correct word—"Oh yes, art opening." She looked pleased with herself. Her smooth, pale skin enhanced her elegant features, and her rather strong Gallic nose was softened by warm brown eyes and a ready smile, a face that could only be French.

"Our other guest is Bill Ingram," Georges said. "You remember him, chap here on sabbatical from an American university, a young professor. I think you met him at our September lunch."

Annie remembered the painful afternoon, all of them trying to keep from dozing off during the delicious meal accompanied by copious amounts of wine. Bill Ingram had monopolized the conversation with endless anecdotes of his research on an obscure eighteenth-century essayist. Now Annie shot Wesley a look, the pleading "do be nice" look understood by long-married couples. Wesley ignored it.

The two guests were seated on the satin-covered sofa opposite the fireplace. The French word *salon* suited this formal, brightly lit room filled with elegant period furniture, shining inlaid tables, and soft velvet draperies. Céleste had inherited much of it. The American professor, a small, neat man in a navy turtleneck sweater tucked tightly into his trousers, stood up and thrust out his hand. "Great to see you both again. I'm headed back to Boston at the end of the month. Isn't that where you met the Verniers?" The light reflected off his thick, dark-rimmed glasses.

"That's right," Wesley answered. "Georges and I were both in gradu-ate school. More than twenty-five years ago. Hard to believe. I was in my final year at Harvard Law and Georges was at the business school." Wes-ley gave Bill's hand a brief shake and then looked down at the English guest still seated on the sofa. "You must be Daphne," he said.

"Daphne Walker." Heavy golden hair swung forward as she stood to shake Wesley's hand. Annie had always thought of herself as tall, but this woman had to be almost six feet. She turned toward Annie, exud-ing a comfortable elegance, the kind of woman at ease in any situation.

Annie drew in her breath, amazed. Daphne was the woman she had seen a few days before in the subway, the woman in the blue cape. An-nie could hardly tell her that she'd watched her in the Métro station. It would be like admitting to eavesdropping.

Céleste and Georges completed all the necessary introductions, ex-plaining to Daphne how Annie and Wesley had taken the Verniers under their wing when they lived in Cambridge during their graduate-school days. Céleste and Georges had been thrilled to reciprocate when the Reeds moved to Paris a few years later. Daphne nodded and turned to Wesley. "What brought you to Paris?"

"I was working at a law firm in New York," he said. "They asked me to join the Paris office." He smiled at the Verniers. "Knowing Céleste and Georges made it an easy choice. Now, I'm practicing here on my own." Annie was pleased to see some of his old charm emerging. He joined Daphne on the sofa.

"Georges, let me help you with the champagne," Bill said, having lost his seat next to Daphne. Georges carefully poured the champagne into sparkling clear flutes. Bill passed the glasses around and then of-fered a toast. "To our thoughtful hosts, to new friends, to Paris."

His words were met with murmured cheers and thanks. Paris would not be an easy city to leave, and Annie felt a little sad for him. She sat in a single chair beside the fireplace, while Bill pulled another chair closer to Daphne. Wesley explained their monthly ritual of joining Céleste and Georges for lunch, directing his comments to Daphne as if he were under some sort of gravitational pull. "It all began when we first moved to Paris," he said.

"Every single month?" Daphne asked.

"Yes. And when the children still lived at home, they joined us."

"The children made it very lively," Georges said. "Sometimes mutual friends from Cambridge stopped in when they were visiting Paris."

"I think they planned their trips so as not to miss the Sunday lunches," Wesley said. "Well worth it, as you'll soon see. Céleste's a wonderful cook."

Céleste shook her head and murmured denial, though she was obviously pleased by the compliment. Annie, sitting apart from the group, had the impression of being set adrift. She wanted to participate in the conversation but for the moment couldn't think of anything to say. She was aware of Daphne's charismatic presence and tried to brush away a niggling sense of envy. She sipped the cool, jewel-like champagne, enjoying the way it tickled her throat.

"I've had some marvelous lunches here too," Bill said. "Céleste and Georges love to collect English-speaking friends. They say they like to practice their English, but they hardly need to. They both speak beautifully. Anyway, you never know who you'll meet here; it's great fun."

"We will miss you, Bill." Céleste's pronunciation drew his name out to sound like "Beel." "Your stories of Boston and Cambridge have brought back many good memories."

"Those were good years," Georges said, beaming at his guests.

"You will excuse me?" Céleste said. "I must see to the oven." She touched Georges on the arm, and Annie noticed the loving glance that flickered between them.

"May I help you?" Annie asked.

"No, no, *ma chérie*, but maybe a little later." Céleste pronounced little like "leetle." Why is it, Annie wondered, that a French accent could sound so charming, while an American speaking French poorly hurt her ears? Céleste left them for the kitchen. The smells of meat roasting in the oven hinted at the delicious meal ahead.

Daphne leaned back against the soft sofa cushions. Annie studied her gray knit dress, stark and simple but immensely feminine. Georges hovered close to his English guest, looking like a delighted school-boy when she accepted more champagne. Daphne watched Bill through heavy-lidded eyes as he rambled on about Boston and his research at the Bibliothèque Nationale, while Wesley, uninterested in Bill's remarks, kept his eyes on Daphne.

Although Daphne said little, she remained the center of attention. What was it that made her so alluring? Annie wondered. It was prob-ably her many curves, most obviously the curves of her figure, but also the waves in her hair, and the curve of her lips, which slipped pe-riodically into a smile. Annie knew that she herself was considered an attractive woman, though she thought of her face as ordinary, with its regular blue eyes, slim, straight nose, and overly wide mouth. Wesley once said she looked like a long-legged Alice in Wonderland. She would have gladly traded her aging-ingénue demeanor for Daphne's indefinable appeal.

When Annie reflected on the luncheon later, she would picture moths fluttering around a porch light on a summer evening. The three men were clearly attracted to Daphne, but Céleste too appeared to make an extra effort that afternoon. Her laughter came more freely, her voice was pitched a little higher, and her generosity assumed a greater weight.

"I'm going to miss the French bubbly," Bill said.

"Certainly there's champagne in Boston," Daphne said.

Bill laughed with some uncertainty. Annie detected a snobbish vein in Daphne's cultured English accent. There was a lull in the conversation. Annie wished she were in her own cozy living room curled up in her chair in the corner working on her poems, but she knew she needed to say something and not fade away from the group entirely. "When you return to Boston, will you go right back to teaching?" she asked Bill.

"Yes, I'm afraid my book will have to be on hold until *les vacances* this summer. *Quel dommage!*" He shrugged and rolled his eyes in an unbe-coming manner. Bill routinely peppered his sentences with French words and expressions. Annie wondered what the students must think of this tiresome young man.

"Professors spend more time out of the classroom than in it, it seems to me," Wesley said. Annie didn't like the tone in his voice, but Bill didn't seem to notice.

"Clearly, you've never been burdened with a full teaching load while trying to write books," Bill said. "You can't imagine the time constraints."

"I'm sure I can't," Wesley said.

Daphne looked across at Annie. "Céleste tells me that you write poetry." She drew her hand through her hair, lifting it away from her face.

Annie, to her annoyance, felt herself blushing. "Yes, I do. I'm trying to get back to it, actually." She felt uncomfortable discussing this in front of everyone. She considered her writing a private part of herself. "I wrote a lot when we were first married and living in Cambridge."

"Annie has published two books," Georges said, nodding with approval. "The first was when she was in college."

"Not books exactly," Annie explained. "Chapbooks, small soft-bound collections. I wrote the second when we lived in New York. I was enrolled in an MFA program there, but it all got to be too much with a baby and then moving to Paris." It continued to surprise Annie the way poetry had crept back into her life. She had never stopped writing, but in the last few years it had taken on a greater importance.

"So, do you write in French now?" Daphne asked.

"No. The poems are mostly about Paris, but I write only in English. It makes it hard to get published here." Annie noticed red lipstick on the rim of Daphne's glass. She wondered if she should try wearing a darker shade too. "I send most of my work to the States, but I'm afraid no one remembers my few successes after so many years."

"You know, I might just be able to help you," Daphne said. "You see, I've come to know this French fellow. He's an editor or publisher, something like that." She pushed her hair off her face again. "He's doing some kind of project that involves poetry. He mentioned needing someone who writes in English."

"Well, I'd certainly be interested in talking to him." Annie doubted this would go anywhere. It was too much of a coincidence. Why would a French publisher be interested in an unknown American?

"Annie's real job is working at the Liberal Arts Abroad program," Wesley said.

"Yes, I work part-time. I'm an administrator." Annie didn't want to talk about her job. The word *administrator* felt as cumbersome and boring as the job itself. She explained her work finding host families for American college students, working with the French university system to enroll them in classes, and then arranging for the transfer of credits to the American schools. She knew it must sound tedious.

"For students doing a gap year?" Daphne asked.

"It's really more of a junior-year-abroad program because the students are still working for their degree." While Annie explained the popularity of studying abroad, she became aware of Daphne's eyes. They were the same color as her dress, chameleon-like, capable of soaking up the color of their surroundings. Annie was conscious of the sound of her own voice—she sounded like she was quoting directly from the Liberal Arts Abroad brochure. "But tell me, what keeps you busy here in France?" Annie asked.

"I'm in the antiques business. I also buy art for clients, now and then, which is how I met the Verniers."

"Yes, Georges told us." Wesley looked at his friend, who was pouring out the final drops from a second bottle of champagne. "My sister in Connecticut sells antiques. Mostly primitive and American of course." Wesley seemed glad to have this connection with Daphne. "We've bought some patchwork quilts from her over the years."

"I'd love to learn more about quilts. Would your sister ever consider selling in France?"

Wesley, recently so silent at home, talked easily about his older sister and her business. Besides Sophie, Madeleine was their only family back in the States. Following her divorce years ago, she threw herself into her thriving business at her country home. She sold simple pine furniture, sturdy crockery, and kitchen implements, the kind of antiques that once had been the everyday necessities of hardworking farm families in New England. Annie imagined Daphne's antiques to be of a more sumptuous sort, objects whose only purpose was to be beautiful.

"*A table, mes amis!*" Céleste called them to the table.

Céleste served a clear soup from an antique Limoges terrine. Steam rose before her face as she lowered the silver ladle into the fragrant broth and told Daphne about the woes of her daughter, who was having trouble finding work in London.

"I haven't lived in London for quite a while, so I'm afraid that any contacts I might have wouldn't do much good," Daphne said. "My brother has moved out to Devon, so he's not much help either." She turned to Georges. "Tell me about this wonderful red wine."

"It's a Burgundy," he said. "My brother brought me a case. One of his better finds in my opinion." Georges, like most Frenchmen, took charge of the wine at all of their parties. Wesley had assumed the same role when they moved to Paris. Annie had never minded.

"It's lovely," Daphne said, taking another sip.

Bill complimented Céleste on the soup. Annie knew how time-consuming it was to prepare such an intensely flavored broth. She'd learned everything she knew about cooking from Céleste. They'd spent many afternoons talking about recipes when they were young brides in America. Annie knew that Céleste relished her life as wife and homemaker now as much as she did then. Even though their children were grown, nothing ever seemed to change in Céleste and Georges's life. Shopping in the open-air markets, finding the best purveyors of cheese, visiting relatives in the country most weekends—their lives seemed to hum along in a predictable pattern.

"How's Jean-Marc?" Bill inquired after the Verniers' son, who was studying at the University of Toulouse. "I wondered if he's ever met Professor Thibault. He's been on the faculty at Toulouse for several years, I believe."

Annie was soon drawn into a discussion with Bill and Céleste on the University of Toulouse and the relative merits of studying outside of Paris. She wished she were talking to Daphne and not stuck with Bill. Wesley was leaning forward over his soup bowl, as if he didn't want to miss anything that Daphne said. Georges too was sitting up very straight, and seemed engrossed in the conversation. Annie could only catch a few words. They seemed to be talking again about antiques or art. It wasn't that Daphne didn't speak loudly enough, but the low timber of her voice required the listener to give her full attention. Annie knew it was not just what Daphne was saying that held her listeners. Beyond her attractiveness and her sex appeal, she seemed complex, as if she was holding something back.

The meal proceeded slowly, as it should on a leisurely Sunday afternoon. Céleste brought the platters of food into the dining room on a brass-wheeled tea trolley and passed them around the table—sliced pork with a tangy mustard sauce; roasted potatoes; and steamed carrots and parsnips, small and sweet with a bit of the green stems still attached, making them look like they came right out of the garden. Annie wondered if her own heightened state of awareness was due to Daphne's presence. It was as if she were dining at the Verniers' for the first time. A dazzling white linen cloth covered the table, and the fine old silverware felt heavy in her hands. The tinkling of plates and glassware added to the elegant party atmosphere. She heard herself taking part in conversations, laughing at anecdotes, complimenting her friend on the delicious meal, all with a strange sensitivity, as if she were outside of the room and looking in through tinted glass.

After the salad course, Céleste brought out a platter of cheeses that she'd arranged artfully on a layer of overlapping green leaves. Annie recognized a chèvre, a creamy blue, and a generous wedge of Saint André. Céleste always remembered to include Wesley's favorite. Next to it, a ripe, runny Camembert gave off an earthy, barnlike scent. Daphne chose that one.

"Tell me about your house in the country," Wesley said.

Georges had gotten up to refill the wineglasses. Enjoying the role of host, he carried a large white linen napkin over his arm like a proper sommelier. Annie felt a little warm, but she nodded when Georges reached for her glass. Thankfully, everyone now turned to Daphne.

"It's called God House."

"What an auspicious name," Bill said. "Did it used to be a convent or monastery?"

"Not at all. It's just a beautiful old house on the Seine, in a small town called Villandry. I inherited it from my French godmother. As a little girl, I called it God House, the house of my godmother. It was a silly childhood name, but we've called it that ever since."

"It's a wonderful name," Annie said. "How did you come to have a French godmother?"

"Antoinette worked in London when she was young. She went there to learn the antiques trade and stayed for nearly ten years." Daphne's face had taken on a dreamy expression, as if she was trying to visualize her godmother at that time in her life. "That's where she met my mother. She came often to our house in Devon, and she and my mother became very dear friends." Daphne lifted her hair again, a gesture that Annie would eventually associate with her.

"Was God House her family home?" Georges asked. Like many traditional Frenchmen, he liked to know about one's roots. He often spoke of his own boyhood in Burgundy, the family rituals, and of his brother, who still lived there and worked as a wine exporter. He'd never understood Wesley's willingness to sell his parents' home in Connecticut after their death or Annie's reluctance to return to her small town in Vermont.

"No. Antoinette grew up in Paris, but when she moved back to France she bought the house in Villandry. She started her antiques business at God House with money she'd inherited."

Annie, always an avid reader, had loved the magic of certain houses in books—like Miss Haversham's, in Dickens; Margaret Mitchell's Tara; or Manderley, which had prompted her to read everything that Daphne du Maurier had ever written. "Did they stay close friends when Antoinette came back to France?"

"Oh yes. My mother adored Antoinette and came to God House frequently. In fact, after I was born, my mother spent months at a time at Villandry. God House was a kind of refuge for both of us." Daphne's expression grew somber. Annie noticed just the hint of violet circles under her eyes. "After Mummy's death, I pretty much moved in with Antoinette," she said. "I was either there or in boarding school in England. My father was never around, but I don't want to bore you with all of that."

Annie wanted to know more, but as Céleste's longtime guest, she needed to be useful. It was time to clear away the cheese and bring out fresh plates for dessert. Annie and Céleste worked together with the easy rhythm of two old friends. Annie cleared the table while Céleste scraped the delicate white plates and lowered them into a dishpan of hot, soapy water. Annie got the dessert plates down from a high shelf, and Céleste divided the plum-and-almond tart into six slices.

Céleste lowered her voice to a whisper. "What do you think of her? Georges was practically drooling over her when we met at the art gallery. It was his idea to invite her."

"I gather she's not married," Annie said.

"Well, she's not wearing a ring. When I invited her to lunch I asked her if there was someone she wanted to bring. She said, 'No thanks.' "

"There's something different about her. Wesley is certainly paying attention." Annie hesitated a moment before confiding in her friend. "Wesley's been so down lately. I hope he gets more work soon." Annie had told Céleste about Wesley's work problems, but she couldn't imagine telling her how their marriage seemed to be deteriorating as well. She worried that she was failing Wesley at some deeper level.

"I'm sure things will improve. Georges says the current government is ruining the business climate, but you know how conservative he is!"

Back at the table, Annie hoped to hear more about God House, but Georges was telling Daphne about his brother's place in Burgundy.

After eating Céleste's homemade tart, they moved back to the living room. Céleste carried in a tray with coffee and demitasse cups.

"I'm afraid I can't stay for coffee," Daphne said. "I'm meeting a client in Passy. She has some chairs for me to appraise. I promised I would stop by before driving back to the country."

"Of course, we understand." Céleste smiled. "We're so pleased that you could come to lunch." Céleste looked to Georges, whose face registered disappointment, and asked him to get Daphne's coat.

"Thanks, Céleste, it was a heavenly lunch," Daphne said. "I so enjoyed it." She kissed Bill on both cheeks and wished him well on his return to the States. "Good luck with all your projects," she said to Wesley, offering him her hand. Then she turned to Annie. "We need to talk more about your poems."

"That would be great." Annie was surprised she remembered.

"Check your diary and give me a ring. I'm in and out of the city all the time." She pulled a card out of her black leather bag and handed it to Annie.

"Céleste, I want you and Georges to come out to God House. Perhaps this spring when the weather warms up."

Georges returned carrying Daphne's coat, the deep blue cape with the black velvet collar. He shook it open and placed it over her shoulders. Daphne brushed past Annie, leaving behind the faintest scent of lilac. Annie felt staid and predictable as she stood in her wake. She loved English expressions like "diary" for calendar and "ringing" people on the phone. She knew it was unlikely that Daphne's connection in publishing would come to anything, but she was pleased that Daphne had taken an interest in her poems.

"Let's walk along the river," Wesley said. "I think the sun's coming out." The strong coffee after lunch had revived them. Annie reached for Wesley's arm. After the good food and lively conversation, his handsome features had regained their definition. They turned down rue Séguier, a narrow side street that led to the Seine. Tourists would be unlikely to stroll this street without any shops or cafés in view. Indeed, like many quiet Paris streets, it looked like a tired old gentleman whose worn but well-tailored elegant clothes were now faded and smelled of closed rooms and tinned soup.

"You seem to have cheered up," Annie said.

"It was a good party. Daphne was different from most of Céleste and Georges's guests."

"You and Georges seemed to like her," she said, smiling up at him.

"What's that supposed to mean, Annie?"

"I'm just teasing." She looked up at the sky. The afternoon light was on the wane. "What did you talk about at your end of the table?"

"Mostly about Daphne's antiques business. Madeleine should get in touch with her." Turning away Wesley breathed in the wet air coming off the Seine. "Georges sure is generous with the red wine."

Annie said nothing. The Seine surged along below them, a dark turbulent gray, but a tough blue sky began to push through the clouds.

"So, are you going to call her?" he asked.

"Maybe." She started to tell him that she'd seen Daphne a few days ago in the Métro, but she decided against it.

"Let me see her card," he said.

Annie pulled it out of her pocket and held it up. The words *God House* stood out in raised black ink against the heavy cream paper. A phone number was printed below. Wesley made a motion to reach for it, and Annie, laughing, leaned into him and kissed him on the lips. His mouth felt warm and soft despite the cold air. He didn't allow his lips to linger but withdrew his arm from hers to turn his collar up against the wind. She thrust the card back into the depths of her coat pocket. Masses of steel-gray clouds had quickly swallowed up the patch of blue sky.

THREE

L' Invitation

"I don't mind the cold, but I'm sick of the dark." Wesley picked up the kettle, stopping the shrill whistle. "It doesn't get light until nearly eight-thirty now." He poured the boiling water over the coffee filter, releasing a nutty warmth as the brown stream trickled into the glass carafe. He preferred his coffee black, unlike Annie, who'd adopted the French custom of drinking café au lait in the morning, half strong coffee and half hot milk. His face had already lost the relaxed, peaceful expression he'd worn in sleep. He looked somewhat disheveled in a faded checked flannel shirt loosely tucked into the corduroy pants he'd worn all week. When he'd worked at Wilson & James, he wore neat dark suits with a crisp white shirt and silk tie, the clothes of a successful attorney in a sophisticated city.

"Speaking of the dark," Annie said, "it's almost the winter solstice." She hoped talking about the party might lift his spirits. "I've asked everyone for the nineteenth this year." The Reeds hosted an annual dinner party to celebrate the winter solstice. Annie had started this tradition when they first moved to Paris. She liked the idea of giving a party just before Christmas and lighting the apartment entirely with candles during this darkest time of the year.

Though she looked forward to more light-filled days, Annie preferred writing poems in winter. Oddly, the fragile winter light fed her spirit more than the brilliant, overblown beauty of summer. She'd gotten up early to work in the alcove off the living room, the small space she'd appropriated for her writing once Sophie had started school. From her favorite chair in the corner she could just make out the tops of the trees as they emerged slowly out of the darkness.

She'd found it hard to write that morning. She still felt the sting of the recent rejection letter. She worried that her poems were too narrative, too direct. Some of the younger poets she'd been reading recently had an edgy quality. The last time she'd attended a reading of American and English poets, held at the American Church in Paris, she'd had a difficult time understanding the work. The words were clear, but the mood was often cruel and angry, quite lacking in heart.

Wesley carried his coffee over to the table while Annie sliced the previous night's baguette for toast. The bread was unusually hard, and crumbs scattered across the counter under the pressure of the knife. She put the slices under the broiler and carried the butter and jam to the table.

"Who's coming?" he asked.

"Céleste and Georges, of course, and Mary and Tom. Just the six of us." Two of Wesley's partners from his old law firm used to come with their wives every year, but they had chosen to go back to New York when the firm closed.

"Our numbers have certainly dwindled." He stared out the window, ignoring his rapidly cooling coffee. "Why don't you ask Daphne? She'd liven things up." He looked back at Annie as if to gauge her reaction. "Wait till Tom gets a look at her."

"Hmm. Maybe." Annie frowned. Mary, her boss at Liberal Arts Abroad, was married to Tom, an unstoppable flirt and a big drinker. The last time they had dinner together, he'd run his hand under Annie's skirt. Annie hadn't told Wesley.

Annie pulled the toast out from the oven, and while they ate they discussed the menu for the party. Wesley enjoyed choosing the wine, but wanted to check with Georges about the négociant of the Burgundy that he'd served last Sunday. He became interested in food when they moved to France, and he took pride in his selection of wines. He would probably spend several hours scouring the local wine merchants for just the right pick. Georges and Wesley had a longtime friendly competition to see who could turn up memorable or undiscovered wines while keeping to an agreed budget. Annie made a mental note to buy more candles, and she thought that place cards this year would be a nice touch.

The telephone rang. Annie reached for the receiver and answered the phone, giving Wesley a questioning look. "Sophie, is that you?" The connection was poor. "It's the middle of the night in New York. Why are you up so late?" Annie's brow furrowed. She imagined her daughter in the tiny studio apartment, miles of gray ocean away from the familiar French neighborhood where she'd grown up. She was relieved to hear from her only child. Sophie's sporadic phone calls were unexpected gifts. If only she could reach out at that very moment and give her daughter a hug.

Sophie's voice came in more clearly. "Mom, we just finished this incredible deal. Our team worked so hard. It really paid off. Marla's thrilled." Sophie had told them about Marla Kellogg, her boss, an accomplished forty-year-old woman who took pride in breaking through the glass ceiling of the corporate world. She was a role model to Sophie. Sophie worked for a large consulting company, a plum job for someone right out of college. Now, despite her enthusiasm, she sounded hollow from fatigue.

"That's great, Sophie, but why aren't you in bed?"

"Mother."

Annie tried to sound more positive. "Dad and I were just talking about the solstice dinner. It's on the nineteenth. Will you be home in time?"

"No. That's why I'm calling. Marla picked me to go to Los Angeles with another group. It's really an honor, the best account that our division has ever landed. I can't say no. I really want to work on this one."

"You've been working nonstop since June." Annie pushed away her plate of dry toast. "Surely they'll give you vacation time at Christmas." She hoped this didn't come out like a whine. She leaned her elbows on the table and clutched the phone tightly against her ear.

"Mom, it's not like France. You know that. They want us out there on the twenty-seventh. There's not enough time to come to Paris. Aunt Madeleine said I could spend Christmas in Connecticut with her."

Annie sighed. She didn't want to hear this.

"This project will take about three weeks, maybe a month." Sophie's voice was brisk and matter-of-fact. "Anyway, I rebooked my flight home for the end of January."

Annie and Wesley would just have to wait. This would be their first Christmas without their daughter. "That's lovely of Madeleine to have you," Annie said. Wesley had stopped drinking his coffee and watched Annie. She could see him trying to guess the other end of the conversation. "Of course I'm disappointed. We'll miss you terribly. I guess this is being a grown-up, putting your job first and all." Right now Annie wished that Sophie was still a small child. She missed being needed, being caught up in family life, and the simple physical pleasure of seeing her daughter every day, smoothing her hair, touching her cheek, tucking her into bed each night with a kiss. "Do try to get enough sleep, sweetie."

"Mom, don't keep saying that."

Annie could hear impatience in her daughter's voice.

"I'll call you again this weekend. How's Dad?"

"He's right here. I'll put him on. Take care. I love you, sweetie." She shook her head and handed the phone to Wesley.

Sophie reminded Annie of Wesley in the early days of his career. Every case was the "big" one, and once it was over, he'd be quickly absorbed in the next. She watched him pace now as he listened to Sophie relate her business adventures. She knew he hated her not coming home as much as she did. Annie had been counting on Sophie to cheer up her father and bring their lives back into balance.

"Well, at least she sounds happy," he said after hanging up. "Says she's working sixty hours a week."

"I think these firms push their young people too hard."

"Annie, you haven't a clue what it's like. Long hours are typical."

"But she has no time for a personal life."

"No time to come home either. At least she can go to Madeleine's." He stood looking out at the glimmer of pearl-gray sky just beginning to lighten, his shoulders rounded.

They were lucky to have Madeleine, who relished any opportunity to be helpful to her family. After Wesley's parents died, she'd assumed the role of family matriarch, stepping in whenever she could and having Sophie visit during breaks from college. The two were very close.

Annie got to her feet and forced a smile. "Well, we're going to have to get used to it." She put her arms around Wesley and drew him into a hug. "Come on, don't be sad, we've got each other. This is supposed to be a good time in life. Maybe we should take a little trip. I'll bet Morocco would be fun." She reached up, touched the planes of his face, and pressed the slight dimples on either side of his mouth.

"You know we can't go spending money like that, especially now."

"I know, but it's a nice idea. I'll never forget that lovely trip when we left Sophie behind, just the two of us."

"Yeah, a long time ago." He brushed her lips in a habitual way, a conciliatory kiss, and stepped out of her grasp. "What are you up to today?"

"I'm meeting Hélène. She's found some more families to house students. I'm hoping one of them can take the new girl we have coming next semester."

Hélène Rocher had been one of the first to host families for Liberal Arts Abroad back in the early days of the program. At that time her husband was still alive and her son, Alexis, was living at home and eager to learn English. Hélène no longer took in students, but she had been invaluable to the program over the years, finding other host families. She seemed to have endless connections: her hairdresser's cousin, her neighbor's sister, the young man who had worked for Hélène's husband, whose wife was a teacher at the lycée. Mary, director of the program, always preferred having the personal recommendations for host families that Hélène could provide. And to Annie, Hélène had become more of a friend than a colleague. Wesley liked her too. "She won't be in Paris for our party either." Annie started to clear the table.

"Umm." Wesley looked distracted, and she could tell his attention was already elsewhere. He poured himself more coffee and went down the hall to his office, the floor creaking in all the familiar places under his step. She wondered what would keep him busy in the solitary hours ahead. She picked up her coffee. By now the milk had congealed, forming a thin skin across the surface. She poured it down the sink.

Later, when Annie put on her coat to leave, she reached into her pockets for her gloves and felt the crisp edge of Daphne's card. She drew it out and ran her finger across the heavy black lettering. Why not? She picked up the hall telephone and dialed. An answering machine clicked on. "God House. Please leave a message."

Annie asked Daphne if she'd like to meet for lunch one day this week and left her number. She thought of telling Wesley, but the door to his office was closed. She grabbed a worn cashmere scarf from the chest by the front door and headed off to see her old friend. Hélène lived in the Sixteenth Arrondissement, an elegant quarter on the other side of Paris. She decided to walk part of the way. She was craving some exercise and wanting to enjoy the sun, which was making a surprise appearance.

"Annie, *ma chérie*. It is a long time since I have seen you." Hélène's English was formal and old-fashioned, but she rarely made a mistake.

"It does get so busy in the fall," Annie said, wishing she had made the time to come and see Hélène sooner. She always loved their little talks.

"I want to hear everything," Hélène said, laughing. "*Les détails des détails.*"

The details of the details. Annie secretly thought of Hélène as a kind of mother to her, an especially lovely French mother. Today Hélène was beautifully dressed in a trim navy suit. Annie admired her vivid dark eyes and neat red lips. Her nails, painted a matching shade of red, stood out against the pale skin of her delicate hands. Annie silently chastised herself for not taking the time to keep her own nails polished. Frenchwomen were so good at paying attention to *les petits soins*, the little details of grooming that kept them looking their best.

Annie brought Hélène up to date on what was happening at the office and the need for a new host family in January. "The couple I had lined up changed their mind and want to wait until fall before taking a student," Annie explained. "I'm running out of time to find someone."

"*Pas de problème*," Hélène said. "I know of just the family. Françoise, from my bridge group, has a niece who lives in the Sixth. She is willing to have a student at any time. Her daughter is studying English and wishes to practice. A good plan, *non?*"

"It sounds perfect." Annie felt a weight lifted. "I'll make arrangements for them to meet Mary at the office."

"*Mais, toi alors.* Tell me more of yourself," Hélène insisted.

"I'm working on my poems again," she said.

"Aha!" Hélène clapped her hands together. "I thought I saw a sparkle in your eye."

It was so easy to talk to her. "It's insane, really," Annie said. "I can't seem to get anything published, but I can't stop myself from trying."

"And you should not stop. Sophie, she has gone; it is your time now."

Her time. How could she enjoy "her time" when Wesley was so miserable, when so many things seemed to be falling out of place? "Sophie isn't coming home for Christmas this year," she said.

"Oh, my dear. This is a disappointment."

Hélène's son was married now and lived in Ireland. Annie sensed that she felt the same all-consuming love for her child as Annie did for Sophie. "Do you miss Alexis?" Annie asked. "Goodness, what a silly question. Of course you do. But does it get any easier?"

"Everything changes when your child leaves home. You had your Sophie so young, so you must face this sooner than most." Hélène turned her neatly coiffed head and looked toward the bare branches bowing gracefully in the winter wind beyond the windows. "And yes, *ma chérie*, you always miss them, but one wants the little birds to leave the nest, *non?*"

"You're right. I know you're right. But it's hard all the same."

"Of course. *C'est difficile.* But you learn to enjoy the children whenever you are together. *Noël*, yes, this is important, but is it not a joy, an occasion for celebration any time you come together?"

Hélène was right. Sophie's return would be cause for celebration on any day of the year. Annie could certainly manage one Christmas without her.

"Besides," Hélène continued, "it is nice to be a couple, *non?* After Alexis moved away, Bertrand and I traveled more. It was a happy time for us. Almost like the early days of our marriage."

Annie looked away. The past months with Wesley were nothing like the early days of her marriage. Annie could put up with his bad moods; they were understandable. But he had grown so distant. A lump formed in her throat, and she couldn't bear to tell Hélène how difficult her life with Wesley had become.

"I do have more time now for my writing with Sophie away."

"Exactly. These days can be a very rich opportunity for you." Hélène paused, as if to reflect. "I won't try to convince you of all of the advantages of growing older." She smiled and the lines around her eyes made her look kind and understanding. "But one gains a kind of freedom in midlife." She laughed and shrugged. "If you have the courage for it."

Annie stood up but hesitated to leave—being with Hélène was so comforting. "Hélène, you make me feel better. You really do." She bent awkwardly to hug her friend. She hoped one day she would have some of the wisdom that this charming French lady possessed. Hélène looked so comfortable and at ease with who she was, a woman who had already surmounted so many of life's hurdles.

Annie opened the door to her apartment and immediately smelled something burning. She found Wesley in the kitchen leaning against the counter with one hand in his pocket, and the other holding the phone. His back to the stove, he appeared oblivious to the open-faced cheese sandwich smoking under the broiler. He smiled over at her, the dimpled smile that unlocked his charm. "Annie just walked in. I'll put her on."

Annie took the receiver and gestured emphatically toward the smoking stove.

"It's Daphne," Wesley informed her, looking pleased. He turned and pulled the ruined sandwich from the oven, then opened the window.

"Hello there," Daphne said, her low English voice sounding friendly. The blue cape flashed into Annie's mind. "Wesley has just invited me to your solstice party. Is that some sort of American tradition? I rather thought it more of a Nordic thing."

"Just a few old friends. I hope you can come. Céleste and Georges will be there." Annie was annoyed that Wesley was listening to her every word. He was starting to cut more cheese for another sandwich.

"Sounds like fun," Daphne replied. "I'd love it. If it's a late night, maybe I could stay with Céleste and Georges instead of going all the way back to the country."

"Why don't you spend the night here? Our daughter's room is free. She won't be home in time for the party this year." Annie surprised herself with this invitation. They rarely had guests for the night.

"Well, that would be lovely. Funny, I was thinking about you too this morning."

"You were?" Annie colored slightly.

"Yes. I talked to the fellow I know in publishing. I'd like to take him some of your poems. He said he'd be willing to look at them."

"My, that sounds extraordinary. He doesn't know anything about me."

"Of course not. But I told him I had a feeling about you, also that you had published in New York."

"I know, but that was a long time ago and—"

"You're not backing out, are you?" Annie detected a note of impatience. "He didn't say he'd publish them, just that he'd look at a few."

"Of course I'd be willing to show him my work."

"Good then. Let's meet for lunch and you can give me the poems then."

They made arrangements to meet the next day. Annie put the phone back and turned her attention to the burned sandwich that Wesley had left in the sink.

"Well?" Wesley said.

"Well, what?" Something about Wesley's interest bothered her.

"Is she coming to the party?"

"She is. And I'm meeting her for lunch tomorrow."

"Aren't you glad I thought of asking her?" Wesley said.

Annie tried to hide her impatience. "Mmm." She was no longer thinking about the solstice party. She needed to decide on which poems to bring to lunch, but that would have to wait. Unfortunately, she had to get back to the office that afternoon. At least she had good news to report to Mary, about the potential host family Hélène had found. She wanted to schedule the interviews as quickly as possible.

And Daphne had remembered her poems. Annie felt her spirits lift. She had a feeling that something good was going to happen, that something might even change for the better. She tossed Wesley's burned sandwich into the trash.

FOUR

Le Café

"Life is filled with all kinds of risks, some you don't know you're taking."

They sat facing the street. Annie had arrived first, securing the table, and Daphne had come twenty minutes later. The noon rush had abated, but the ever-fashionable Café de Flore was still filled with cell-phone-wielding business patrons, trendy Left Bank women, and a scattering of tourists seeking the literary ambience for which the café was once known. Their intense voices melded with the clatter of plates and glasses as busy waiters cleared tables and readied places for the next wave of diners.

Annie, feeling a draft on the back of her neck, pulled her scarf more closely. She had just explained to Daphne how taking on a big project after all these years seemed like quite a leap. "Even if this editor liked my work and wanted me to write the poems, I'm not certain I could do it." She wanted to be honest.

The sidewalk tables were enclosed by glass walls, allowing one to sit and watch the bustling crowd in any season. A meager winter sun was trying to break through a smoky gray cloud cover, but supplemental heaters blew out a dry heat and kept the cold at bay. Daphne, with the signature blue cape draped over the back of her chair, thumbed through the folder of poems. Her hands could have been those of a young man, with long tapered fingers and short square nails, but the soft pale skin was delicate and feminine.

"It's mostly new work," Annie said uncertainly. "I enjoyed doing that series on French churches. Right now I'm doing a group of poems inspired by Courbet." Perhaps she should remain silent as Daphne read. Annie felt suddenly exposed and fragile. She still couldn't quite believe that Daphne was truly interested in her.

The waiter, in a flapping long white apron, arrived with the carafe of red wine that Daphne had ordered. He poured the wine into their glasses, casting an appreciative glance toward Daphne. She wore her allure like an old sweater, easy to toss on and fend off a chill.

"I like this line, 'Dust motes in the arc of light, sprinkling grace on ragged souls below.'" She nodded approvingly. "Well, I'll take these to him and we'll just have to see." Daphne raised her glass. "To your success!" she said. Annie rarely drank wine at lunch, certainly not during the week, but she didn't need to go back to the office that afternoon. For some reason, she didn't feel like being her usual careful self. Besides, the red wine would warm her on this cold winter day.

"Tell me more about your friend in publishing," Annie said. She was still puzzled that a French publisher would be willing to read work of an unknown American poet.

"He's a client actually, named Paul Valmont, but we're getting to be friends. Good-looking man. You'll see." Daphne took another sip of wine and looked at Annie across the top of her glass. "Anyway, he has a small publishing business, edits some books himself. His wife died recently, and he called me because he wants to sell some of her furniture. She collected antiques. I think that having her things around makes him sad."

Daphne leaned her elbows on the table, drawing closer to Annie. "He's doing a book of François Naudin's photographs. Have you heard of him?" Annie shook her head. "He's old now, at one time quite well known for his scenes of Paris. Naudin is an old family friend. They want to do a book together with poems in English to go with a collection of pictures of Paris. You know, a kind of art book, but one English-speaking tourists could take home to remember their trip."

"I love writing about Paris. So many of my poems are about the city." Annie felt encouraged, almost ready to believe she was up to the task.

"It would mean writing specific poems for each photograph."

"You mean all the poems for the book?" Annie leaned back in her chair. "I've never tried to do anything like that before."

"Like I said, we're faced with risks every day."

"Well, it's too soon to worry about that. It all depends on whether or not he likes my poems."

"I have a feeling he will." Daphne smiled.

Annie wanted to believe this. But Daphne was not a poet herself and she'd glanced at only a few of her poems. Annie wondered why Daphne would try to help someone she'd met only once. Until today, they'd had only the briefest conversations. Still, Annie had an uncanny feeling about Daphne. Something compelled her to pay attention to this woman, but also to be wary.

Today Daphne's eyes had a green tinge like her sweater, a loosely woven affair with a shawl collar, belted at the waist. Under this she wore a silk shirt, a paler shade of green. Her collar was turned up, but the top two buttons were left undone, revealing the creamy skin of her throat. Annie felt prim beside her. She'd worn her hair pulled back and tied with a velvet ribbon in the style that made her think of the French actress Catherine Deneuve. The beige skirt and matching wool turtleneck that had seemed understated and chic when she chose them that morning now felt colorless and dull. Everything about Daphne suggested nonchalance. Perhaps a calculated nonchalance.

The waiter appeared with their lunch. He placed a large golden omelet filled with wild mushrooms in front of Daphne. She'd ordered her omelet "*baveuse*," and rivulets of warm, barely cooked egg oozed out toward the vivid green parsley garnish. Annie had ordered a bowl of onion soup. It came topped with pale yellow Gruyère cheese melting onto the crisp toasted slice of French bread floating in the center. The buttery, woodsy smell made Annie feel better. Daphne picked up her knife and fork and started eating lunch. Annie, suddenly ravenous, tried to sip the steaming soup without burning the roof of her mouth.

"So, when was the last time you took a risk?" Daphne asked. Their conversation was veering off into unfamiliar territory. Céleste talked only about family, food, or plans for the weekend. She and Georges often went to the country to see Georges's family and to escape the hurried pace of Paris. Céleste worried about "*le stress*." Their most intimate talks went only as far as family health, or worries about their grown children. Over the years, most of Annie's American friends in Paris had moved back to the States. Her closest friends had been the mothers of Sophie's classmates, wives of Wesley's colleagues, and a few poets she'd met at readings. She had never shared that same kind of intimacy with her French women friends—except for Hélène.

Risk. Annie didn't even like the sound of the word. Her first serious boyfriend, Luke Walters, wanted her to leave college and move with him to New York. She was nineteen then and he only twenty-three. Perhaps that's the kind of risk Daphne had in mind. "I almost left school and ran off with a playwright," she said. "Now and then I wonder what my life would have been like." She hadn't thought about Luke for years.

"What was he like?"

"Very artistic, typical in a funny way. He had dark, thick hair, good-looking. Sort of brooding, painfully sensitive, but his voice was the amazing thing. I think I fell in love with his voice. It's funny, I can almost remember it now. It was soothing and very clear. I could hear him, the sound of him, years later, long after I forgot almost everything else."

"So why didn't you go with him? Sounds dishy to me."

Annie liked dishy, one of those charming Brit words but not in the least appropriate for Luke. "He was too sullen to be dishy." The word sounded odd in her mouth. "I think he was talented, though I can't remember anything he wrote. He probably should have been an actor; he was intense, very dramatic. Passionate too. In any case, I didn't go with him."

"Going off to New York with a handsome young man doesn't seem like a terrible risk to me."

"Believe me, it was. My father was a professor. My finishing college and getting a degree from a good school was one of the few things he cared about. Also, I didn't like Luke's friends. I would spend the weekend with him and his theater friends and return to school utterly wrung out. It was Luke mostly. He was draining. I felt like I was constantly trying to be someone I wasn't. It's hard to explain."

"So marrying Wesley wasn't a risk?"

"Oh no. I guess it was risky to get married so young, and I did turn to him on the rebound." Annie smiled. She liked thinking about the early years of their marriage. "Wesley was sunny, positive, like he had the whole world figured out. Being with him was a relief."

"And that's a commendation?"

"I guess relief isn't the right word. It's just that with Luke it was like walking on a high wire, giddy and exhilarating when I was up there, but there was this incredible tension, you know, the possibility of falling off."

"You'd rather get off gracefully while you could."

"Exactly. But what about you? Tell me about the men in your life." The wine was loosening Annie's tongue. She didn't want to be the only one dredging up old loves.

"Let's just say it's been a series of short high-wire acts." A closed expression fell across Daphne's face. She reached for the carafe and divided the rest of the wine between them. Her lipstick had worn off her full lips, and her teeth appeared surprisingly small for such a generous mouth.

"Tell me more about God House." It seemed strange to Annie that a younger single person would prefer living out in the country instead of in Paris. "Is it very remote?"

"Yes and no." Daphne took a long final sip of wine. The town isn't even an hour outside the city, that's without traffic of course. Only fifty minutes on the train. The house is just a kilometer outside the town, but once you go down the drive"—Daphne gestured toward the traffic in front of the café—"it's like leaving the world behind. A large stand of chestnut trees blocks the house from the road, and the house itself sits up on a rise facing the river and the fields beyond."

"It sounds lovely." Annie tried to envision this place. "You don't get lonely?"

"Never. Have you ever lived in a place where you feel like of all places on earth that is where you are meant to be?"

"That's how I felt when we came to Paris."

"I love Paris too, but when I go through the gates to God House, it's home, where I'm truly alive." Daphne had finished eating. Her face had taken on a luminous expression, her eyes focused on a distant pleasure. "When I lived there with Mummy and Antoinette, it seemed like life was quite perfect, the happiest days of my life really. God House has made me who I am. You'll see." She looked at Annie. "Funny, neither of us wanting to live in our native land. Where were you born anyway?"

"New York City. But I don't remember it as a child. We left for Vermont when I was four. My mother had died. My father moved there so we could live with his sister, my aunt Kate. He'd been a professor at Columbia. He never recovered from my mother's death. It was aunt Kate who raised me, and Daddy took a job teaching history at a small local college."

"No brothers or sisters?"

Annie shook her head.

"I see. So you were the poor, lonely, sensitive only child," Daphne said in a slightly mocking tone.

Annie didn't know how to respond to this, but just then the waiter came to clear their dishes and deliver their salads. The earthy aroma of garlic rose from the wavy greens that glistened in an olive oil sheen. Daphne nodded with pleasure after taking a large bite and licked the corner of her mouth. "Marvelous salad here, maybe not as good as Céleste's, but close. What was your aunt Kate like?"

"Wonderful. I miss her terribly. She died two years ago. We used to go to Vermont to see her every summer." Annie wondered if this breed of spinster aunt still existed: maiden aunts, they were called then. Aunt Kate, much older than her father, lived for her animals and gardens. She raised a small herd of sheep for wool that she traded to a co-op of weavers. She tended a large vegetable garden during the short summer months, and she studied with the local painting society during the winter. Annie had several of her whimsical watercolors of vegetables and gourds hanging in her Paris kitchen. She could still picture Aunt Kate bustling around the kitchen, cookies baking in the oven and pots of jam boiling on the sticky spattered stovetop. She'd encouraged Annie in all her pursuits. "Maybe you'll be an actress like your mother," she had once said.

"Do you still have the house?"

"No. We sold it. It was hard to look after, so far away."

"And your father?"

"My father?"

"Yes. What was he like, besides insisting on a college education?"

"Quiet. A sweet man underneath. He died just before Sophie was born. I wish he'd known her. Aunt Kate said he was brilliant, but he suffered from depression."

When Annie was a teenager, she'd overheard a woman talking about her father in the local IGA. "Damaged goods" were her words, and to this day Annie could still remember the worn linoleum floor of that grocery store with its shelves of dented cans and day-old bread.

"Is your father still living?" she asked Daphne.

"I haven't a clue. He left my mother before I was born. I've erased him from my life." Her voice made it clear that this topic was closed. Daphne gestured for the waiter. "*Deux cafés, s'il vous plaît.*" He hurried off and returned almost immediately with two black coffees. Daphne added a dark brown cube of sugar, stirred with the diminutive spoon, and leaned into her chair, arching her back in one languid movement. She didn't seem to be in any hurry, and a comfortable silence fell between them.

The two women seated at the next table were getting up to leave. They retied scarves, found gloves, and headed outside. Annie had noticed them during lunch. They looked like mother and daughter, laughing and sharing intimate confidences, much the way she and Daphne had been comparing life stories. She could see them now out on the street, walking arm in arm, perhaps off to do some shopping for Christmas. Annie felt a momentary longing for Sophie.

She took a sip of strong coffee and pulled her shoulders back. She didn't know if it was the good meal or Daphne's interest in her, but she felt promise. She wanted this editor, this Valmont, to like her work. She knew she could write those poems. It was the power of this place. Paris had inspired her writing from the moment she'd arrived in the city and it still did. All these years of putting Sophie first and now brooding over Wesley. She'd had enough of that. Maybe it was her turn now. She knew that when she was writing, falling into her poems, all her day-to-day troubles bothered her less.

She glanced at her watch. It was nearly three. She could feel the encroaching darkness, but today it didn't seem to matter. Later, they paid the bill, dividing it in half like two friends accustomed to a longtime ritual. They said good-bye out on the street, and Daphne kissed Annie

on both cheeks. Annie caught the faint scent of lilacs and wondered if
there were lilacs planted in the gardens of God House.

"Until the solstice, then," Daphne said. Her hand lingered for a
moment on Annie's arm.

Annie could hear Wesley on the phone in his office when she arrived
home. She hadn't bothered to shop for dinner. Instead, she'd taken the
remaining afternoon to look in some of the small boutiques in the
Latin Quarter. She hoped to find something special to send Sophie for
Christmas, and there wasn't much time left. Tonight they could always
heat some soup, or better yet, go out for dinner. She put her coat away
and stretched. She wasn't hungry, and she knew she wouldn't be for
quite some time.

She kept thinking of Daphne and their afternoon together. It had
been fun to share stories about their lives, but there was something a
trifle unsettling as well. Spending time with Daphne reminded Annie
of being with Lydia, her best friend when she was eleven or twelve.
Lydia was always talking Annie into trying new things.

One summer night Lydia had persuaded Annie to climb out onto
the roof of her house to smoke her first cigarette. She had talked Annie
into spying on her parents' raucous parties and stealing sips of unfinished drinks. Annie had thrown up in the rhododendron hedge before
she had any idea she was tipsy. She and Lydia had become blood sisters by pricking their fingers with needles taken from Aunt Kate's
sewing basket. Annie both loved and feared their adventures, and she
had missed Lydia when her family moved to California a few years
later.

Lydia was the daring one, and Annie never understood why Lydia
had paid any attention to her at all. And now, standing here in the
calm of her own home, Annie wondered again why Daphne had taken
an interest in her. Did she really care about her poetry, or did she
merely want to help her client, Valmont?

Annie put her head in the office doorway. Now off the phone, Wesley
remained focused on a document on the computer screen. "I'll be
with you in a minute," he said.

She liked seeing him bent in concentration, the neat firm line of his jaw. She entered the office, Sophie's old room, and sat on what had been Sophie's bed. When they'd changed the room to an office for Wesley, she'd moved the bed against the wall and covered it with pillows to make it look more like a daybed. She watched him tapping the keys, scrolling down, and frowning. She couldn't imagine Daphne's fingers on a computer keyboard; instead, closing her eyes, she pictured the pale hands buttoning the soft mohair sweater, turning up the collar of her blouse, and unbuttoning the top button for just the right effect. She relaxed into the pillows.

"That was Charlie on the phone," he said.

Annie opened her eyes. "Charlie, who used to be at the firm?"

"Yeah. He works for a small British firm now. Over near the Opéra. He asked me to help with a project he's doing for the U.S. Commerce Department."

"Great. See, you are getting more business." She sat up on her elbows.

"It's a small project. Where've you been all afternoon? I thought you weren't going to the office."

Annie told him about her afternoon with Daphne, holding back some of the details of the long lunch at the Flore. "It's amazing. I feel like I've known her forever. And she's taking my poems to a French publisher, Paul Valmont." Just saying his name made the project sound like a real possibility. "It's a small press, but well respected."

"I wouldn't get your hopes up." He'd shut down the computer and swiveled his office chair to face her. Despite his somber mood, he looked attractive to her, vulnerable, but in a sexy way, like some of the brooding French poets she'd studied in college.

"I'm not going to get my hopes up," she said. But she did feel a new kind of energy. A subtle positive force had come over her. She felt a looseness in her limbs and a flush of warmth in her veins. She knew it wasn't only the wine. "Wesley, I had fun this afternoon. Fun. Something I think you need more of." She stood up and pulled the velvet bow from her hair, allowing it to fall loosely about her face.

"Yeah, right." He looked away from her. "I have other things to think about besides fun."

"You shouldn't think about work so much."

"You mean lack of work." He turned the chair back to face the desk.

She went over to him. "Take off your glasses," she said, starting to massage the muscles in his neck. His skin was warm. She bent to kiss his head, his shaggy hair softer than it appeared.

He pulled his head away. "Come on, leave me alone."

"You don't mean that." She moved around and lowered herself into his lap. A small pile of papers slid onto the floor.

"Annie, look at what you're doing." He tried to lean away and reach for the papers scattered across the rug. "Annie, please."

"Please what?"

"Please, not now."

"I know what you need." She ran her fingers through his hair and down to his shoulders.

"Listen to me. I said, not now." His words felt like a slap.

"Well, when? Will you tell me that?" She reached to unbutton his shirt, but he took her hands in his own with a determined grip. She felt hot and embarrassed, but she couldn't stop. "What is it? You don't want sex?" The powerful word echoed in her ears. "There I've said it. You haven't touched me in months." He looked away, still holding her hands. Now her words poured forth in a torrent. "What's happening to us? You're not old; certainly I'm not. I still need you, Wes. This coldness, it's changing everything."

"I don't want to talk about it." He let go of her hands.

"We need to talk about it." She reached for his face, trying to get him to look her in the eye. "You don't want sex? Or is it me? You don't want me?"

"It's not about sex." He wouldn't look at her, and his tall, slender body remained rigid and inert.

"Maybe you should talk to someone?" She spoke softly, as if coaxing a difficult child.

"God, Annie. It's not that."

"I know what depression is. You remember my father."

"Look, I'm stuck inside here all day long trying to hang on to the few clients I've got, and trying to get new ones. It's not easy." His blue eyes darkened to the slate color of a rough sea. "This is not some kind of mental illness. It's very simple. I can't stand not having enough work to do. I feel like a goddamned failure, and it just keeps getting worse."

"You're not a failure."

"What would you call it then?"

"Wesley." She decided to take a different tack. "This is not just about you. We're in this together. This problem belongs to both of us, and you're shutting me out."

"Annie, just give me time. Everyone has their own way of coping." Now he sounded angry. He stood, nearly knocking her to the floor with the sudden movement. "I'm going out. I want to get some air." He clicked off the desk light and left her alone, standing in the dark.

Annie crossed the shadowed room and sank back onto the bed. At first she felt only shame. She curled into a ball, pulling her knees to her chest. Her hair fell lank around her face. Wesley didn't want her. He wouldn't allow her to help. She heard the front door close and his footsteps fading in retreat. The old familiar ache set in, the girlhood loneliness she'd endured when her father closed the door to his study, the way he used to shut her out. He had refused to talk about her mother, refused to reveal his sadness, refused to share their loss. She'd been powerless then, a mere child, unable to change her parent. Now, as she lay on the faded bedspread, a similar helplessness weighed upon her. She listened to her own breathing, the silence heavy. Part of her wanted to fall asleep and forget, but she could feel anger creeping in and taking over her body.

She would not let it happen again. She got up, went to the alcove off the living room, and turned on the lamp by her chair. The light fell across the fine old maple drop-front desk that had belonged to her mother. A photograph of her mother sat on top of the desk, along with a bud vase that she kept filled with seasonal blooms. It contained a sprig of holly, shiny dark green leaves and red berries. She studied the wide grin, the smooth forehead and straight nose, her mother's spirited expression that, along with the tilt of her head, said, "I dare you."

Annie sat down, picked up her notebook, and began to write. She jotted down words and phrases that helped to summon the still-imaginary place, God House. It already existed in her mind. A house where you would come alive—what had Daphne said? Annie didn't want to be an actress, like her mother, but she would be a poet. She gripped her pen more tightly and watched as the words spilled across the page.

FIVE

Le Bureau

"Perhaps you'd like to look at the photographs while we wait for François. I expect him soon."

Paul Valmont was younger than Annie expected. In the cool morning light she could detect flecks of gray in his dark hair, but he was not the aging widower who had occupied her imagination since his phone call. Daphne was right. He was good-looking, but in the French way, with strong features, deeply set eyes, and angles defining his face. His lips were full, capable of dangling the ubiquitous cigarette. He stood behind an elegant antique desk that looked nothing like the sleek modern furniture in the outer office where she had arrived. Loose papers, stacks of manuscripts, and books covered every inch of the surface, and a fountain pen lay in the crease of an open volume. Black ink markings still appeared wet on the page.

He reached for a well-worn leather portfolio that leaned against the side of his desk. "Let's go over to the table by the window. The light is better. I'm afraid that my desk is never clear."

"It's a beautiful desk," she said, noticing the carved legs and delicate inlaid wood along the edge.

"The desk of my father. The business belonged to him as well." He gestured to the wall of books. "My family has been in the book business for generations." The shelves on the wall behind him were filled with old leather books, finely tooled gold lettering glimmering on the spines. The shelves within reach of Valmont's desk chair overflowed with more modern volumes in colorful jackets, along with paperback editions squeezed horizontally into every available space.

Valmont pushed aside several manuscripts on the narrow table to make room for the portfolio. Annie stood beside him while he unfastened the worn black ribbon that held the two sides together and revealed a stack of black-and-white photographs separated by sheer creamy vellum sheets. His wide, pale hands shook slightly as he drew back the first page.

Annie looked down at the picture of an old woman, a cloth coat pulled tightly across her rounded back, sitting on a bench in what looked like the Luxembourg Gardens. Her swollen ankles were crossed, and her feet were barely contained in worn, unfashionable shoes. The light, soft and ethereal, was dreamlike. The photographer had captured her either in the first moments of dawn or at dusk. More likely dawn, as there was a freshness, a tenderness to the scene that implied the start of something. The photograph of this woman, alone on the bench, the row of trees behind her, and in the background a glimpse of an ornate marble statue from a more glorious era, infused Annie with a terrible feeling of loss.

"What do you think?" Valmont asked her.

"Lovely, sad . . . no, that's too simple." Her voice came out in a whisper. She tried to pull herself back together. "It's an extraordinary photograph," she said in a more normal voice.

He nodded, turned it over, and lifted another vellum sheet. The next photograph depicted three children playing on a merry-go-round, the old-fashioned kind, with benches set around a circular frame. Two of the children sat and held the center bar as the third, a boy with knee socks puddled around his ankles, held the wooden frame and ran beside it to keep it in motion. His legs looked airborne. The playground was tucked in a small park behind Notre-Dame Cathedral. Annie knew this park; she had taken Sophie there when she was a little girl. Again, the light was astounding. The picture was both intimate and grand, balancing the sweetness of children at play against the majesty of the cathedral.

"The light—there's such a tangible softness," she said.

He stood back from the table. "It makes me think of the Italian word *sfumato*. François achieves that same smoky edge in his photographs. Leonardo da Vinci was the first painter to create that effect."

Annie met his intense gaze. "Yes, that's it exactly," she said.

"Here's the one of Saint-Eustache. When I read your poem I thought immediately of François's photo. Your words and his image are in"—he hesitated—"harmony, yes, perfect harmony." He didn't pronounce the h. This made her smile.

His deep voice seemed gentler than when he'd telephoned. His accented English reminded her of the typical seductive Frenchmen in American movies, but his serious demeanor quickly dismantled this impression. "Please, take some time and study the others." He motioned to the portfolio. I'll go and see if François has arrived."

"Thank you," she said. "I've been anxious to look at them."

Annie was glad to have a few minutes alone to gather her thoughts. She hoped that over time he would become easier to talk to. Was it her own reserve or his formal nature that colored their conversation? He'd called her Madame when he telephoned to set up their appointment, but today she asked him to call her Annie. She liked the way he pronounced her name. It fell easily from his lips. He told her to call him Paul.

She had been struck by their difference in height when he stood next to her looking at the photographs—he was shorter by several inches. His upper body appeared strong and well muscled, but his legs looked thin under his heavy corduroy trousers. She noticed the hint of a limp when he left the office to look for the photographer. Annie wondered if he was recovering from an injury. Maybe it was the result of polio or some childhood illness.

She looked back at the pictures, turning them over one by one. They captured Paris in all her shades of beauty, all her moods, the traditional Paris along with the modern city that throbbed to a contemporary beat. They also had an introspective quality. On one level, the images told a story, but they held something back as well. Annie found herself trying to see beyond the edges of the photographs, as if there was something more the photographer was keeping from view. While not exactly secretive, they had a suggestive quality.

She stopped at the last two pictures, pulling in her breath. They were nudes, and while the previous scenes of the people and places of Paris had a sensual energy, they had not prepared her for these. The pictures worked as a pair and depicted a female torso from both sides. More abstract than the photographs of the city, they were still breathtakingly lifelike, and the breasts, rounded and petal soft, made Annie think of her own breasts, untouched for so long. The woman's back was long and serpentine, a fluid line. She felt flushed and imagined Valmont whispering *sfumato*. What was she thinking? She inserted the final sheet of vellum and closed the portfolio.

Annie could hear muffled voices beyond the closed door. Something about this man captured her imagination. She looked around his office again, hoping to discover more about him. She went behind the desk and studied some of the titles on the bookshelves. Unable to erase the image of the nude torsos, she closed her eyes, amazed at the powerful effect of those photographs. Turning back to the desk, she noticed an arresting photograph in a silver frame. She picked it up. The lovely heart-shaped face of a young woman with dark hair falling to one shoulder and huge doelike eyes stared back at her. From her clothing, Annie guessed it had been taken at least twenty years before. Nonetheless, the woman's energy seemed to pulse right through the frame. Paul had positioned it on the desk so the photograph would be in view any time he paused to look up from his work. It must be his wife. Judging from the picture, she would have been about Annie's own age if she were still alive. Annie was embarrassed to be found holding the picture when the door opened a moment later.

"A portrait of my wife," Valmont said.

Annie put the picture down. "I'm terribly sorry." She felt like she'd been caught trespassing. "She's very beautiful. I—"

He didn't let her complete her sentence, but he didn't appear angry. "Now you can meet the man responsible for that one as well as the others." He walked toward her, this time his limp more apparent, with his arm drawn around the shoulders of an elderly gentleman. "Madame Reed, Annie, I'd like to present François Naudin. He's eager to meet you."

"Indeed, madame, I have been longing to make your acquaintance."

Annie came from behind the desk and offered her hand. "I am delighted to meet you, Monsieur." Instead of shaking her hand, he bowed graciously and kissed it. "Please, call me Annie."

"And you must call me François."

Despite his advanced years, François walked with a jaunty step. Paul led him over to another chair near the desk, helping him the way a son would a father, François's eyes shone through his glasses, a clear hyacinth blue. His thick wiry hair, smoothed back behind his ears, was the same color as his neatly trimmed salt-and-pepper mustache. Annie sat beside him and Paul returned to his desk.

"So what do you think?" Paul asked.

"I loved them all." Annie looked over at the portfolio. "They are extraordinary photographs."

"I am pleased that you like them," François said.

"I envision the final book composed of twenty-five to thirty photographs with the poems on the facing page." He looked at Annie. "François has had many photographs published over the years, but this would be the first time an entire series would appear in one book."

"Paul is so kind to indulge me."

"Nonsense. This project is long overdue." Paul smiled warmly at the old man. First we must decide which photographs to include and—"

"Oh, I leave that to you," François said excitedly. "You are the one making the book."

Annie found it hard to believe that she was sitting here in this office. Daphne had given Paul her poems as promised, and to her amazement, he'd called almost immediately to arrange this meeting.

"Well, of course the photographs speak for themselves," Paul said, "but I think that the poems need to reflect the beauty of the images and in some way reinforce the visual message. Do you agree?" He looked at Annie.

"Oh, certainly." She could see that the project meant a great deal to him.

"A good idea, non?" François said. "Pictures and poems together?"

"I think it's a terrific idea," she said. "François, you are truly an artist, the very best. You capture the essence of Paris."

"François and I have talked about this book for many years. My father had wanted to do a book of François's photographs, but in those years when my father was still alive, François was too busy traveling and taking pictures for the newspapers."

"You're a photojournalist?" Annie asked.

"Not for many years, but that is how I spent my working life. A long time of living from the *valise*, you say—ah, yes, suitcase."

"How fascinating."

"I loved it, *mais oui*, but when I was a young man I wanted to make pictures as art. I had not thought of journalism then. You know of Eugene Atget? He began in the 1890s and photographed Paris every day for more than twenty years. Some call him the architectural historian of Paris. He influenced me greatly, *enormément*. But then came the war, and I used my camera for the army and later for the newspapers. There was no time for my art."

"It was not all bad, the war, I mean," Paul said. "After all, that is when you met Eileen. Sometimes good things come of bad situations."

"*Oui, oui, ma belle Eileen*. Paul is right. I met my wife during the war. She was a nurse, American, like you. Life is not the same without her."

"Oh, I'm sorry," Annie said.

"She died fifteen years ago." François became more subdued. "I think of her every day. She left a hole in my heart."

Annie saw that Paul was no longer paying attention to them but staring at the picture of his wife. François noticed too. "Paul, I am sorry," he said. "I know it is still very painful."

"I am fine, François." Paul appeared weary, drained of the enthusiasm he'd shown earlier. He looked at Annie. "You must excuse me. My wife and I were in an accident. On the *autoroute*, last spring. She did not survive." He folded his hands together and rested them on the desk as if trying to pull himself together.

Annie ached for this man. "Yes, Daphne told me that your wife had died. I'm so very sorry. I can't think of anything worse." Her words sounded inadequate and empty in her ears. To lose his wife in a grisly car crash seemed so cruel. His wife had been yanked away, taken from him while still in her prime.

"Tell me about your work, Annie," François said. "When did you discover you were a poet?"

"I've always loved writing." Annie liked the way he asked the question. She'd always known that it wasn't a matter of deciding to become a poet. Writing poetry had been part of her life for as long as she could remember. "When I was a little girl I wrote mostly stories. I was an only child and I loved to create stories about imaginary brothers and sisters. My aunt Kate saved them all, saying one day they would make up a book. Just childish scribblings, and they've since been lost. Her encouragement kept me going though. By the time I was in high school I knew that poetry was my first love."

"How do you begin a poem? Do you know right away where to start? I wonder if the process, the artistic process I mean, is the same as photography." François had removed his glasses and waited for her answer.

"I imagine it might be like when you decide to take a picture. It's usually something I see that triggers a new poem. It could be a place or an object. If it's a person, it might be the slightest gesture, a movement or glance, that becomes the kernel of an idea."

"And then what do you do?" Paul asked.

"I'm always making notes, and if the image keeps appearing, if it won't go away, I know that's it's worth continuing."

"That must take time," Paul said.

"Sometimes the idea and the images evolve very quickly, and other times I may linger on a piece for weeks. It's an organic process. I guess you could say that some poems grow more quickly than others. After that, there's the endless process of revising."

"François's photographs should lend themselves very well to your process," he said.

"Paris has always inspired me to write," she said. "I would love to try writing poems based on your pictures, François. They are already a poetic form."

"You are very kind, my dear." He bowed his head.

"What I suggest," said Paul in a more businesslike tone, "is that you select four or five photographs from this group and write about them. We like very much the poems you gave us, but we need to see if you can work from the pictures. Maybe you could send me a few poems early in the new year."

"I'd be happy to."

"Here are some copies of the originals," François said, handing her a thick brown envelope. "If you please, choose a few from this group. You can take them with you today."

Annie accepted the envelope. She had passed the first hurdle, but now she would have to prove that she could create the poems. Could she finish several poems in just a few weeks? And would they be good enough for those incredible photographs?

"It is quite amazing," Paul said. "If I hadn't told Daphne about looking for a poet, I never would have found you."

"I'm certainly grateful to her as well." Annie wondered how well he knew Daphne.

"Have you been to God House?" Paul asked.

"No. But I love the name. Daphne talks so much about it."

"I can see you there. It's a poet's kind of place."

"We must thank this English lady for bringing us together," François said, getting to his feet. "But enough talk of business. Now that I have met this charming poet, it would give me great pleasure to take you both to lunch. We will mark this day with *un bon repas*, a good meal. Are you free, Paul?"

Paul looked surprised at his suggestion but laughed. "It's a fine idea. François, you are a true Frenchman, never forgetting your appetite."

"*Et Madame Annie?*" François bowed in her direction.

"*Avec plaisir.*" Annie smiled. And it was with pleasure that she accepted this unexpected invitation. They hadn't even decided on whether to use her poems for the book, but she sensed that François was hungry for company and probably wanted to prolong his visit. She could see how he enjoyed being with Paul.

"Annie?" Wesley's voice boomed from the front hall.

"I'm in the kitchen." She pulled a steaming casserole from the oven and set it on the counter. Her anger at Wesley had slowly diffused over the last few days, and she'd grown accustomed to their silent truce. She had been deeply hurt by Wesley's rejection the afternoon she'd returned from her long lunch with Daphne. That scene was humiliating to her;

his pushing her away had seemed so cruel at the time. She knew his self-esteem was at an all-time low, and she wanted to be patient, but it was becoming more difficult. Poor Wesley. It seemed like his life was closing down on him, just as hers was starting to take off in a new direction.

Since that afternoon, he had been courteous, almost to a fault, and she accepted the distance he seemed to want to keep between them. Now she was excited to tell him about the possibility of the book and her meeting with the two men that morning. Already she felt a glimmer of hope. François and Paul had been charming at lunch, and they had,spoken so positively of the poems she had submitted.

When she'd come home, still buoyed by the glimpse of their literary world, she decided to make an especially nice meal for Wesley. As she chopped and sautéed, she thought back to everything that had happened during the lunch. François had kept them both laughing by telling stories about Paul as a little boy. Both families spent summers together in the south of France in a charming village called La Motte in the hills above Saint-Tropez. She enjoyed hearing about their shared history. But later, when the waiter brought their coffees, a shadow fell across Paul's face. He looked older, and the pleasure of their conversation seemed to fade as the weight of grief fell again across his shoulders. Everyone had his share of troubles, it seemed.

"There you are." Wesley came into the kitchen and drew her into an awkward hug. "I've got some good news." He grinned, clutching a bag from Petit Robert, the wine shop around the corner. He had more color in his face, perhaps from a long walk in the fresh air. He pulled out a bottle of champagne. "Let's have a toast. Can dinner wait a few minutes?"

"Where've you been?" she asked. He looked breathless and his glasses had steamed up when he came in from the cold to the warm kitchen. "This must be great news." Her heart started to lift, as she imagined a new client or some new case. She pulled off her apron. "I'll get the glasses." Wesley twisted the bottle with one hand while holding the cork steady with the other. He was rewarded with the festive *pop*, and she followed him into the living room.

"Our luck is changing. Wait till you hear." He sat on the sofa and Annie set the champagne flutes before him on the coffee table. He poured, and Annie watched as the sparkling wine danced into the glasses. She reached across and smoothed his hair. He took her hand and drew it to his lips, kissing the tips of her fingers, then lifted his glass and touched hers. He still remembered the easy, affectionate gestures that she thought had disappeared along with his job at the firm.

"Here's to our future," he said. His voice was light and happy, as if nothing had fallen between them, nothing had weighed on them month after month.

"Tell me, Wes, what is it?" She took a big sip, relieved that Wesley was back, the sunny, dynamic Wesley she had married. She could hardly believe the sudden change. She moved closer to him.

"Hal called this morning."

"Well good." She smiled. "I'm glad to hear that."

"His firm has agreed to a lateral hire, and he said I would be the ideal candidate." He grinned and leaned back into the cushions. "He waited to call me until he got the go-ahead from the hiring committee."

"Why, that's wonderful! Great news." So many good things had happened in one day! "Did he offer you the job?"

"Not exactly. I need to go to Washington and meet the other partners. Hal says it's just a formality. I'm the kind of attorney they're looking for. I have all the right credentials. He's setting up interviews with the other partners. I'm going over right after New Year's."

"So would you be opening a Paris office for them?"

"Annie, no. I told you. It would mean a job in Washington." He sipped his champagne.

She put her glass down. She didn't remember him telling her this. "What do you mean?"

"I told you it was a possibility. That we might need to move if I found a job somewhere else." He reached for her again, but she moved forward to the edge of the sofa.

"I thought Hal was just going to give you some business here in Paris. That you were waiting to hear about that."

"That's how it started, but now they want me to join the firm. Don't worry. We don't have to move right away. I could go over and find a place to live, and you could come later."

"Later?"

"In the spring. Whenever."

"What did you tell him?"

"Hal?"

"Yes, Hal. What did you tell him?"

"Well, if the meetings go well in January, and there's no reason they shouldn't, that I could start right away."

Annie felt like she'd been carried up onto a cloud, floated momentarily, and then dropped to earth.

"I can't believe you're telling me this. When the firm closed we both made the decision to stay in Paris. I love it here. I thought you loved it here even more." She hardly knew where to begin. "Why didn't you talk to me first? I feel like this is so sudden, so . . . out of the blue."

"Christ, Annie. It's not out of the blue. You know what it's been like. I don't love it here when I don't have any work, or even the prospect of a job. I'm sick of scrambling for work. This firm is perfect. I have the expertise they need. They want me. Did you ever consider that?"

"Of course I understand all that. It's just so sudden. You told me you were going to look for more work here, try to build your practice again."

"Well, it hasn't been working."

"You said it would take time." She took another sip of champagne. It no longer tasted the same.

"Well, it's taking too much time and it's just too damned uncertain. Look, Annie, this is a job. It's a job that I want."

"And just because you want it, I'm supposed to want it too?"

"Look. You wanted me to find a job." His voice took on a sharp edge. "You wanted me to work again. Well, I've found a way. I don't see why you're so upset."

"It's just a lot to get used to, that's all. We made the decision not to move last spring. You were actually quite adamant about wanting to stay in Paris."

"Well, I've changed my mind. I'm trying to make a living, you know."

"I know that. I just wish you'd think about what this is like for me." She put her glass down. "I met with the editor today, Daphne's friend.

Both he and the photographer liked my work, and they want me to do some poems based on the photographs—sort of on a trial basis." The dream of doing the book was fading fast. Even if she got an offer, how could she write the poems in all this upheaval?

"So, write the poems."

"What's the point now? I'd need much more time here. It's not that simple. If they agree to hire me, I'd have to meet with them. There would be editing and—"

"Come on, Annie. If you did the book, you can fax back and forth. Look, we're moving to Washington, not the end of the earth. You can write poems anywhere. Plus we'll be so much closer to Sophie."

How could she argue with that? She missed her daughter terribly.

"See, Annie, everything is going to change now. I feel so much better knowing I have a future. It will be like it used to." He set his glass down and put his arm around her.

Could it ever be like it used to be? she wondered. "But I hate the thought of leaving," she said. His arm weighed on her shoulder. "We've been here so long."

"Paris will always be here." He stroked her face and pulled her closer.

All of this made sense, but her heart felt heavy. Wesley's familiar hug didn't feel the way it used to.

"Come on, Annie. I want this job, and I want things to be better for us." He tipped her chin up and looked into her eyes.

Here was the man she thought she knew better than anyone else on earth, and yet it was like she was sitting next to a stranger. She couldn't believe how easily he'd made this decision. She turned her head away. "So, we erase the last six months and do whatever you want to fix it?" She pulled away and stood up.

"You're being unreasonable now," he said, his voice cool.

Perhaps she was, but she felt suddenly powerless. She tried to push her angry reaction aside. "I don't know. I just don't know." She left her glass of champagne on the coffee table and walked back to the kitchen to resurrect the casserole for dinner.

SIX

Le Solstice d'Hiver

The morning of the solstice party Annie awoke with a sore throat, a raw dryness that indicated a cold coming on. She didn't want to get sick. She needed all her energy to finish getting the semester grades for the students at Liberal Arts Abroad, and that meant tracking down stodgy French university officials who saw no need to supply this information promptly. She wanted to get this work behind her so she could give her full attention to writing the poems for Valmont. Even if she and Wesley had to leave Paris, she still wanted the chance to do the book.

She had started work on two of the photographs. The poem about the merry-go-round was going well, but it wasn't going to be easy to finish three or four poems by the start of the year. While she walked on the street, rode the subway, even while she loaded the dishwasher, words and phrases played out in her head. The scenes in the photographs kept reappearing before her, and her small notebook was filling quickly with ideas.

Later that morning, after swallowing two aspirin, she drew a steaming hot bath, hoping a good soak would make her feel better. Wesley was out on a wine-buying mission, and she'd given him a list of several ingredients she'd forgotten. She bent her knees and eased lower into the hot water. The tap at her feet dripped slow fat drops like the quiet, even ticking of a clock. She was glad for this time alone. The book project felt like a lifeline to her, something she could wrap her mind around, something to focus on besides the probable move to America.

Wesley kept trying to convince her of the benefits of moving. He would be earning more money and she wouldn't have to work. She could write full-time. His arguments were valid. Would things return to normal once he had a job in a firm, a job with more security? Sometimes Annie had a difficult time remembering what their lives were like before the law firm had closed. Wesley had been busy, sometimes distracted even then, a level of tension often coloring his behavior. But the stresses of his job, demanding at times, were like dark clouds that frequently lifted and allowed his kind, loving nature to shine through. They used to spend winter evenings together, each at one end of the living room sofa, he with papers in his lap, his glasses sliding down his face, she with her nose in a book. "Wesley, listen to this"—and she'd read him a few lines of a poem. He'd push his papers aside, close his eyes, and reach over to rest his hand on her shoulder or her neck, touching her lightly and giving her his full attention. They used to talk, laugh about inconsequential things, and ultimately he'd pull her up from the cushions and they'd walk arm in arm to bed, their lovemaking smoothing out any unpleasantness from the day.

Wesley refused to discuss what they would be giving up if they moved to Washington, what it would be like to leave. They'd lived in Paris for more than twenty years, and it felt like home. The rhythm of their days, enriched with everything Paris had to offer, had fueled Annie's creative life and made her happy. If Wesley got the job in Washington, he would immediately have the challenging, interesting world of his office, whereas she would be alone in a new place, setting up a home, starting over. He ignored her doubts and reservations. This infuriated Annie.

Last spring, when Wilson & James closed their doors, they had had many long talks about the future and had made a joint decision to stay in Paris. Now Wesley was making this decision without her. When she'd asked him about interviewing with other American firms in Paris, he said it was impossible, that law firms were cutting back, that American companies turned to French law firms to handle their business problems.

"But have you interviewed anywhere recently? Have you called anyone? Wesley, I just wish you wouldn't give up so soon. The decision you make affects both of us."

"So you want me to turn this down? You want me to stay here and be miserable?"

"Of course not. If we have to move, we'll move."

She secretly hoped that the job in Washington wouldn't come through. She knew this way of thinking was uncharitable, but perhaps all of a sudden some new client would appear. Wesley just needed a few good clients to get his practice going.

Annie placed the hot washcloth over her face. The moist heat felt good and blocked out the day ahead. Normally she looked forward to parties. She enjoyed the preparation and the planning almost as much as the main event. Now, with her bad throat and aching head, she viewed the solstice dinner as something to get through. She breathed into the soap-scented cloth. At least there was Daphne. Knowing that she was coming tonight made the party more exciting. They'd talked several times, and Daphne had been delighted that Paul wanted her to try writing some of the poems. "Paul's quite taken with you. He says the work you submitted was really good. Now you both have me to thank." Her throaty British laugh had pleased Annie. "You'll be forever in my debt," she had joked.

"I still have to show him I can write poems for specific photographs. He hasn't made an offer yet."

"Oh. He will."

"How can you be so sure?"

But Daphne had simply laughed and offered no reply.

Annie thought again of Paul. This would be his first Christmas without his wife. She took the cloth off her face and began to scrub her shoulders and back. When she and Wesley were first married, she always called him into the bathroom to wash her back. She shivered in the cooling water. She mustn't linger any longer. There was much to do to be ready for her guests. She would get through this party and somehow she would get through Christmas.

Annie treasured all the Christmases they had spent in Paris. The emphasis was on lovely family meals and finding the very best delicacies: rich foie gras from the Dordogne, vintage champagnes, smoky wild mushrooms to stuff the turkey, and a gorgeous bûche de Noël, the cake shaped like a yule log that tasted as wonderful as it looked.

Annie did not look back on her childhood Christmases with nostalgia. The old clapboard farmhouse in Vermont should have been an idyllic setting, and eccentric Aunt Kate, wisps of gray hair escaping her bun, wrapping packages in hand-decorated brown paper, should have completed the image of a charming old-fashioned holiday scene. Annie knew her father tried to be more cheerful at Christmas, but there were years when he rarely came out of his study, leaving it to his sister to create the magic of the season.

Aunt Kate was heroic in her efforts. They tromped through the woods, cutting greens and gathering berries and cones to decorate the house. Updyke, the old Dutch gardener who helped Kate with the heavier work, cut them a tree from his farm and set it up in the front parlor. Annie remembered, during the best years, her father standing on a ladder and putting up the lights. "Can I start to decorate? Please, Daddy, can I put up the ornaments?" The answer was always the same. "One thing at a time, Anne Louise; you need to do things in their proper order. You can put up the ornaments after I finish the lights."

Annie was in charge of place cards for their ritual Christmas Eve dinners. She printed out each name in her best grammar school penmanship and decorated the cards with glue and glitter. Aunt Kate had her write a little poem—she called them verses—for each guest. They invited their nearest neighbors and usually a few teachers from the college. Aunt Kate referred to some of them as the lonely hearts. "Keep the verses for the lonely hearts nice and jolly." Everyone read their poems, predictable childish rhymes, aloud during dessert, and Annie loved hearing her own words come alive.

Despite the often large gatherings of guests, Annie knew that someone was missing from the holiday table. The old feeling of longing would come back like the flurries of snow that announced the season. She wanted her mother. Her father felt it too, and at many Christmas dinners he excused himself and left the table before the meal was over. Then the joyous clatter of Aunt Kate's preparations paled and the old wooden house became hollow, silent, and cold.

It had been a relief to celebrate Christmas in France with a completely different set of rituals. Annie loved going to midnight mass in one of the great churches. Saint-Eustache had been their favorite. The forest of Gothic columns and the vaulted ceiling throwing back the voluminous sounds of the organ made the Christmas story come alive for Annie. The powerful beauty of that place made her believe in God. When Sophie was old enough, Annie had made Christmas a child-centered holiday. Each year she sewed a new dress for Sophie and made a matching one for her doll. She tied red bows on Sophie's teddy bears and filled a stocking with trinkets for her to find on Christmas morning.

Wesley had loved their holidays together too. He adored reading to Sophie, and after " 'Twas the Night Before Christmas," he bundled her up for midnight mass. She would sleep between them, her head nuzzled in the crook of his arm. On Christmas morning they would open their presents and go to the Verniers' for a wonderful lunch. When Sophie came home from college for the holidays, Wesley would take her off on special shopping expeditions, just the two of them. Last year, when Sophie was twenty-one, he took her to the Ritz for lunch and a glass of champagne. He'd wanted her twenty-first Christmas to be a memorable one. He was the kind of attentive father that Annie had always wished for.

Now she had guests coming to dinner, the beginning of a rotten cold, and Sophie wasn't coming home for Christmas at all. Annie stepped out of the bath, shivered, and reached for the towel.

"Fascinating, the way you've used the patchwork quilts, even one for a tablecloth," Daphne said. She fingered the soft old fabric on the table.

"This one is just a quilt top," Annie said. "It's never been backed or pieced together." Annie was pleased that Daphne had praised the way she'd decorated the apartment. It was less formal than the Verniers' living room, but Annie thought the large beige linen sofa and deep armchairs were elegant as well as comfortable. She'd used soft floral fabrics and pieces of antique linens to cover pillows and to skirt the two round tables on either side of the sofa. The walls were painted a warm cream, the color of buttermilk.

"Marvelous how these French Country pieces blend so well with your quilts," Daphne said.

"The quilts on the walls make me think of medieval times, when they hung tapestries on the walls of the châteaux," Céleste said. She nodded toward the log-cabin pattern that hung behind the sofa. The soft teal, pinks, and beige patchwork picked up the colors of the room. "And look at the beautiful bowl of white roses. A feast for the eyes on a winter night."

Annie was proud of her table decorations. She'd chosen white roses because they reminded her of the snow in Vermont, and she'd tied bundles of holly to the pair of candelabra with wide satin ribbons. She liked the way the ornate twisting silver contrasted with the simple patchwork and her French pottery dishes. Besides the candles burning on the table, Wesley had lit more than a dozen candles in the living room and hall. Annie had collected the candlesticks over the years, and they ranged from the fancy French candelabra she'd found at the Paris flea markets to some humble wooden spools she'd discovered one summer in Vermont. The apartment did look pretty in the soft flickering light.

The first guests had arrived within a few minutes of one another: Céleste and Georges bearing a sumptuous box of chocolates and Mary and Tom, who gave Wesley an expensive bottle of Cognac. Georges, looking like an Old World French gentleman, wore a dark suit, and Céleste looked pretty and festive in a red silk dress, a departure from her usually understated clothes.

Mary, a petite woman with dark straight hair, looked a little tired to Annie—perhaps she was coming down with a cold too. Usually so lively and talkative, she seemed subdued. Tom and Mary did not have children, and Annie wondered if Mary, now close to forty, ever would. Tom was ten years her senior and had the handsome, energetic looks of a man who knew how to have a good time, the kind of man who would have been the center of attention at college fraternity parties. Annie knew his bravado and charm had a lot to do with his success in international sales.

Daphne had come later, once the others had settled comfortably by the fire. When Annie answered the door, Daphne had entered the hall with flushed cheeks, her golden hair sprinkled lightly by the wet evening mist, and smelling of cold. She offered Annie a small, beautifully wrapped gift. "Something just for you," she said, giving Annie a hug. Annie took the now-familiar blue cape, and they joined the others in the living room.

The party began well, and by the time they gathered around the table for dinner, Annie was relaxed and had begun to enjoy herself. They started into the first course while the filet of beef roasted in the oven and a mushroom shallot red wine sauce simmered on the stove. Wesley looked handsome to her in his tweed sport coat and festive red bow tie on a crisp blue shirt. At moments like this, she forgot her anger. She liked seeing him at the opposite end of their table. It felt like some kind of balance had been restored to their marriage. He was a charming host, talking and laughing easily with their guests. The echo of their angry words that had hung about the apartment all week was fading away in the convivial chatter.

Annie had seated Céleste and Mary on either side of her husband. Georges, who sat at Annie's left, was already joking with Wesley about the merits of that night's wine. "I think you've finally outdone your-self on this pick," he said. He swirled the wine and lowered his nose into the glass to capture the bouquet. "Indeed, it's a good one, but I don't believe it was only thirty euros." He shook his head. "I think I'll need the receipt for proof."

"They challenge each other to find the most beautiful wine for a price," Céleste explained to the others. She looked across the table and met her husband's eyes, smiling affectionately. Annie couldn't imagine Georges and Céleste having an argument. She'd never heard her utter a critical word about her husband.

"You know I play by the rules." Wesley laughed. "Wait until you try the Sauternes I have for dessert." They continued to banter about which wine merchants you could trust.

Annie worried about Mary, who talked and laughed politely along with the others, all while keeping an attentive eye on Tom. He sat across the table from her, between Céleste and Daphne. Tom had given Daphne an appreciative glance when he first arrived. He also compli-mented her on her dress when he took his place beside her at dinner, but so far he was keeping his flirtatious tendencies in check. Mary had told Annie about a huge fight they'd had recently. She worried that Tom was seeing another woman. Annie had found it unsettling to hear about her boss's unhappy marriage. Mary had enumerated the symp-toms, as if describing a disease where powerful germs had infected their once happy lives. Just listening to Mary's woes made Annie fearful, as though it could be contagious. She had no intention of sharing her own troubles. Telling Mary about the strain in her marriage would make it all too real. She didn't want to put her doubts into words.

Daphne, who appeared to be enjoying herself, looked beautiful in the candlelight. She wore a dress of rich plum velvet, cut high in front, scooped low in back, with long, tightly fitted sleeves that came to a point at the wrists. Annie wondered how long it would be before Tom would find some excuse to put his hands on her. In Annie's experience, his friendly hugs had always seemed a little too close, a little too long.

Annie wore a simple black V-neck dress that was several years old. She had pulled her hair back and wore Aunt Kate's string of garnet beads. She felt her cold moving into her sinuses and knew that she was paler than usual. "Are you trying to look like Emily Dickinson?" Wesley had said when she dressed. He gave her a teasing grin.

Annie pictured the New England poet with her serious face and prim appearance. "That's not funny. You know I feel terrible." She turned to have him finish pulling the zipper on her dress. "You should be glad I didn't spend money on something new."

"We won't have to think so much about money when I get the job in Washington." He fastened the top hook.

"We agreed not to discuss it anymore." She frowned and smoothed the front panel of her dress.

"I think Miss Dickinson needs a kiss." He reached for her. "I think a little love would cheer her up." Wesley had been trying to humor her for days. She stepped away from him and went to her dressing table to put on more blush.

Now, sitting next to Daphne, she wished she had bought a new dress, something that would make her feel younger, sexier. The decongestant she had taken earlier made her head feel packed with cotton. Her ears rang.

"God, this fish thing is delicious," Daphne said, referring to the first course. "You must tell us how you did it."

Making the fish mousse had almost put Annie back to bed. By the middle of the afternoon her headache had returned, her throat was noticeably sore, and she had dirtied every bowl in the kitchen. Wesley had gone out again on some unnamed errand, and she still had to make the sauce for the main course.

"I'm so glad you like it." Annie was used to making an effort for good meals. Cooking was so much a part of French life. Everything revolved around good food, creating the perfect dish, whether it was making your mother-in-law's *coq au vin* or trying to replicate a fresh asparagus soup you tasted at a country inn. Food was continually shopped for, discussed, debated, and argued over.

Céleste helped Annie clear the table and bring out the main course. The meat looked too rare to Annie, so she covered each serving liberally with the mushroom sauce and hoped no one would notice. Thankfully, the candlelight made it difficult to see.

"Let's have more of that red wine, Wesley," Tom said, louder than necessary. "It's a winner in my book." Mary shot him a warning look.

"So it seems we're both in sales," Tom said, leaning toward Daphne. "Opposite ends of the spectrum. You're in antiques, and I'm in emerging technologies."

"I must confess, I'm not very high-tech, and I don't have a clue as to what's emerging." Daphne looked away from him and handed Annie the basket of bread.

"Nothing you need to know," he said. "It's apparent you have other talents." He fingered her sleeve. "Your dress is the exact color of tonight's wine. Great Burgundy. Great bouquet." He swirled the wine in his glass.

Wesley, who was making his way around the table pouring the wine, leaned in between Daphne and Tom, putting a protective hand on her shoulder. She looked up at him, ignoring Tom. "I would love to talk to your sister about buying some of her quilts," she said. She tilted her head so that her hair brushed across Wesley's hand. "I have several clients who might be interested."

"I'll put Madeleine in touch with you," Wesley said. "I'll probably be seeing her soon anyway. I'm going to the States right after the holidays." Wesley removed his hand from her shoulder and reached for Tom's glass.

"I think Tom's already enjoyed too much of your winning wine," Mary said, forcing a quick laugh. The lines across her forehead deepened. Tom had downed several large glasses of Scotch before dinner. Wesley hesitated but Tom lifted his glass defiantly.

"I'll be the judge of that," Tom said. Mary said nothing, but Annie could see the tension in her jaw. Wesley filled his glass and, after serving the others, returned to his place at the head of the table.

"*Qu'est-ce que tu dis?* What are you saying?" Georges asked. "Did I hear something about going to America?" He looked over his glasses at his friend.

Annie rested her fork on the side of her plate. The beef was too rare and difficult to chew. It had needed more time in the oven. She glanced at Wesley; he smiled, met her gaze, and looked away.

"I'm going to Washington to see about a job." Wesley spoke easily, as if going to America to interview for a job were an everyday occurrence. "I'll probably stop in New York on the way home." He looked down the table at Daphne. "Madeleine lives an hour outside the city."

"What job is this?" Georges asked. "Have you some kind of news?"

Céleste had stopped eating and looked at Annie as if she should have forewarned her of information of this magnitude. Everyone stopped talking and looked expectantly at Wesley.

"I'm going over for the last round of interviews." He told them about the job, what he would be doing for the firm in Washington, and how important the move was for his career. He sounded sure of himself, sure that he would get the offer. Annie couldn't believe he was telling everyone now. It wasn't like Wesley to speak prematurely about such a major decision.

"But can you not work for them in Paris?" Georges asked. "Continue in your office here?"

"I'll still travel to Paris, but they need me there, based in the home office," he explained.

"But Wesley, *mon chéri*, how can you leave Paris?" Céleste asked with earnest concern. "You and Annie are like our family."

"We'll still be like family. You and Georges can come over and visit, and we'll come back as well."

"My, this is big news," Daphne said. She gave Annie a strange look, as though Annie had misled her in some way.

Annie felt the evening going sour. The candlesticks dripped globules of wax, some of which pooled on the quilt-covered table. The roses, now fully open, dropped spent petals, but she could not smell their hothouse scent or taste the dinner that cooled before her.

"Sounds like a great opportunity to me," Tom said. His speech slurred and his eyelids drooped. Mary glared across the table at her husband. "Looks like you'll have to find a new assistant, Mary." He slumped in his chair.

"That's just one of my problems," his wife said flatly.

"We will miss you, my dears," Céleste said, having regained her composure. "Georges said the other day we need to start to travel more. So you can be sure we'll come to see you."

"Of course," Georges said. "Your career is important. We must become accustomed to this." He looked around the table in a paternal manner as if it was everyone's duty to pull together and support their friends. Céleste agreed with Georges that Wesley's job was certainly the priority.

Mary turned to Annie. "Don't worry about Liberal Arts Abroad. We'll try to figure something out. It just won't be the same without you in the office."

"But we're not moving for sure." Annie didn't recognize the sound of her own voice. Her words sounded rough and squeaky, out of her control. "I mean, Wesley hasn't been offered this job yet, not officially anyway."

"Annie," Wesley said. His tone of voice was that of a father about to scold a child.

"It's not something we should be discussing yet," Annie said. Everyone looked at her. It was if she had spoken out of turn, as if she were at fault.

"Annie is right. We don't want to spoil the chances." Céleste smiled down at Annie and patted Wesley's arm. "Wesley, chéri, you will tell us when you know something, and for now we will keep good thoughts. I'm sure that soon there will be something to celebrate and then we will toast your good fortune."

"*Mais, oui*," Georges said. "You've had a fine career in Paris, but if they need you in Washington, we will just have to accept our loss."

"Annie, you must tell everyone about Valmont and the book," Daphne said. Her clear voice immediately drew their attention. "Wesley, isn't it terrific?" She lifted her wineglass in his direction. "It looks like Annie may have a new job too."

Annie paled. She had hoped to become invisible after her outburst, and all she wanted now was to crawl into bed. Daphne leaned in next to her and put her arm around her shoulders. Annie felt the soft velvet sleeve against her neck.

"Go on, tell them," Daphne said.

"I've been asked to submit some poems for a book of photographs," she began, and told them that if the editor and photographer liked her work, she might be asked to collaborate with them on the project. She explained the concept for the book.

"Annie, that's great news." Mary smiled. "I know how much time you've been spending on your writing lately. This sounds like a wonderful opportunity."

"*Oui, oui, Annie, c'est fantastique.*" Céleste smiled at Annie with admiration.

"Yes," Daphne said. "It's quite an extraordinary coincidence. Paul Valmont, Naudin's editor and the man publishing the book, is a friend of mine. I showed him Annie's poems, and *voilà*, it was a perfect arrangement."

"It's not definite yet." Annie wanted to put an end to this topic. "They still have to approve of the new poems."

"You know they will," Daphne said.

"Here, here," Georges said, coming to his feet. "Let's offer a toast to Annie, our poet."

Everyone lifted their glasses. Annie managed to smile at the faces turning toward her in the shadowy light.

"And to Daphne," Wesley said, "who managed to bring Annie and Valmont together." The next few minutes were a blur of clinking glasses, more pouring of wine, and the clatter of silverware as everyone resumed their dinners.

"Come," Daphne whispered later in Annie's ear, "I know you aren't feeling well. Let me help you with dessert."

Daphne followed Annie into the kitchen. "Have you noticed," Daphne said quietly, "men never do a bloody thing in this country, except maybe pour the wine." Annie took the chocolate mousse out of the refrigerator. "It's true, isn't it?" Daphne said. "And we can pour our own wine—so who needs them?" She laughed and carried the dessert plates to the dining room.

The morning after the party Annie awoke to the sounds of distant voices. She pulled up the down comforter and rolled over, hoping to go back to sleep. She was glad the winter solstice was behind them. She looked forward to the lengthening days and wondered if this bleak stretch in her marriage would start to lighten as well. Perhaps when Wesley got to Washington he would come to understand the magnitude of this decision and the reality that a move would entail. She hoped he would change his mind.

When she awoke for the second time, she realized that she heard Wesley talking to Daphne. She felt worse than ever, a combination of too much wine, her dreadful cold, and not enough sleep. She and Daphne had stayed up talking until nearly three. After Wesley had gone to bed they shared a pot of herbal tea at the kitchen table. Daphne sat in Wesley's place.

"That's the trouble with marriage," Daphne had said. "It's always getting in the way and holding one person back."

"What do you mean?"

"I can tell you don't want to leave Paris."

"You're right. I don't. But Wesley wants the job in Washington."

"I can see that, but if you had a job offer in New York or someplace, do you think Wesley would drop everything and follow?"

"Of course not, but it's never come up."

"So you're prepared to leave everything behind to make his life easier?"

"When you marry someone, you're in it together. You have to compromise."

"So someone loses." She shook her head.

"That's not the way to look at it." Annie's voice wavered. "Marriage is just like that. You make concessions all the time."

"He's asking for a pretty big concession." Daphne yawned and stretched. "I guess the bottom line is that I'm not for marriage."

"What about Antoinette?" Annie asked, curious about Daphne's godmother. "Did she ever marry?"

"Never. She was a beautiful woman, extremely independent and a serious feminist at heart. For her it was a question of power. She relished making her own choices. No man would ever hold her back."

Now, remembering those words, Annie decided it was time to get up. She pulled on her robe, went to the kitchen for coffee, and carried her cup down the hall toward their voices, which came from Wesley's office.

"I hope we didn't wake you, Annie." Wesley looked up at her. "You deserved to sleep in after all the work for the dinner. It was a great party."

"Your darling husband heard me shuffling about and brought me coffee in bed." Daphne sounded groggy, her voice lower, a sexy pitch. "We've been having a good rehash of last night's events. Tom Sanders is a handful. Poor Mary." Daphne laughed and leaned back against the pillows, wearing what appeared to be a man's white shirt. The upper buttons were undone and her breasts were easily seen through the fine material. Annie was reminded briefly of François's photograph of the female nude. Daphne's knees, covered in blankets, were drawn up in an attempt at modesty, and her thick hair was tousled from sleep. Wesley sat at the foot of the bed holding his mug of coffee. He had pulled on jeans and wore an old gray sweater. From the doorway, despite his graying hair, he looked like the rumpled law student Annie had fallen in love with.

For a brief moment Annie felt forgotten. She was the one on the edge of the photograph, the one cropped out and discarded. Then a feeling of uneasiness rushed through her like a deep blush reaching all the way to the roots of her hair. She thought she saw desire on Wesley's face, desire for that ripe young woman at arm's reach. Mixed in with this came her own sense of longing. She didn't want to be the one left out. This woman sitting in bed in Wesley's office no longer felt like her friend, her understanding ally in the war with her husband. They looked too comfortable together, sharing intimate words while she had slept down the hall.

"Come and sit, darling." Wesley seemed glad to see her, which annoyed Annie all the more. "I'm going to go out and get croissants."

What was she thinking? Wesley and Daphne had merely been talking, allowing her to sleep longer and recover from the party.

"Croissants would be marvelous," Daphne said. "Thanks, Wesley. I love talking over a successful party. Really fun people, and the food was spectacular."

Annie tried to smile and took Wesley's place at the foot of the bed. He leaned down and kissed the top of her head. "I won't be long." Annie found his departing kiss irritating. She knew it was an empty gesture. He was trying to look like the good husband.

Daphne lowered her legs, not bothering with modesty, looking lovely in the sheer nightshirt. She didn't look like she'd had only a few hours sleep. "So how are things going with the poems?"

"Pretty well. Paul wants to see a few after the new year." Annie felt her doubt return. "I don't know what I think now. None of this is going to be easy, especially if we have to move right away."

"Don't look so glum. I know he's going to ask you to do the book. As for the rest, I bet everything will work out." Daphne pulled her knees up again and smiled. "I've had a brilliant idea. You and Wesley must come out to God House for New Year's Eve."

"You mean for the night?" Annie asked.

"Not just the night. The entire weekend." Daphne swung her legs to the floor and came over to Annie, still perched at the foot of the bed. She took Annie's face in her hands. "But now, dear friend, you are a sick girl and you must get back to bed and stay there." Her hands were warm and gentle on Annie's pale cheeks. "And, I want you to open your present."

SEVEN

Le Réveillon

Wesley closed the trunk of their car, which he had double-parked in front of
their building on the rue des Archives. The old Fiat, dusty from sitting
in a garage a few blocks away, hummed along as if ready for a stretch
on the open road. He and Annie rarely used their car in the city, letting
it sit idle except for weekend trips to the country or their annual summer vacation. This year they hadn't taken a vacation, and the Fiat had
remained unused for months. Maybe a few trips to the country would
have lifted Wesley's spirits. Annie hadn't thought of that. He wore his
old camel hair topcoat, a bit worn and gently frayed at the cuffs, but it
still looked elegant on his tall frame. The scarf around his neck was the
color of his eyes, a cool blue.

"I think I've got everything." Annie clutched a heavy canvas satchel
in one arm and carried a large, beautifully wrapped package in the
other along with a lush bouquet of flowers. The canvas bag held two
bottles of champagne, a side of smoked salmon from their favorite
specialty shop, and a fine bottle of port that Wesley had put aside for
a special occasion. The package contained a mohair lap robe in a smoky
shade of green. Annie had thought of Daphne when she saw it in a
boutique on the rue Saint-Honoré.

"Isn't that an awfully expensive present?" Wesley had said.

"Christmas isn't the time of year to be frugal," she'd told him.

Wesley maneuvered the car carefully in and out of the narrow
streets toward the Péripherique that would carry them around Paris
and onto the Autoroute du Nord. At last they were headed to God
House. It was the final day of the year. It felt good to be going on

a trip, if only for a few nights in the country. A momentary hush hung over the city, as if the busy world was holding its breath.

Traffic was light. They need not worry about *bouchons*. Annie loved that French word, meaning bottle stopper or cork, to indicate a traffic jam. The French always found a way to get back to wine. The afternoon was what Annie began to think of as Naudin gray, the soft, shadowless light that François captured in his photographs. Less cold than usual, it seemed a mild, harmless afternoon.

"Will anyone else be there?" Wesley asked, his voice just audible over the roar of the motor.

"I thought it was just us," Annie said. "But Daphne told me a friend was visiting from England. Tim something."

"Just a friend?" Wesley asked the question that Annie had been mulling over. In all their talks Daphne had never mentioned this man. She'd led Annie to believe that there was no one special in her life at the moment.

"I think he's an old friend. Maybe someone from her childhood."

Wesley remained quiet for the next few minutes of the trip. He took an exit off the main highway. Daphne had suggested they take a secondary road, a more scenic route, once they were away from the city. Annie held the directions and map on her lap.

Riding in the small car together created an intimacy that neither of them could escape. They had made it through Christmas. The days following the party Wesley had retreated to his office for hours at a time. Annie knew he was working on materials to take to the firm in Washington. She'd finished her work at Liberal Arts Abroad and used the final days before Christmas for her writing. When she'd asked Wesley one evening to look over a draft, he had refused.

"I don't see why you're spending all your time on those poems. This guy may not even choose you to do the book."

"I think I have a chance. Besides, I love the photographs. They inspire me to write."

"But what's the point? We're going to be moving. I'm going to need you to get the apartment ready to sell."

Need. There it was again. Annie had loved creating a family and being needed by her husband and daughter, but more and more she could feel the seeds of resentment take hold. She also felt the need to write, to make these the best poems possible. The inevitable move to Washington hung between them. She was hurt that Wesley showed no interest in her poems. He was angry that she showed no enthusiasm for starting a new life back in the States. Something in his antagonism made Annie all the more determined to succeed with her poems.

Now, traveling through the bleak outskirts of Paris, they passed industrial sites and blocks of public housing. The light was flat, the scenery uninteresting. Eventually the landscape opened up and they saw farmhouses, barns, and the open fields. The small farms formed a patchwork of geometric shapes, fallow fields of brown, gray, and dusty gold, much like the colors in the Reeds' antique quilts. The sky had also changed, the steady gray giving way to shifting clouds that revealed hints of blue far above.

Annie felt her spirits lift. She'd finally recovered from her cold, and Liberal Arts Abroad was closed for the next few weeks. She'd spent hours in her alcove chair writing as well as reading the delicate leather volume of poems that was Daphne's present to her on the night of the solstice. A collection of poems by Paul Verlaine—a perfect gift. She had told Daphne that Verlaine was her favorite French poet. Before beginning her own work, she liked to read a few of his poems. His clarity of language, melodic verses, and painterly images always inspired her.

"I thought Sophie sounded stressed yesterday," Wesley said. They had called, waking her in Los Angeles, still groggy in her efficiency apartment after she'd worked long into the night. Wesley kept his eyes intently on the road. He'd never grown accustomed to the wild French drivers. He'd been complaining lately about other typically French things, like noisy motorbikes, heavy smoking in restaurants, and a recent transit strike, all attempts to make his case for a new life in America.

"I'm glad I'm not the only one who worries about her," Annie said.

"Of course I worry about her. You don't have the right to say that."

"I wish you'd told her to ease up a bit. You know she's working too hard. What is she trying to prove?"

"I think being the youngest one on this assignment makes her insecure." He glanced up at the rearview mirror. "She's trying to show them she can manage."

Wesley put on the brake and slowed, allowing a black diesel Mercedes to pass. "Can't these idiots ever take their time?" His jaw was clenched and he looked pale in the winter light. The exhaust fumes seeped into their car like the ill will that had settled around them.

"Annie, if we lived closer, it would make a difference. If I took the job in Washington, we could travel more, see Sophie on weekends."

"You've said it over and over." She tried to keep from getting angry again. "Please, let's not talk about it all the time. After all, nothing's decided yet." Annie stared out across a flat field with a farmhouse in the distance. It looked uninhabited, mournful.

"They will offer me the job. Hal is convinced of it."

"Okay, fine. You're getting the job." Why did everything have to go back to this? It would be nice to be closer to Sophie. She would concentrate on that; it was the only positive aspect of moving.

Annie cracked her window open, suddenly hungry for a burst of country air. It was not as cold as she expected. The road curved and Wesley slowed. "There's the sign for Villandry," she said.

"I see it."

"It'll be a right turn." She smoothed out the map and looked at the directions she'd written on the back of an envelope. Wesley downshifted and turned off the main road following the signs for centre ville. "Go past the train station, make a left turn onto the road along the river," she read from her notes. "Watch for the iron gates about a kilometer on the right."

A few minutes later they wound along a small country road. Annie caught brief glimpses of the river that shimmered beyond wide fields and lightly forested landscape. Then the trees thickened and the road climbed, hiding the river from view. The first rays of sun she'd seen in weeks peeked through the clouds.

"There's the entrance," she said, pointing to a pair of open iron gates set in moss-covered stone pillars. Wesley turned and the car crunched onto the gravel drive. The grounds were heavily planted with evergreens and shrubs, and as the drive curved to the left, the house came into view.

God House. Annie was enchanted immediately. They approached the house, a gray two-story building dressed in ivy with three tall windows on either side of the front door. While not enormous, this house with its faded sage green shutters was perfectly proportioned. Its beauty came from an understated charm, like a well-groomed Frenchwoman of a certain age, perfectly suited to her surroundings. Wesley pulled up in front of what must have been a coach house but now served as the garage. A fairly large building, mottled gray stucco like the house, it had two sets of double doors, painted the same green as the shutters, and heavy iron hinges. A shiny dark blue sports car with English plates sat in front of one set of doors, and Wesley stopped their car in front of the others. "What a lovely house," Annie said. They sat for a moment in silence.

"Look," Wesley said, "let's put the rest of our lives on hold for a bit and just enjoy this." He reached out and touched her cheek. His hand was warm, familiar. Annie looked at him and nodded. He turned and got out and she opened her door, carefully disentangling herself from the packages around her feet. The air, while still winter cold, was softer and seemed to hold promise. Wesley came around and helped lift the satchel of wine while Annie extracted the bouquet of flowers and her present for Daphne.

"Welcome to God House. You're here at last." Daphne emerged from the front door. She wore jeans, a baggy navy pullover sweater, and a large white apron. Her hair was clipped up on her head with a large yellow plastic barrette, and her cheeks were flushed, as if she'd been cooking over a hot stove. Annie handed her the flowers.

"God, they are truly gorgeous." Daphne bent her head and breathed in the springtime scent of the white flowers tinged with green. "Viburnum, my favorite. Such extravagance. You are a dear." She hugged Annie and then Wesley. "What can I carry?"

"Not a thing," Wesley said. "Annie, if you can take the wine bag, I'll get our suitcases from the trunk."

Annie gave Daphne the wrapped package and picked up the wine.

"What, more presents?" Daphne said.

"Your Christmas gift. That's all."

"Now you're spoiling me." She tucked the package under her arm and cradled the white flowers. "Follow me and I'll show you where to put your things."

Daphne led the way up the wide curved front steps and into the hall. Annie was instantly transported. The hall, painted a pale peach with a black-and-white stone floor, reminded her of a Vermeer painting. A wide curved staircase led to the floor above. On the right was a low fruitwood chest that smelled of lemon oil. On it sat a big silver bowl of fresh pears and a Chinese lamp decorated with coral-colored dragons. Beyond the chest Annie saw a long wooden bench under which several pairs of boots and shoes were lined up. Light flooded in from double doors at the opposite end of the hall, balancing the entranceway.

Wesley set the bags down at the foot of the stairs. "What a great house," he said.

"Daphne, it's so beautiful," Annie said. "I had no idea."

Daphne put her arm around Annie. "Yes, it is beautiful, and it's the sort of beauty that never fades." She looked directly at Annie. "I think you'll see that when you spend more time here." She released her arm. "Well now, let's take all this to the kitchen."

They followed her through another set of double doors opening into the dining room and beyond into the kitchen, a huge old-fashioned room dominated by a well-worn pine table in the middle.

"It smells wonderful in here," Wesley said. "I had a feeling you'd be a terrific cook."

"I'm terrible on my own, but I love to cook for friends." Daphne set the flowers down on the sink and came over to Wesley, drawing her arm around his waist. "I'm going to put you to work too, my sweet," she said in a joking voice. "As a matter of fact, there are some bottles of Haut-Brion on the sideboard in the dining room that need to be decanted before dinner." She handed Wesley a corkscrew and a dish towel.

"I'm happy to help," he said. He left them together and went to see about the wine.

"And what can I do?" Annie asked.

"Let's get everything in the fridge first," Daphne answered. "Later, I'll let you arrange the salmon on the platter. I think it would be quite nice to have it with cocktails in the drawing room before dinner."

Annie saw that Daphne had put a long silver tray on the kitchen table. "It looks like you've been polishing as well as cooking."

"I have Berthe to help me. You can use that for the salmon." Daphne opened the oven door, bathing them in the scent of garlic, wine, and roasting meat. She adjusted the heat.

"Who's Berthe?" Annie could feel her mouth water.

"Believe it or not, she's my nanny. Actually, my nanny when I was a little girl at God House. She has always lived here. She looked after me when I was young and she took care of Antoinette until she died. She lives in the apartment above the garage." Daphne moved about the kitchen with a relaxed ease, sliding the salmon onto a shelf in the refrigerator and removing a platter of cheeses to warm to room temperature.

"Does she help with the cooking?" Annie asked, looking toward the oven.

"I don't let her do as much now. She's pretty old. I made the stew. It's called *daube provençal*. It's like a beef stew, but with tons of garlic and orange peel. It simmers all day in this gorgeous Burgundy."

"You're the one spoiling us. It smells divine."

"Let's go put your things upstairs, and then I thought a walk might be nice. First we'll get that darling husband of yours to carry the bags."

"You even arranged to have the sun come out for us," Wesley said. He wore a sweater and a sport coat with the collar pulled up, his blue scarf tied loosely around his neck. His favorite corduroy trousers looked suitable for a country walk. Annie had borrowed a pair of rubber boots from the collection in the front hall. She'd put on heavy socks and now clomped along with a childish gait, the boots slipping loosely on her feet. The ground was wet from several days of rain.

"Not bad for a winter's day," Daphne said. She wore a man's gray overcoat that almost reached her ankles. Annie had never seen such a masculine outfit look so feminine, but Daphne seemed to have a way with clothes, making the sloppiest old things come alive. Daphne thrust her hands in the pockets and led them through the garden. "Tim decided not to join us. Felt he needed a nap. I'm afraid we started celebrating the new year a little early last night." She laughed and shook her head. "He wants to be in good form for tonight."

Annie left her coat unbuttoned and enjoyed feeling the soft breeze as it touched her face and throat. This weather was a reprieve from the cold, brittle weeks before Christmas. They were barely into winter, but Annie wondered often where she would be when spring finally arrived. They followed Daphne along a gravel path through the back garden toward the river. "It's absolutely lovely," Annie said. "It must be heaven in the summer."

"I'm afraid I like to let it go wild." Daphne surveyed the garden. "The French are so damned ordered in their plantings. All those parterres and such." She frowned. "I like the plants to have their way."

"Sounds like a nice form of rebellion," Wesley said.

Annie could see that this garden, even in its present state, had great bones. Although she admired the restrained classical lines of French gardens, she loved this random beauty too. They walked past the ragged winter borders and overgrown shrubs that swayed seductively in the breeze. The colors of the dormant plants were still muted—gray-greens, soft heathers, shades of honey and wheat. Annie reached up and unfastened her barrette, allowing her hair to fall to her shoulders and blow freely.

At the foot of the garden they came to a well-trod path along the river. As they walked, their conversation became intermittent. Annie drank in the mellow beauty of this last day of the year. The river pulsed along, very much a live creature in the bucolic landscape. She tossed a small stick into the cold, dark water and watched as the current carried it along until it floated into a gentle pool close to shore. There it swirled gently for a moment before the larger stream pulled it out to deeper waters.

They faced into the wind when they turned to go back to the house. Annie liked the way the breeze lifted her hair, and she felt her old energy return. She reached for Wesley's arm, but Daphne stepped between them, hooking her arms into both of theirs. They fell into step and made their way back to the house. The sun was quickly going down. The sky took on a pewter cast, and the temperature began to drop. Wesley reached up to retie his scarf. "I guess I should have worn my overcoat," he said.

"You'll warm up at God House," Daphne replied. She linked her arm back in his.

Later, after reading by the window in their bedroom while Wesley napped, Annie got dressed for the evening and went down to help with dinner. She stepped into the living room, a large rectangular room softened with ample sofas, faded oriental rugs, and windows draped in heavy silk. Its pale shades of green and gold matched those in the winter garden.

"Why, hello. You must be the lovely Annie that Daphne's talked so much about." The voice startled her. She had forgotten about Daphne's friend. He stood up from the fireplace, where he had been arranging logs. He was a slight man of medium height, and the first thing Annie noticed was his handsome, deeply tanned face. He must have spent his Christmas holiday in some tropical climate.

"Tim Fortney." He grinned, revealing the white teeth of a movie star. "I'd shake your hand, but as you see"—he lifted his soot-covered hands and shrugged.

"Yes, I'm Annie. So nice to meet you." She was glad to be wearing her dressy silver sweater and her mother's pearls. He seemed to be studying her carefully. He had tossed his navy blazer onto the sofa, and the sleeves of his pristine white shirt had been rolled back for his task.

"Daphne always gives me the jobs she knows I'll hate. Building fires is not my thing." He bent once again and lit a match to the crumpled paper in the grate. The flame curled up, lapping at the heavier logs stacked above.

"It looks like it's going to work," she said. They stood side by side watching the flames spread.

"It's just the paper right now. Let's give it a minute, and then I'll mix a pitcher of martinis." He flashed a grin. "Gin is something I know how to do."

"I'm going to get the salmon out of the fridge," Annie said. "That's my assignment for the evening." She smiled and headed toward the kitchen. "Then I'll be back for one of your drinks." She felt him watching her as she left the room.

Annie paused in the dining room to admire the table. Daphne had arranged the richly scented viburnum along with shiny dark green holly in a long silver trough. She'd added strands of variegated ivy, which trailed onto the dark wooden table. The table itself was set simply with starched white linen napkins and heavy silver cutlery. The sideboard, where Wesley had lined up the bottles of red wine, was of the same dark, highly polished wood, and above it hung a medieval tapestry in blues, green, and gold. Annie could picture Old World French aristocrats seated in this room.

In the kitchen she arranged the smoked salmon on the long silver tray. She placed paper-thin slices of lemon around the edges and sprinkled capers across the pink fish. Daphne had left a silver fork for the platter and a basket of toast. Annie liked having a moment to herself. She was able to take in the details and savor the unique presence of God House. In a strange way, she felt like she had been there before. The house seemed to have taken hold of her, making her feel comfortable and at home. Being there made her want to shed all the disquiet of the past months with Wesley. She felt like this was a place where she could start over, reinvent herself.

Annie heard laughter and a crackling fire when she returned to the living room with her platter of salmon.

"There's the lovely lady who left me for a fish." Tim came over to Annie and took the platter, setting it down on the coffee table in front of the fire. "Now I'll give you a proper greeting." He kissed Annie on both cheeks in the French tradition.

"Annie, you do look lovely." Daphne got up from the sofa she had been sharing with Wesley. She wore a midnight-blue velvet sheath, more like a nightgown than a dress. "Tim mixes a mean martini." She lifted her glass. "We also have champagne."

"Champagne would be great." She saw that Wesley had chosen champagne over gin. Tim promptly handed her a flute and took a seat beside her on the sofa across from Wesley and Daphne. Wesley looked so much younger this evening, as if he had shed years since coming through the gates and up the gravel drive to God House. He looked more American in this setting, but in the best way: even-featured, long-legged, healthy, very male. She could tell he enjoyed sitting beside Daphne, who carried off her sensuous state of dishabille without any problem.

"Daphne, is that your mother?" Wesley asked, looking at the portrait above the mantel. The woman in the picture looked out at them with gray eyes, a strongly defined jaw, and shimmering hair styled in the pageboy of an earlier era. She wore trousers and a finely cut tweed jacket and looked very at home in this richly appointed but somewhat faded room.

"Yes," she said. "Her name was Nora. My father had it painted when she turned thirty. One of the few periods of happiness in their lives, or so I'm told. Ten years later he left for New York. Another woman, or some business scheme he couldn't miss out on." Daphne shrugged. "Only problem was he left my mother pregnant with me."

"Oh, how terrible," Annie said.

"Not one of my favorite topics. Is it, Tim darling?"

Tim said nothing and sipped his drink.

"It's a fine portrait," Wesley said.

Annie studied the face. She did resemble Daphne; though, with shorter hair, this could be the portrait of a poetic young man. It had a certain masculine quality.

"Mother gave it to Antoinette, and it's been hanging there as long as I remember." Daphne eased back into the sofa and rested her head on a cushion. Her hair looked freshly washed and fell in loose, golden strands against the navy velvet of her dress.

"So what brings you to God House?" Wesley asked Tim.

"I'm on my way to Nice, a business trip. Daphne's always a good sport about putting me up. We've known each other for eons." He looked at Daphne, a smile playing around the corners of his mouth. "It certainly beats a hotel."

"No question about that," Wesley said.

"What sort of business?" Annie asked.

"I'm a yacht broker. I've been in the Bahamas all fall, but I have a Greek client meeting me in Nice." He drank the last of his martini and reached for the pitcher on the table. "Say, Daph, I saw Roger in London. He says he's coming to France in a few weeks."

"Roger is my older brother." Daphne wore a closed expression. "He thinks he's an investment manager, but let's just say that family and money don't mix very well."

"Now, Daphne, you're sounding like a cranky baby sister," Tim said, though he didn't seem surprised at her disapproval.

Daphne put her empty martini glass on the coffee table. "Tim, be a darling and entertain Annie while Wesley helps me in the kitchen." She stood up and gave a hand to Wesley as if to draw him up out of the deep cushions.

"You're sure you don't want my help?" Annie asked.

"Not right now, thanks. The rest is easy, and Berthe's going to do the washing up tomorrow. Enjoy the fire. Tim will take care of you for a few minutes."

"I'm good at that," Tim said leaning back and crossing his legs.

Annie could smell the spicy sweetness of his cologne.

It was after nine when they went in to dinner. The viburnum blossoms on the table released their heady fragrance, and Wesley had lit the tall, creamy tapers in the center of the table. They began with oysters that Tim had picked up in a seaside town on his way to God House. The cold ocean saltiness shocked Annie's tongue. Looking at them, limpid and wet in their shells, made Annie think of the lustrous Dutch still lifes that hung in the Louvre. Indeed, the entire dinner would have suited an artist's eye.

Annie loved having recovered her sense of taste; in fact she felt like all her senses had come alive again. She savored every detail of the evening: the finely minced orange rind floating in the wine-flavored sauce, the sharp tang of a Roquefort cheese contrasting with a luscious Saint Alembert, and the velvety smoothness of chocolate mousse on her tongue. The glimmering candles dripped onto the table like the final minutes of the year ticking away. She noticed that each time Tim got up to pour more wine, he touched Daphne in some way: a hand on her shoulder, fingers lifting a lock of hair, and finally, a kiss planted on the back of her neck. Daphne seemed to ignore these flirtatious gestures.

During dessert, he directed his attention to Annie. "Gorgeous pearls," he said, fingering the triple strand around her neck. Then he took a sprig of viburnum from the bouquet and placed it behind her ear. "Now you look like the medieval princess in the tapestry." He laughed, as if he no longer cared about propriety. She saw Wesley's mouth tighten across the table.

After dinner in the drawing room, Tim poured Cognac into a glass, swirled it, and held it to her lips. Annie took the glass. The amber liquid felt like an explosion in her throat. Wesley moved beside her and slipped his hand around her waist. Annie leaned into him, allowing her head to fall back against his neck.

"My dears," Daphne said, "we need to toast the New Year quickly. I think it's already past midnight." Annie heard the slur of wine in her voice. They had all drunk a lot during dinner. "Wesley, darling, would you mind?"

Wesley withdrew his arm and went over to the drinks table where Daphne had set another bottle of champagne. He opened the final bottle, and the evening became a blur of toasts, silly stories, laughter, and finally kisses all around to celebrate the new year. Tim's body felt hard and unfamiliar when he pulled Annie to him. Daphne hugged Annie and whispered in her ear, "Here's to Annie, the new Annie," and then Wesley kissed her deeply in front of all of them before leading her upstairs for the night.

Annie's head swirled when she climbed the stairs. Wesley did not release her hand, and when they reached the landing, their shadows fell as one in the dimly lit hall. He opened the door to their room, and she heard it click shut behind her as they crossed the darkness to the bed. She collapsed back onto the fluffy duvet. She saw the outline of Wesley above her and the shimmer of moonlight on the ceiling. Then the almost-forgotten warmth of his body covered hers.

"Annie, my Annie." The quiet, rhythmic refrain hummed in her ears as her name crossed his lips. Did he need to remind himself that it was she moving under him? Or could he be thinking of Daphne without her velvet dress?

Later, as they lay skin to skin, his lips on the back of her neck, she let herself dream. She saw herself being carried down a river. She floated freely, her hair loosely splayed like the reeds that caressed her skin and tickled her legs. A voice called her, a woman's voice. She tried to answer but no sound came out. The water became turbulent, the current stronger, and the voice slowly faded, lost in the roar of water.

EIGHT

La Pluie

Tim Fortney did not look as handsome or as tanned in the morning. It was still early when Annie slipped out of bed and left Wesley in the depths of sleep. She had come downstairs and found Tim standing in the living room staring out the front windows at the slow, steady drizzle falling onto the drive.

"Are you leaving?" She'd seen a duffel bag and briefcase next to the bench in the hall.

"Did we wake you?" He sipped from a mug of coffee. "I'm afraid Daphne and I had a bit of a row." He turned away from the window. He had deep circles under his eyes.

"I didn't hear anything." Annie shifted uneasily, not quite sure what was expected of her. "I'm sorry you had a disagreement."

"History tends to repeat itself in this house," he said.

"What do you mean?" Annie asked. She wished she had some coffee. Her head felt fuzzy, not quite clear of sleep.

"Daphne's a lot like her mother." He offered no movie-star grin today. "That's not always a good thing."

"You've known Daphne a long time," she said.

"Her brother and I were at school together."

"Roger?"

"Yes. He's not the villain she'd have you believe, by the way. They've had their arguments over money, but it's more complicated than that."

"What do you mean?" Annie had a stale taste in her mouth. She hadn't anticipated this kind of conversation so early in the day.

Tim studied her face as though trying to decide how much to tell her. He set his coffee down. "I met Daphne when she was sixteen.

I was twenty-one." He closed his eyes for an instant, perhaps trying to see that moment all over again. "It was a sort of golden summer—long, endless fair days—there's never been another like it, none that I can remember. I was besotted. There's no other word for it."

"This was in England?" Annie asked.

"Yes. Their country home in Devon. Roger was wonderful to Daphne. They did everything together. She adored him." He paused and looked up at the portrait of Nora. "She was pretty wild."

"You mean Daphne?"

"Both of them, really." He exhaled, blowing his breath out through his teeth. "Nora wanted everyone to be happy. She gave Roger and Daphne free rein. It was the kind of summer when everyone let down their guard. One party flowed into the next. We migrated from house to house. At the end of the summer Nora hosted a group of young people, friends of Roger's and mine from university. There was a girl."

"A friend of Daphne's?"

"No. That was part of the problem." His face hardened. "Tessa Hardwick. She'd been part of the group all summer. For some reason Daphne never liked her. None of us knew then how serious Roger was, how important this girl had become to him. Except maybe Daphne."

Tim went over to one of the sofas and sat down with the weariness of an old man. Someone had straightened the living room, and the down cushions, crushed from the weight of their bodies the night before, were plumped up, ready for a new day, a new year. The lingering wineglasses, blurred with sediment, had been taken away, the liquor bottles securely corked and placed neatly in a row on the drinks table. The fireplace gaped, cold and empty, the ashes swept back under the grate.

Tim remained silent for a moment, as if lacking the energy to go on. He leaned forward, rested his elbows on his knees, and clasped his hands. Annie felt the presence of the portrait. The artist had painted Nora so that her eyes watched you everywhere you went in the room. It was as if she were listening to Tim's account years after some event.

"There was an accident." Tim stood. "Everything changed after that."

"What sort of accident?"

"There was the drinking; probably drugs too." He walked back to the window.

The rain was heavy now, coursing down in sheets. Annie watched Tim, waiting for some sort of revelation. She folded her arms across her chest. The room was cold.

"You should ask Daphne," he said. "You should ask her to tell the story." He looked angry, the lines around his mouth tight. "Roger turned against his sister, naturally. Poor bloke. What would you expect? Then Daphne kind of went off the deep end. Depression, breakdown, whatever you want to call it. Nora brought Daphne here to recover. Daphne always made her escapes to God House. Just like Nora. I thought I could help her through it," he said bitterly. "I loved her still." He lowered his head.

"So you came to God House then?" Annie was now totally confused. "What sort of accident?"

"Jesus. Talk about cruelty. The way she treats people . . ."

"Surely Daphne had friends who cared about her? Other boyfriends?"

"Oh yeah. Boyfriends. Girlfriends too." He stood up. He face was pinched and angry. "Maybe you should ask her about that." His tone was sarcastic.

Annie couldn't think why any of this would matter now. Whatever had upset Tim had happened years ago. He obviously cared for Daphne. But last night she'd made it pretty clear that she wasn't interested, at least not in the way he'd hoped.

"Are you still in love with Daphne?" The question popped out.

"Let's just say I can't seem to stay away. I don't think Daphne knows what she wants." He shook his head. "Part of the problem is this house. She'd never give this up. I know it's lovely. But don't let it fool you," he said with disgust. "This place is in a time warp." He got up and walked back to the hall. Annie followed him.

"Well, I'm sorry," she said, leaning against the door frame, "I mean I'm sorry things didn't work out as you'd hoped." She watched him pull on his coat and carry his bags to the door. She wondered where Daphne was now.

He turned back and looked at Annie once more. "Are you in love with Wesley?"

"He's my husband," she said. She wished he would go. She'd had enough of his angry ranting.

"I'd be careful," he said. "You seem like a nice person." He hesitated, then spoke again. "You don't want to get entangled in all this." He pulled the heavy door shut behind him.

Annie stood still in the silent hall. Tim's words hung in the air, sinister. What he'd described sounded terrible. Be careful of what? Tim made it sound like Daphne posed some kind of threat. Ridiculous. Thanks to Daphne, she had found someone who might publish her poems, and Daphne had done nothing but encourage Annie to do what she loved.

And how dare he question her about loving Wesley? What had given him that idea? Wesley hadn't been easy to love lately, but that would change; she knew it would.

Annie buttoned her cardigan sweater and went into the kitchen toward the welcoming aroma of coffee. Her hands trembled when she poured the black liquid into a heavy porcelain cup. She added hot milk from a saucepan on the stove, drew her hands around the smooth warmth, and drank, determined to ignore Tim's ugly words.

Daphne called the long conservatory that stretched across the back of the house the glass room. Another childhood name, like God House. Annie stood there watching the rain, still heavy, patter and splash onto the flagstone terrace outside the French doors. Some of the gutters backed up, causing the rain to gush in torrents off the corners of the roof, but the wide stone floor beneath her remained dry. God House felt like a sturdy ship that had seen rough weather before and was prepared for combat, come what may. She held a second cup of coffee and looked out at the river at the foot of the garden. Even at this distance, it looked threatening. It surged along with a mind of its own.

"I see you found the coffee." Daphne's voice jarred Annie out of her reverie.

"Thank you. It's delicious. Just what I need."

"I hope your head isn't as bad as mine." This morning Daphne's face was strained, the skin below her eyes looked gently bruised and the lines around her wide mouth deeper. She looked older.

"The kitchen is totally cleaned up," Annie said. "Your Berthe is like a fairy godmother."

"It makes her happy to be helpful." Daphne looked over at the iron garden table in the corner. "Have you eaten anything yet?"

"No, but I was about to." She had only just thought about eating.

"Have you been up long?" Daphne asked.

Annie thought she saw a shadow of concern cross Daphne's face. "No. Not long. Wesley is still asleep." Annie followed Daphne over to the table where Berthe had set out the breakfast. Beside the basket of croissants, there were butter and jam and a platter of cheeses and fruit.

"See, she's an angel," Daphne said. "She gets these divine buttery croissants from the village, and it's my idea to have cheese."

"I saw Tim just before he left," Annie said.

"He wanted to get an early start," Daphne said. "With all this rain it'll be rough going. I'm glad you aren't leaving until tomorrow." They sat down in the dark green wicker chairs that looked like they belonged in a garden. Daphne passed Annie the basket of croissants.

A lurking uncertainty made Annie persist. "I thought he was staying until tomorrow as well. He said you'd had an argument."

"Oh, God." Daphne leaned back in her chair. "To make a long story short, we've been together off and on. More off than on, really. I told him this morning that it just wasn't going to work." She rubbed her eyes. "He didn't want to hear that, of course."

Annie paused and considered whether or not she should continue. She thought again of Tim's parting words. He'd spoken about Daphne as if she'd been some kind of mental case. "He told me about the summer when you met and that there had been some kind of accident—"

"What did he tell you?" Her voice was sharp.

"He said I should ask you about it."

"Oh Christ. I can't believe he started dredging all that up again—just because I won't fall in love with him. A lot happened that summer, not all very happy. But it's ancient history and doesn't do any of us any good to talk about it. We've all managed to move on." She shook her head. "He's totally ridiculous. I am fond of Tim, but I'm not in love with him. I certainly don't want to traipse around the globe watching him sell sailboats." Daphne put her elbows on the table and cradled her chin in her hands. She stared out beyond the breakfast table toward the river. Her face, last night so beautiful and animated, was slack and void of expression, offering no clues, no hint of the truth.

"Look," Annie said. "This is no way to start a new year. I'm sorry I brought it up." She reached out and fingered a basket filled with forced narcissus in the center of the table. "The flowers are lovely. The scent fills the whole room."

"You really are sweet," Daphne said, and she reached across the table and squeezed Annie's hand. "Look, what shall we do today? Lunch out, a walk, what do you think?"

"I don't mean to be rude, but I'd love to spend some time today writing," Annie said. "I sent Paul a few poems before we left Paris, but I need to finish the last two."

"Well then, of course, that's what you should do. I didn't plan anything, thinking we'd sleep in this morning and maybe take another big walk later. You can have the entire day to write."

"You're sure?"

"Of course." She smiled. "We'll finish our coffee and I'll set you up in the library. There's a small fireplace in there and a lovely big desk facing the window." Daphne leaned back in her chair and seemed pleased with this plan. Annie was ready for some time to herself. She heard footsteps in the kitchen, and a moment later Wesley appeared.

"There you are. The poet and her muse?" Wesley carried a cup of coffee and came to join them. He looked boyishly happy in a rumpled shirt and baggy corduroy trousers. "Happy new year, Daphne." He bowed in mock politeness. "How are you, Annie sweet?" He met her eyes, bent to kiss her cheek, and touched the back of her neck lightly as he slid into the chair across from them.

"You look like a contented man," Daphne said.

"I think the year's off to a good start." He grinned and reached for a croissant. "More good things to eat. Does it ever end?"

"Not today anyway. Berthe's making a wonderful bouillabaisse for supper. Her parents were from Marseilles. It's an old family recipe."

"I love bouillabaisse," Annie said.

"Your wife is going to spend the day in the library. She has an editor she needs to impress." She looked across at Wesley. "You appear to be in good form today. Maybe later you and I could hike over to the next village. There's an old coach house that's been turned into an inn. We could have a quick bite. You wouldn't mind, would you, Annie?"

"You want to go out in this rain?" Annie asked.

"I think it's going to let up," Daphne said. The sky did appear lighter. "Right now I'm going to go check in with Berthe. The library's ready when you are. Oh, and the matches are on the mantel if you want a fire." She pushed her chair back and smiled at them. There was more color in her face. "I'll see you later."

Daphne left the glass room, and Wesley reached for Annie's hand.

Annie put down her pen. She sat curled on the love seat next to the fire. The embers glowed. She'd already burned most of the logs in the basket near the grate. At first it felt strange to be sitting alone on that somber winter day, but then she'd become absorbed in her work. The small library, just beyond the living room, appealed to her more than any other room in the house. The writing desk felt welcoming, and while working there she would look up intermittently to watch the shifting weather. One entire wall was covered with bookshelves, and on the opposite wall, above a table laden with books and magazines, was a series of black-and-white drawings, genre scenes and quiet interiors, that begged further study.

After several hours at the desk, Annie carried her notebooks to the love seat and covered her legs with the paisley shawl she'd found draped over its back. She didn't know what time it was, but the sky was darkening and it looked as if the rain that had let up that afternoon was spitting lightly onto the terrace in the garden.

Earlier that afternoon, she'd watched Daphne and Wesley layer up with sweaters and rain gear. Daphne found a pair of foul-weather boots large enough for Wesley. Their easy banter diminished as they walked down the drive. Annie didn't mind seeing them go. The house itself offered a kind of solace. She didn't feel lonely, and a curious detachment had settled over her when she sat down to work.

The final two poems were nearly finished, but now she was finding it difficult to concentrate. The leather volume of Verlaine's poems was on the table beside her. She looked again at the inscription Daphne had written in black ink with a wide-nib pen. "To Annie, to inspire you in the days ahead . . . Daphne—" Indeed. The days ahead. Where would this new year lead?

The book fell open to her favorite poem, "Il pleure dans mon coeur." The last two lines in the first stanza had been running through her head for days. *"Quelle est cette langueur qui pénètre mon coeur?"* What was this feeling making its way into her heart? Wesley had finally made love to her on that last cold night of the year, but she felt plagued by an uncertainty that wouldn't go away. Some days she didn't care if she ever recaptured the joy in her marriage; on others, she physically ached to have Wesley back the way he used to be.

"Now, there's a serious face." Daphne stood in the doorway to the library. She was flushed, and damp strands of hair clung to her cheeks.

Annie hadn't heard her come in. "You're back," she said, consciously trying to look more cheerful.

"Did you finish?"

"Finished for now, anyway. Where's Wesley?"

"I sent him to the kitchen to make tea. He's soaked too. It started raining about a mile from the house. We should have carried umbrellas, but it didn't matter." She fingered her wet hair. "We'll warm up."

"Did you have a nice lunch?" Annie asked.

"Not great. The inn was closed, so we ended up in a nasty little café down the road. We each had a beer and a poor excuse for a cheese sandwich. What about you?"

"I had some cheese and fruit. I'm saving room for dinner."

"Berthe will be over at about six. Listen, I'm going to run a tub. When Wesley brings the tea in here, would you bring a cup up to me?"

"I'd be glad to. How do you like it?"

"No sugar, just a splat of milk. Shall I put on another log?" Daphne moved about the room turning on a few lights.

"That's okay," Annie said. "I'll do it." She got up and took the last log from the basket.

"I'll ask Wesley to bring in some more wood. I showed him where the firewood is kept." Daphne stopped before leaving the room. "I thought you might like to look at this." She pulled a leather-bound photo album from a low shelf. "These are photographs of my mother, Antoinette, and me when I was little. Also, the gardens in summer. Antoinette was an incredible gardener." She handed Annie the maroon-covered book that was rimmed in a delicate border of fleur-de-lis tooled in gold leaf. "I hear the kettle whistling. See you in a bit."

Annie sat down again close to the fire, the book in her lap. The log flamed heartily and crackled in the grate, sending out renewed warmth. She was glad that tea was on the way. She opened to the first page and studied the petite, dark-haired woman smiling into the camera. *Feminine* was the first word that came to mind. Her features were small and delicate, the eyes wide open as if she'd been suddenly caught unaware, her chin tilted up in a teasing pose. She wore a flowered print dress with a row of ruffles at the neck and a deeper ruffle at the hem. She stood on the front steps of God House, the shrubbery on either side in full bloom. It must be Antoinette.

This pretty woman looked almost fragile in the next photograph, where she stood next to Daphne's mother, who looked exactly like the portrait in the living room. "Nora et moi 1958" was printed neatly below in faded block letters. Nora looked strong and glamorous in a simple white shirt and wide pleated trousers. Her glistening fair hair reached her shoulders and fell seductively across one eye. Her arm draped across Antoinette's shoulder, and she looked very much at home. In fact, Nora looked more like the owner of the house than the young woman in her shadow. Annie turned the pages, watching them in the garden, on trips to the beach, and with a group of friends all in tennis whites at a fashionable club. Daphne appeared toward the end. First an enchanting robust baby and later a tomboyish schoolgirl with scuffed shoes and unruly hair escaping her barrettes. There were no photographs of Daphne's brother. Annie wondered if he ever came to this house.

"How's my poetess?" Wesley came in carrying a large tray. The cups and saucers clattered lightly as he set it down on the table behind the love seat where Annie sat. It looked like he'd put on dry clothes, and his hair was damp and neatly combed.

"Did you get very wet?" she asked.

His eyes sparkled appealingly and his entire demeanor said the world was all right. She had been drawn to this very quality when they'd first met.

"Not bad. I've dried off and this fire feels great. I want to get an early start tomorrow." He lifted the pot of tea. "Shall I pour you a cup?"

"Thanks. What's the rush?" Annie hated to think it was almost time to leave.

"Nothing really. I just want to get back. Where's Daphne?"

"She's gone up to have a bath. I'll take her a cup in a few minutes."

He handed Annie her tea, plain, the way she liked it, and poured his own, adding sugar and a generous amount of milk. He came and sat beside her on the tufted leather love seat. "What are you looking at?" He slid closer and leaned in to kiss the nape of her neck. This proprietary gesture annoyed her. He acted as if last night's lovemaking was an immediate cure, as if sex could solve everything.

She opened the album onto his lap. "Who do you think this is?" She pointed to one of Nora seated on the bow of a boat, her legs hanging over, her toes skimming the water.

"Daphne looks so much like her," he said. He turned the page and pointed to the petite woman at Nora's side. "Antoinette?" She nodded. "She looks very sweet," he said. "Not the sort of person suited for the hard-bargaining world of antiques."

"Daphne told me she was very good that way. Quietly talking people out of old treasures they thought of as dust-catching junk."

Wesley leafed through more pages. "I don't feel like looking at these now." He shut the book, stretched his legs, and leaned in close to Annie to rest his head on her shoulder. She could smell his skin, his clothes, his hair. There had been a time when just breathing in the scent of Wesley had made her feel safe, loved, as if all was well with the world. She felt the warmth of him against her while she sipped her tea. It all seemed more complicated now.

"I'd better take Daphne her tea," she said. He withdrew his hand that rested on her thigh. "Don't forget to bring in more logs." She stood up, leaving him to gaze at the dwindling embers.

"Come in." Daphne's voice came from the bathroom off the bedroom. "Bring it in here, please. I'm having a wonderful soak." Daphne's room, decorated in shades of pale blue, was the same shape and size as the one she and Wesley shared across the hall. Annie noticed a dear little fruit-wood desk with a drop front over by the window. The desk was open, and Annie could see letter paper with Daphne's emphatic bold script. Daphne had proudly told her that she always wrote everything by hand, even business correspondence.

Annie did as she was told and pushed open the bathroom door. Daphne sat in the enormous old tub filled almost to the brim with steaming water.

"Just put it here," she said pointing to the rack that spanned both sides of the tub. "Please stay for a bit. We can have a little talk."

Annie sat on the rush-seated stool at the foot of the tub. It felt strange to be in a bathroom with another woman, like being back in college again when the girls trooped in and out of the huge bathrooms in various degrees of undress, trying not to notice one another. Daphne smiled up at her through the steam. Her hair was piled on her head and fastened with the yellow clip.

"You look like one of those luscious bathers painted by Renoir," Annie said. She looked at Daphne's firm pink flesh, the lovely breasts only hinted at in her clothes.

"I hope that's a compliment," Daphne laughed loudly. "Ah yes, Renoir. He loved any excuse to paint naked ladies for rich old men to ogle in their leisure."

How different this was from the austere old bathroom back in Vermont. Aunt Kate, ever frugal, allowed only three inches of water for a tub. Daphne sipped her tea and water dripped from her fingers.

Her expression became more serious when she spoke again. "Wesley wishes you were more enthusiastic about moving back to America."

That was the one topic that Annie wished to avoid. She stood up to go back to Wesley downstairs by the fire.

"No, don't leave. Look, I don't blame you." She picked up her washcloth and a fragrant bar of white soap. She rubbed the soap across the cloth, her hands pink from the hot water. "Would you be a dear?" She lifted the cloth toward Annie. "There's usually no one here to wash my back. One disadvantage of living alone."

Annie took the soapy cloth and knelt down beside the tub. She moved the cloth up and down Daphne's long spine. She had a beautiful back, like the one in François's photograph. Annie had the odd sensation that she was about to discover something forbidden, something she was not supposed to see. Annie knew European woman were more relaxed about their bodies; she was accustomed to French-women going topless at the beach, and she was used to breasts and buttocks of all contours displayed in magazine ads and on subway posters. But seeing Daphne alone in the steaming bath seemed different, making her feel stifled and uneasy.

"Wesley talked to me about the law firm in Washington," Daphne said. "You know, I think he's viewing this job as his last chance. Having his career cut short has been tough on him."

"I don't want to talk about this," Annie said. "It sounds like he's persuaded you and now I'm the selfish one who doesn't understand." Annie dipped the cloth back into the water and rinsed the soap from Daphne's back. She pictured Daphne walking in the rain with Wesley, discussing this matter without her. She was furious with him, with both of them, for talking about something that was none of Daphne's business. Still on her knees, she wrung out the cloth and handed it back.

"Annie. Annie, I'm on your side. I'm your friend." Daphne put a moist hand on Annie's arm.

"It sounds like you and Wesley see eye to eye." She hated this stupid trite phrase as it flew from her mouth.

"He just needed to talk. I was there to listen. That's all. I think I know how you feel. I need to be here, I need God House, so your needing to stay in Paris is somewhat the same."

"But it's different for you. You're on your own, and how you live affects only you."

"That's not entirely true. I'm not always alone, and there's Berthe. I take care of her now. She's spent so much of her life taking care of me."

Daphne spoke softly, with the tenderness of a dear friend. Annie looked into her eyes, the eyes that melted from gray to green and could darken with her mood, and thought she saw compassion.

"I know the job makes sense for him." Annie's voice came out resolutely. "It's not easy for someone his age to find a job, much less one that would really utilize his experience, one that would challenge him. I also know it's less likely in Paris, but not impossible." Annie lowered her head. She didn't care now what Daphne thought. "I guess I'm afraid of what would happen to us. I worry that we are who we are because of Paris."

Daphne turned toward her, and with her other hand she stroked Annie's hair, gently drawing it away from her face.

"I know I love Wesley, but is it enough?" Annie said. "Things aren't the same as before. Do I want to give up everything and live where I don't know anyone? There's also my writing." She closed her eyes. "It's odd. It's like I'm a piece in a puzzle whose shape has changed, a piece that no longer fits into the space it's always occupied." She felt Daphne's fingers stroking her hair, the way Wesley used to when they first met. Annie opened her eyes, suddenly feeling disloyal. It was like she'd given Daphne a glance at something private, something she shouldn't have shared.

"You need to take your time," Daphne said. "There is nothing to decide now. Let him go. Just wait and see what happens." She withdrew her hand. "Now, will you be a love and hand me my robe? I think it's time for drinks by the fire."

Later, at the kitchen table, eating the delicious fish stew, Annie faced Daphne and Wesley with a strange sense of calm. She felt like she was the photographer looking at them, at all of their lives, through a lens. This imagined distance provided an emotional calm.

"This is incredible," Wesley said. "I've never had better." He rested his spoon on the rim of the serving plate and reached for another hunk of bread. Berthe had carried in the yellow pottery tureen filled with the steaming fish soup as if presenting a father with his firstborn son. She had spent the afternoon cooking in her little apartment above the garage, preferring not to disturb them in the big house. Sweet pieces of white fish, shiny black mussels, and succulent morsels of lobster floated in the fragrant tomato-based broth. Wesley asked Berthe, a tiny but strong woman who had to be in her eighties, what the magic ingredient was.

"Oh, monsieur, it's not just the ingredients, it's where you get them, the freshness of the fish, mussels from a certain bay. These things take many years to know. And"—her black eyes crinkled in amusement—"you must also put your heart into the preparation. That I think, is the magic." She spoke with the accent of someone from the south of France, slowly, with robust rolling r's and a singsong fluidity. Daphne gave her a hug and walked her to the door with a protective arm around her. She looked so vibrant and young beside the bent older woman with steely gray hair.

When they finished the soup, Daphne brought the platter of cheeses to the table. "Try this one." Daphne pointed to a small round cheese. "It's a *chevrot*. One of my favorites." She passed the platter to Wesley and turned to Annie. "I'm glad you found it so easy to write here."

"Yes, I really did. I think it helps to get away; it gives you a fresh perspective."

"Well then, you must come back, and I mean soon."

"We'd love that," Annie said.

"No, I mean it." Daphne caught Annie's eye. "Why don't you come visit when Wesley's in the States?"

"What, without me?" Wesley laughed and Annie thought he looked uneasy, even displeased.

"I'm sure I could find my way back without you, Wesley."

Daphne nodded. "I'm certain of it," she said.

NINE

Le Départ

The unusual bitter cold had returned. When they pulled out of the driveway at God House the small puddles, left by yesterday's rain, had become miniature frozen lakes. Like a child, Annie had thrust her foot into one, shattering the mirrorlike surface into sparkling shards. Daphne had stood on the top of the steps waving them off. "Come back soon!" she called, her voice buffeted by the wind. Annie watched Daphne's face grow smaller in the rear window as they pulled away, leaving God House behind.

Now, entering the outskirts of Paris, they were entangled in a web of traffic as far as they could see. Taillights pulsed on and off as the masses of vehicles pushed forward. Strains of jazz from the car radio sounded above the engine and the roar of traffic around them. Annie ignored it. She wasn't in the mood for jazz; in the bold clarity of midday, it only added to the traffic-induced tension. Wesley had selected the station, and she refrained from showing her displeasure in his choice. With the car in first gear, he eased his foot on and off the clutch as they crept along toward the center of Paris.

Annie leaned back against the headrest and looked out at the row of cheap shops and the grimy windows of ordinary cafés and restaurants. Not far from their car, an old woman shuffled along the sidewalk toting a plastic bag in one hand. She wore a thin raincoat pulled tightly over bulging sweaters, and the hem of her skirt drooped below her coat and fluttered in the winter air. Her bag looked ready to split and spill its contents onto the hard pavement. She would have been a pathetic sight but for the fat little dog she held by a leash in her other hand. Annie could imagine the dreary little flat the two would call home, but she was comforted that the old lady would not be alone and that whatever sad meager supper awaited her, some of her scraps would end up in her dog's bowl. The woman reminded her of François's photograph of the old lady in the park.

"There's something we need to talk about," Wesley said.

Annie turned toward him. She didn't think she could muster the energy to talk about anything serious just now, but she could see from the set of his jaw that his mind was made up. At least she would have a reprieve from all their weighty discussions when he left for Washington. With him away, she would have more time to write, and time to think. "I'm listening," she said.

"It's about money," he said. The light changed but they moved forward only a few car lengths.

She sat up a little straighter. They never had had reason to argue about money. She and Wesley both spent sensibly and agreed on the same luxuries—meals out from time to time, nice trips once or twice a year—and they took pleasure in splurging on special gifts to mark momentous occasions. He gave her a cashmere coat one Christmas; she gave him a set of gold cuff links from a fine jeweler in the Place Vendôme for his fiftieth birthday. Wesley's salary at Wilson & James had afforded them a comfortable life, and the money she earned at Liberal Arts Abroad gave them even greater financial ease.

"The checking account is getting low and I didn't have any billings in December. I'm going to arrange for a monthly transfer from our investment account. We need to be careful for a while."

"But that's the money from your parents' estate. You said it was for our retirement. Couldn't we manage on my salary for the next few months?"

"It's not enough." Wesley looked unhappy. He'd never liked talking about money.

"I'm sure if we were careful—"

"If you want me to go through it in detail when we get home, I will." He slammed on the brakes, nearly hitting a motorbike that cut abruptly in front of them. The driver looked like a young boy. "Damn." The car nearly stalled, then lurched forward. "Annie, we live in one of

the most expensive cities in the world, and we choose to live very
nicely. This will help us for a while. It's just temporary."

He shifted into second gear. The traffic was starting to move again.
The shops and restaurants in this neighborhood looked more prosperous and attractive. The city became more beautiful the closer you came
to its center. They passed a flower shop, a bakery with an elegant display of pastries in the window, and a hotel whose striped awning
flapped in the breeze; here they slowed to a stop.

"We seem to get every light. I appreciate your driving." She tried to
restore some small measure of goodwill. "I'll be careful with our
money."

"I know you will." The light changed to green. Wesley accelerated
and Annie spotted a familiar man coming out of a hotel. Annie recognized the athletic swagger, the broad shoulders of a former football
player, the well-cut slicked-back hair. He wore a double-breasted topcoat, gray flannel pants, and a plaid Burberry scarf—a well-heeled
American businessman abroad.

"Wesley, look! There, in front of that hotel. It's Tom Sanders."

Wesley glanced quickly in the direction of the hotel. It was indeed
Tom; the same man who only a few weeks before had sat at their table
for the solstice dinner now stood in front of a hotel with his arm
around a young woman with short curly hennaed hair, wearing a
leather jacket with a fur collar. A young woman, not his wife.

Annie sat at a table upstairs at Ladurée, the lovely pastry shop near the
Madeleine. Hélène Rocher had invited her to tea. Annie had arrived a
few minutes before they were scheduled to meet, happy to escape the
bustling sidewalk of late-afternoon shoppers. The charming, old-
fashioned tearoom, filled with the rush of female voices, decorated
with apple-green walls, pink tablecloths, and tufted velvet chairs, was
known for its heavenly macaroons, layered with creamy fillings in soft
pastel shades: raspberry, peach, pistachio. The pastries, displayed in
glass cases just inside the entrance, were elaborate and fanciful, much
like the ladies who dined there with their poufed hair and artfully
made-up faces.

She and Céleste had come here several times, once years ago with their daughters, who were then ten and twelve. Annie smiled. She could still see Sophie in her neat blond braids consuming every bite of an enormous chocolate éclair, working hard not to spill any on her best party dress. She tried to picture her now, in some office building in L.A., the land of freeways, fit bodies, and perpetual sunshine. That all-revealing, brilliant light would be the antithesis of Paris on a winter afternoon, one shade of gray blending into the next. Yet Annie would pick Paris any day, with its sophisticated subtlety and rich history.

She was glad to sit down. She'd been shopping on the rue Saint-Honoré, enjoying the upscale shops and plush boutiques. It was the glorious allotted two-week period in January when merchants were allowed to put merchandise on sale. French law allowed only two sale periods a year. There were incredible bargains, especially in the higher-priced shops. She had wanted to find a present for Sophie; she knew Wesley would understand that expenditure, but when the sales clerk had seen the black sweater she picked out she'd said, "But Madame, it would be lovely on you." She tried it on. It was amazing how something so soft, so beautifully cut, could make you feel like an entirely different person. She bought it for herself. It was the kind of thing that Daphne would wear, and she knew she had to have it. There would be other ways to cut corners.

Wesley had been gone for two days. Annie had mailed Paul her completed poems, and now she would just have to wait. It had all seemed so improbable when Daphne first mentioned Paul and his book project, but strangely, Annie felt more confident since the weekend at God House. Maybe some of Daphne's commanding presence had worn off on her.

Since Wesley's departure Annie had tried to put her marital worries aside. He'd been in a positive mood the day he left, making Annie feel hopeful that their marriage might recover its sweetness. But she knew that the slightest movement could also throw them back into misery. They had both been saddened to have their suspicions about Tom played out in the broad light of day. Annie wondered what still held Mary and Tom together. How long could a marriage survive the strain of infidelity?

"Ah, there you are. *Bonjour. Ça va?*" Hélène greeted Annie and sat down, pushing her coat onto the back of the chair. Hélène did look well. Her nails and lips glowed in the same riveting shade of red that Annie remembered from their last meeting, and she smelled of gardenias, the lush scent of a winter hothouse flower. She kept her heavy silk scarf around her shoulders while she studied the long list of teas on the menu through gold-rimmed half-glasses. Annie followed her lead, also choosing Earl Grey and an apricot tart.

They spent a few minutes exchanging news. Hélène told Annie about her Christmas visit with her son, Alexis, his wife and children. She'd loved every minute but was happy to come home to her peaceful apartment. Annie explained that Wesley had just left for the United States to interview for a new job and that the law firm would most likely extend an offer. "It's good for him, but sadly, it would mean we'd have to move," Annie said.

"I can see from your face that you do not wish that."

"I'm still hopeful that he'll find something here." She took a sip of tea, savoring the smoky warmth on her tongue. "In the meantime I'm enjoying being on my own."

"It is nice being by oneself," Hélène said. "I miss Bertrand. I still find it hard to call myself a widow. *Hélas*, such a dreadful word. But there are some little pleasures." She smiled and cut neatly into her pastry. "Tonight, for example, I will have just cheese and fruit for dinner."

"Me too. I love not having to cook dinner. I always felt that Wesley expected a nice hot meal, especially after a trying day at work. Funny, how you get into habits like that."

"I often wonder, looking back, if Bertrand expected what I thought he expected." Helene looked into the distance for a moment. "We don't always know the real person even if we think that we do."

Annie imagined that Hélène thought often about her husband. So many shared years. How could she not? "You are so right," she agreed. Twenty-four years with Wesley. Did she truly know him? For the moment, she was enjoying this time without him, a reprieve. She didn't want to think about him for a while.

"But tell me, did you finish your poems?"

Annie had told Hélène about the possible book project when she had phoned to make the date for tea. She nodded. "I've never felt so good about any of my work." She told Hélène about the weekend at God House and how easy it had been to write there. "Even since I've been home, I feel like I'm under a kind of spell. Everything I see is feeding my writing. Sometimes I feel like I'm capturing the very pulse of this city and getting it on the page."

"I am so happy for you." Helene reached across the table and patted Annie's arm. "Do you know the expression 'Être bien dans sa peau?'"

"To feel good in one's skin?"

"This is how I see you now. Exactly." She poured them both some more tea. "Now, tell me more about this man. He is French, non?" Hélène raised her eyebrows and waited eagerly for Annie's response.

Annie leaned forward. She found it easy in this happy female place to forget about her office job and the stack of boring documents that awaited her. All the reports from the French universities had arrived and needed to be translated and reformatted for the transcripts going to the colleges in the United States. It was tedious work, what she hated most about her job, but she knew it had to be done. Mary wanted it completed by the end of January.

"His name is Paul," she said. The rest of her life would have to wait.

His call had come at the end of the week. Annie had just come in the door, carrying a bag of groceries and her dry cleaning. She thought it might be Wesley with news about the job in Washington. He'd called only once, to let her know that he'd arrived safely and to give her the number of his hotel.

"Yes," she'd answered, breathless from rushing to get to the phone.

"This is Paul." The French voice had sounded serious.

"Oh, hello," she'd said, surprised to hear from him so promptly.

He'd wasted no time. "I met with François last night. We both agree. We hope you will write the rest of the poems."

"Of course," she'd said. "I'd love to. I'm so glad you like them . . ." She'd watched as her dry-cleaning bags fell from her hand and slithered to the floor. She forgot what else she'd said in the excitement of the moment.

Now, on this darkening January afternoon in his office, she could hardly believe this turn of events. "But you must have dinner with me," Paul said at the end of this first meeting.

"Well, I . . ." Annie didn't know how to answer. They'd spent hours looking over François's photographs, each one seductive, revealing Paris in her many guises. How to decide? Paul insisted that he didn't want a book that showed only the predictable story, the café scenes, the churches, the parks. Yet the book required a certain degree of familiarity.

"I want the reader to recognize a place, or the feel of a place," he said, "and then the poem will bring them back to that place. The reader will feel like he has been there or that he wants to be there still." He was decisive when he talked about the book. He looked happier that day, seeming to enjoy himself.

Annie had a sudden urge to reach out and run her finger along the crease of his deeply set eyes or to brush his hair back from his forehead the way she used to with Wesley. She imagined that intimate gesture and wondered if his skin would be warm to her touch, if his hair, dark and coarse, would feel strange compared with Wesley's. She sandwiched her hands between her knees and tried to focus on the black-and-white images. She was thinking like a schoolgirl with a crush. He simply wanted to continue their meeting over dinner. He was waiting for an answer.

"There is a good place *en face*"—he had spoken to her in French all afternoon—"I go there often." He knew that Wesley was away, that she was on her own, and it seemed logical to finish their work over dinner. Annie wanted to talk more about the book. She also wanted to continue to watch his lips as they moved in his native tongue.

"I must confess to being hungry," she said.

He laughed. "It is also time for a glass of wine, and I would love to hear you read your poems *à haute voix*, out loud. I want to hear them in order."

Sometimes when Annie spoke French she felt like she was taking on a second skin, becoming someone else. It made her think of playing

dress-up when she was a child. When she put on one of Aunt Kate's ancient crinoline petticoats and spike-heeled shoes, both relics of the
1950s, she walked with a swing in her hips, tilted her head at a different angle, became a different Annie, someone wild and glamorous.
Now, speaking French all afternoon with Paul, a language almost second nature to her, gave her a similar sensation. "Dinner is a good idea."

Later that evening, seated side by side on a leather banquette, they
studied the menu. A small lamp cast a warm glow on the center of
their table and set them apart from the surrounding darkness. Paul
studied the wine list.

"*Qu'est-ce que tu préfères? Le blanc ou le rouge?*"

She told him she liked red better, particularly on a winter evening.
He signaled to the waiter and asked for a vin de Cahors. The waiter
had recommended the cassoulet, a rich bean stew with sausages,
lamb, and duck confit. They took his suggestion.

"My grandmother used to make a wonderful cassoulet." Paul talked
easily about his family. "She was from the Languedoc." He explained
that he was the only one living in Paris, but he went frequently to see
his elderly mother, who lived in the south of France. His parents had
retired there after Paul took over their publishing business.

The waiter returned with their wine and offered Paul the ritual
tasting. The wine, an inky purple, looked dark in his glass.

"They call this *le vin noir de Cahors*," Paul pointed out, referring to its
almost black color.

The waiter looked at Annie and said, "*Pour vous, Madame?*" Annie nodded, indicating she wanted some wine, and while the waiter poured,
it occurred to her that he might assume that she was Madame Valmont, Paul's wife. What would it be like to be married to him? At this
moment he looked gentle, kind, somewhat rumpled but attractive.
She thought of the pretty woman in the photograph on his desk. Had
he ever turned away from his wife, shut her out, or refused to love
her?

Paul lifted his glass. "To our book," he said, and Annie clinked her
glass against his, returning his gaze. His eyes were a deeper blue than
Wesley's, the pupils rimmed with brown. Sitting next to him on the
banquette felt romantic. She took a sip of her wine, set it down, and

smoothed her hair back behind her ears in a nervous gesture. "Do you like it?" he asked.

She nodded.

"Please, will you read to me now?" He spoke in English, perhaps to switch his brain over to the other language. "I want to get a sense of what we have so far." He'd been enthusiastic about this first group of poems. His questions had been thoughtful, and the one change he'd suggested—in the Notre-Dame poem—hadn't bothered her. She'd worried about the final line herself, and his suggestion was a minor one.

Annie opened the folder and began to read the poems that she'd written so far. She knew most of them by heart, and lifting her eyes from the pages, she was able to watch his reaction. He was an attentive listener, nodding periodically, and he smiled when she read about an old dog in a café. When she got to the fourth poem, called "Parting Moment," he closed his eyes. The poem was based on the picture of young lovers, arm in arm on the Pont Neuf, watching a barge pass on the river below them. She lowered her voice at the last stanza.

> They will hold close the memory
> Of nascent love begun,
> The sound of fragile hearts still
> Beating as one.

Paul opened his eyes and sadness transformed his face, making him look tired and alone.

"I'm sorry," she said. "I didn't mean to upset you."

"A good poem should do that." He lifted his hands and brought one to his heart. "If it does not make you feel, well then, it is not doing what it should."

Annie nodded. The longing for his wife seemed to have settled over him like a cloud cover, damp and opaque. His grief belonged to him like the cold dark days belonged to a Paris winter. She tried to think of what to say. "You still miss her very much." The words sounded pointless to her ears.

"Terribly." He picked up the bottle and poured more wine in their glasses.

"You must have had a very happy marriage," Annie said. "How many years?"

"Not quite twenty. And yes, we were happy." He averted his face and drew his fingers across his forehead as if to erase certain thoughts. "Mostly, I remember the good times. She was so lively, full of energy. She often worked late into the night. You see, Marie Laure was a very ambitious woman."

"Was she in publishing too?"

"She was a journalist. Wrote about politics. We did not agree on everything." He shook his head and looked again at Annie. "She did not want to have children."

"And you did?"

"Yes. It was a great disappointment, but I respected her wishes." He drew his lips into a pucker, exhaled, and leaned back against the banquette. "I have never told anyone about this."

Why wouldn't Marie Laure have wanted a child from this man? Her photograph portrayed a loving, warmhearted woman, but there was obviously a lot it didn't tell. "I'm very sorry," she said.

"People assumed we were busy with our work, our careers, and that that was enough." His expression darkened. "So many incorrect assumptions." He reached for his glass of wine. "You told me you have a daughter?"

"Yes. But she's grown and living on her own now." Annie told Paul about Sophie and her gradual departure from her life. "At least when she was in college she came home for long vacations. Now that she's working we hardly ever see her."

"Ah, yes. The American system of only two weeks of vacation a year." He shook his head. "Those terrible Puritans left your countrymen with a bad idea."

Annie laughed. "It's not as bad as that. And eventually she'll have more time off. Actually, that's not really the problem. It's more getting used to the idea that she has her own life now; she won't come home again in quite the same way."

"But you do not want that? Her living her own life?"

"Of course I do. We're very proud of Sophie." She thought of Wesley. "It changes things within the family."

"In what way?" he asked.

Annie considered his question. "I've been asking myself that. It's kind of like a balanced composition in a work of art. Think of the strength of the triangle in classical painting—each side pulls the picture together and makes it strong. The family is like that too, each person helping to create the balance." Annie moved slightly on the bench, putting more distance between them. "When one person leaves, it can throw things off."

He looked at her and shrugged. "But in art, you can also think in terms of two. One half balances the other half. So, all you need is two."

"You're right. That makes sense." She smiled again. "I think Wesley and I are just getting used to it. That's all."

The waiter brought their dinner. The cassoulet tasted of garlic and rich, meaty broth. Both hearty and rustic, it was a comfortable dish to eat while sharing stories. Annie decided to direct the conversation to safer waters. She talked about Vermont and her life with Aunt Kate.

"We didn't eat a lot of cassoulet in Vermont," she joked.

"Vermont," he said with the French pronunciation. "Green mountain. I cannot picture you living there." His accent made it sound remote and exotic, truly a lifetime away. When she spoke of her father, his depression and quiet death in old age, he reached over and patted her hand, a sweet attempt to console her years after the fact.

Later, in front of the restaurant, he helped her into a taxi. She wondered if he was going back to his office or home to his apartment, the new place he'd moved to to escape the memories of Marie Laure. Paul gave the driver her address, and before shutting the taxi door he reached in and drew his hand along the line of her jaw, the way a blind person would explore a face by touch.

Just as suddenly, he withdrew his hand, turned, and walked into the January night. The driver pulled away from the curb and drove toward the bridge that would take Annie across the river to her side of the Seine.

Annie sat propped up against the pillows in the middle of their bed, really her bed now. After just a few days, she was getting used to deciding things on her own. She could turn out the light at night when she wanted to. If she awoke early, she could stay in bed and write. She had stopped cooking dinner since Wesley's departure and sometimes made a tray with soup, bread, and cheese for supper and carried it to her chair in the living room. She adapted happily to these small freedoms.

Wesley planned to be gone for close to three weeks, and he had timed his return to coincide with Sophie's visit at the end of January. He had been kind, not discussing the impending move, as if he knew that saying anything would upset her. They both had acted as if he were taking an ordinary business trip and not making a journey that might determine their future. He had told her that there would be a whirlwind of meetings and that any of his spare time would be taken up with a small project that he and the partners had already agreed upon.

Wesley had taken business trips when he worked for Wilson & James. They occurred infrequently, but Annie had come to enjoy the few brief periods of being on her own. When Sophie still lived at home, they called it their "girl time." Having married Wesley immediately after her graduation from college, Annie had never lived by herself. There had been moments, particularly when her writing had been pushed aside to make room for family responsibilities, when she wished that she had waited longer before getting married. She used to imagine the luxury of time to herself when her only alone time was spent in an alcove off her living room. Now she did have time to herself and the kind of project that she never could have imagined. The thrill of the book had not worn off.

Her writing was going well. Since her visit to God House, it was like she'd discovered a vein of gold. Each photograph served as the beginning, the experience that launched her into the larger idea that would become the poem. From there the metaphors took shape and the images that carried her line by line brought the poem to life. Some days the words almost poured out. She felt like a marathon runner hitting a plateau.

Tonight she'd dined on a plate of pâté, bread, and apple slices along with a chilled glass of Sancerre she'd found already open in the fridge. The wind rattled the windows, so she put her dinner on a tray and brought it into the bedroom, placing it on one side of the bed. Wesley didn't like eating in bed. She remembered visiting his family when they were first married. All the meals were served in the large formal dining room, painted dark green with white crown moldings and chair rails. There were portraits of narrow-nosed relatives staring down from within gilt frames above the sideboard and a worn Oriental carpet. The rest of the house, while cheerful, reeked of stiff-upper-lip propriety. At breakfast the entire family—mother, father, sister, brother—would appear exactly at eight, dressed, smiling, and ready for the day. No one questioned this routine.

When they got to Paris, Wesley had agreed that on weekends they could start the day with coffee in bed, but that was as far as he would go. This evening she'd surrounded herself with her poetry notebooks, the folder of François's photographs, a basket of mail, and a novel that Madeleine, Wesley's sister, had sent her for Christmas. She got under the covers, sipped her wine, and considered where to start. The mail contained nothing but bills. She remembered Wesley's admonition to be careful with money. Of course she'd be careful. If anything, she wished she could be more reckless. Being careful had been drummed into her for as long as she could remember.

She opened the folder of photographs and leafed through. She needed to start another poem but hadn't decided on which photograph to focus on next. She had copies of the entire set, now a total of twenty-one. When she and Paul had spent the afternoon narrowing the choices for the book, she hadn't seen the pair of nudes that had been there the time before. Had François taken them back, or had Paul? She leaned against the pillows. Paul Valmont had stroked her face. She closed her eyes and tried to remember the sensation. His gesture had been a shock to her, so unexpected that she almost wondered if it had really happened. The telephone rang.

"Annie, I haven't heard from you all week." Daphne's voice carried clearly across the line. "I thought you were coming back to God House while Wesley was away."

"I've been meaning to call."

"Now that you're the famous poet, are you going to ignore me?"

"Daphne, don't be silly."

"I'm joking, darling. I just hope you haven't forgotten how you loved working out here."

"Of course not. And thanks to you, I have work to do." Annie had called Daphne immediately when Paul asked her to do the book. Daphne had been thrilled for her. She had also left a message for Wesley in Washington, but he hadn't called yet to congratulate her.

"Well, come tomorrow then."

"Tomorrow's not good." She thought of all the work at the office. "How about the day after?"

"Super. I hope you're writing lots."

"It's amazing. Having this project is so energizing."

"See, I knew you could do it. How did your meeting with Paul go?"

"Great." Annie could feel herself redden. "He's really pleased with the work so far. I'll tell you more when I see you." The beautiful old house loomed once again in her mind. "I'll get up early and take a morning train on Wednesday."

"Lovely. I'll fetch you at the station."

Annie hung up the phone and tried to go back to the pictures in her lap. But now she saw only God House, the sturdy gray walls covered in ivy, the perfectly symmetrical house perched on the hill above the river. Here in Paris, the night was clear. Maybe there, the moon was shimmering on the river. She imagined walking into the peach-colored front hall; she could hear the echo of her footsteps on the black-and-white stone floor before going up the gracious staircase that led to what she thought of as her room, across the hall from Daphne. She wondered what Daphne would be doing on a night like this, all alone in the country.

TEN

La Coiffure

Annie spent the following day at the Liberal Arts Abroad offices. The students were on winter break. Mary was still away and there was no one to interrupt her, for which she was grateful. By the end of the afternoon she was totally discouraged. She'd forgotten what a huge task it was to prepare the transcripts, made all the more discouraging because some of the necessary documents appeared to be missing. She'd had a terrible time keeping her mind on her work, and when she heard the neighboring church bells ringing at six, she knew she couldn't stand it another minute. It would be good to get out to God House, to see Daphne and forget about her job for a while.

On her way home she'd stopped at Saint-Eustache church. She loved the beauty and grandeur of Notre-Dame Cathedral, but it was Saint-Eustache that lured her for reflective moments in her largely secular life. She walked up the center aisle of the nave, now fairly empty, only a few people in the pews. The building revealed years of love and abuse: stained-glass windows in need of repair since the Second World War, the stone floor worn and gritty from tired feet, and the soot-darkened walls reaching for the heavens. Pigeons fluttered high above, trespassers in the sacred space. Annie breathed in the smell of ancient stone, burning candles, and a faint odor of incense.

She sat down in one of the creaking rush-seated chairs lined up like pews. Her thoughts mingled with the hushed voices and low murmured prayers of those around her. The architecture, a glorious mix of Gothic and Renaissance, rivaled that of Notre-Dame, but unlike Notre-Dame, which was constantly encroached on by tourists, this was a hardworking place of worship, a truly comforting church, that embraced all who entered. Writing the poem about this church had eventually brought her to Paul Valmont and the chance to write many more poems.

Saint-Eustache was Wesley's favorite church. Annie bent her head and folded her hands in her lap. How could she and Wesley, happy for so many years, suddenly feel so differently? Or was she the only one who had changed? Certainly people survived career changes and moving to new places. She knew that. But there were other factors too. There was Daphne. "You've got to do what's right for you, Annie. You don't go anywhere in life without taking a few risks."

Annie considered Daphne's life. Could she live like that, in a world free of husband or family? Perhaps after some time apart, she could be more patient with Wesley; maybe she would feel better about moving and setting up a new life in Washington.

A dark figure in layers of rags shuffled by, mumbling to himself. He smelled of urine and the sickening ripeness of the unwashed. Honestly, what was she worrying about? Annie got up and looked at the rose window high above the nave. Barely visible in the evening darkness, there it was, a forgotten jewel right before her eyes, offering her a glimpse of peace.

Annie couldn't see. Her eyes no longer worked. The blackness was fierce, confusing. She tried to push her hair off her face. Then the sharp noise, where was the noise? She needed to find it. She was suddenly awake. The phone, on Wesley's side of the bed, was ringing. She must have been dreaming. She crawled across the covers, pushing aside magazines, notebooks, typed manuscript pages, and a pot of herbal tea on a tray. Her legs were tangled in the sheets. Something clattered to the floor. She found the receiver.

"Annie?"

"Yes," she said. Her mouth was dry, sandpapery. It must be the middle of the night. She pushed herself up onto her elbows and reached for the light. Two in the morning. She'd been dead asleep. "Wesley, why are you calling so late? Is something wrong?"

"Sorry, sweetie. We just got back from dinner. You're never there when I call."

She tried to think. What did he mean by that? He hadn't left a message. He continued on, animated, explaining some kind of long complicated brief, something he had done for the Washington law firm. It had gone well. He had brought in a new client. The senior partner was due back from Hong Kong next week. He was the last person that Wesley needed to meet—a final formality.

Annie tried to focus on what he was saying. It was evening in Washington. She tried to imagine Wesley in his hotel room, seated on the edge of a vast bed, a room in dull shades of maroon and brown. For a moment she couldn't even picture his face. She sat up further. The tray with her cup of tea had overturned onto the rug.

"You woke me up," she mumbled into the phone. What was he talking about?

"The firm isn't as big as Wilson & James, but it's right for me. The other partners are terrific." He sounded like a stranger. "Please try to understand how important this is for me."

"I know it's important. I'm glad you like it. Wesley, it's late." She tried to clear her head. "Did you get my message? Valmont wants me to write the poems for the book."

"I don't see how you're going to have time to do that. Once this is definite, I'll need to be here full-time. We'll need to find a place here, sell the apartment—"

"You said we didn't need to move right away." Now she was totally awake.

"Look, Annie. There will be other opportunities."

"You mean not write the poems for Valmont?"

"I didn't say that. Let's talk tomorrow."

"I'm leaving early for God House. I'll be there for the rest of the week."

"Why are you going out there?"

She looked again at the clock. It would be difficult to get back to sleep. "I plan to work. Daphne said I could have the days to myself. It's where I need to be right now. No interruptions."

"What about your job?"

"I was at the office all day. All I have to do is finish the transcripts for Mary."

"That's a huge job. How are you going to do that and write poems? Listen." He sounded businesslike, as if he were talking to a young associate in his law firm. "I think you're taking on too much."

"I'll be able to get it done."

"I don't know."

"You . . ." She was furious. What did he have to do with this? "Wesley. This is my job, my life. I don't need your advice. For that matter, I don't want your advice."

"You don't need to get so angry. For Christ's sake, I only called to tell you about this job. I thought you'd be happy for me. It's going to change everything for us."

It already has, she thought. "Look, in case you've forgotten, it's the middle of the night."

"We need to talk, Annie."

"We'll talk when you come back." She tried to regain her composure. "This is not the time for this."

"Annie—"

"Please, Wesley," she said quietly. "Good night." Annie put the phone back in its cradle and bent down to pick up the teacup and pot still on the floor. Thankfully, the pot hadn't broken. The cup looked fine, but when she ran her finger around the rim, she felt a jagged edge where it had chipped.

Annie closed her eyes. The pressure of a passing train thundering toward Paris seemed to suck the air right out of the railway car where she sat. Once past, she listened to the steady rumble as they shot over steel tracks. Her train carried her in the opposite direction, and at midmorning it was almost empty. She shared the compartment with a young mother holding a sleeping infant. She looked tired but content, and she held her baby close in her arms, rocking with the gentle rhythm of the train. Annie opened her book and tried to read. She didn't want to sleep, fearful of missing the stop for Villandry.

She looked out the window. The high-speed train created a monotonous gray ribbon of landscape, making it impossible to focus on any particular scenic detail. When she awoke that morning, her fury at Wesley had been replaced by sadness. She watched the young mother across from her. The baby slept deeply and the mother periodically kissed the top of the downy little head.

She remembered her own pregnancy. She and Wesley had planned to have children one day, but it had happened sooner than expected. She had worried about Wesley's reaction to her news.

She'd left the doctor's office on a glorious October afternoon. The results were conclusive. She was healthy and she felt wonderful. She had gone to find Wesley in the library. She would never forget that day. The sky was an intense blue, and the leaves of rich crimson, bold yellow, and gold sailed to her feet. She hurried along the sidewalk by the Charles River. The water glimmered with an intensity of almost unbearable beauty. A day of pure magic.

She ran up the endless marble steps of the library and headed to the place where he usually studied. She found him at a heavy oak table, books and papers piled high about him. She was out of breath. Her heart fluttered in her chest. He smiled when he saw her, took off his glasses, leaned back, and stretched.

"What's up?" He whispered. "You look funny." He grinned fully, the dimpled smile she loved.

"I can't tell you here." She panted.

"Shh." Someone hissed from the next table.

"Write it down." He pushed his notebook across the table to her. She scribbled the news and slid it back. Wesley looked down at the pad. His hair was longer then and she couldn't see his face. He looked up and, with his lips sealed, motioned for her to follow him. He led her out the door and into the stairwell to the stacks below. Then he turned, pushed her gently to the wall, and gave her the deepest and most passionate kiss ever.

Annie descended from the train carrying a flower-printed duffel bag in one hand and clutching her worn leather briefcase in the other.

Knowing that her poems and photographs were inside renewed her confidence. The very weight of the bag gave her a sense of purpose. She loved the intensity of this project. It was so much more interesting than working on one poem, then another, sending them off, then waiting months and months for a response.

Although it was still early January, the air was fresher in Villandry, and Annie thought she detected a hint of spring in the brisk wind and almost cloudless sky. She'd forgotten how a blue sky could lighten her spirit and lift the worry from her heart. She turned off the main street lined with small shops, a post office, and a real estate business, all closed for the noon hour, and began the short walk toward God House. The buildings grew farther apart and the street turned into a country road. The sidewalk became a gravel path. Her comfortable brown walking boots crunched on the pebbles. She avoided the puddles that had so recently been icy reminders of winter. Under her green loden coat she wore jeans and the new black sweater. Her stride became longer and more relaxed as she neared her destination, enjoying the walk.

Turning into the drive at God House she heard Daphne's car come up behind her.

Daphne opened her window and called out, "Well, my timing is off. I'd meant to get you at the station."

Annie leaned down and spoke through the open window, "I never told you my exact arrival time. How are you?"

"I'm great. I figured you'd be on this train or the next. Hop in. I left a pot of Berthe's soup on while I fetched bread from the village. Let's hope I haven't burned the house down."

Annie came around, tossed her things into the backseat, and got in beside Daphne for the last few hundred feet up the drive. The car smelled of old leather and a fresh citruslike perfume she didn't recognize. Daphne's thick hair was tucked behind her ears, and she wore the same baggy pants and sweater that Annie remembered from her last visit.

"I'm so glad you're back," Daphne said. "You'll have plenty of time to work. It's just you and me, and we don't have to answer to anyone. No guests, and Berthe has gone to her sister's house in Aix."

Annie smiled. She did feel better. The image of the mother and baby on the train remained with her, and she wondered what her baby, her Sophie, was doing now. Daphne drew the car to a stop in front of the house. The old gray walls looked warm and inviting, less imposing than on her first visit.

Annie followed Daphne up the front steps. The black-and-white floor, the peach walls, and the antique chest were now all bathed in a softer light, infused with sunshine. Today there was a round pot of rosemary sitting on the chest. Annie brushed her hand across the spiky branches, releasing the pungent fresh scent.

"Nice, isn't it?" Daphne said.

"Rosemary for remembrance. It always makes me think of Aunt Kate. She had a dear little herb garden just outside the kitchen door." For a fleeting moment Annie regretted having sold the old house in Vermont.

They pulled off their boots in the hall and hung their coats on the pegs under the staircase. This time Annie savored the familiarity of it all.

"Go ahead and put your things upstairs while I go and serve the soup."

Annie went up to her room, the one she had recently shared with Wesley. She looked at it with new eyes; the walls covered in the pale pink floral paper and the fabrics of cream-colored taffeta were so distinctly feminine. She hadn't thought of this on their last visit. Other than the library with its leather sofa and mahogany desk, God House had clearly been decorated with the comfort of women in mind.

She stood at the window and looked down at the garden and the river, now glimmering in the sun. This room, now hers alone, felt like a sort of sanctuary. Deep down she must have needed this space. Suddenly she wanted to cry. She was relieved to be away, and yet she wondered if it could solve anything. She brought her hand to her face and could still smell the rosemary on her fingers. Aunt Kate wouldn't have accepted this kind of brooding.

Annie got her brush out of her bag, swept her hair back into a ponytail at the nape of her neck, and fastened it with a tortoiseshell barrette. She frowned in the mirror, noting the circles under her eyes and the fine lines around her mouth. She needed a good night's sleep, though she knew it would only go so far.

Daphne had set the table in the glass room off the kitchen, and a large bowl of vegetable soup steamed at each place. There was a basket of freshly sliced bread and a dish of grated Parmesan cheese on the table beside it. Daphne carried a bottle of red wine in from the kitchen and poured some into their glasses. The soup was thick and delicious, and in no time Annie was in a better mood. The wine brought color to her cheeks, and when they finished eating, they agreed on a big walk along the river. Annie started to clear the dishes but Daphne pulled her away. "Come on. The sun is out now. We can do these later."

Later, as the afternoon ebbed into evening, they sat sipping tea by the fire in the library. Annie felt refreshed from their long walk in the fresh air and stimulated by Daphne's questions and ongoing enthusiasm for the book. She couldn't quite fathom Daphne's interest, and she was somewhat surprised by the intensity of such a recent friendship. They seemed to have reached a kind of understanding that usually took months or even years to develop.

"Wait until we take the river walk in the spring," Daphne said. "The banks will be covered with daffodils."

"Who knows where I'll be then." Annie set her cup down and drew her feet up under herself on the sofa.

"You'll be right here, writing more poems for Paul's book."

"You forget. Wesley's off in America, probably accepting a job there as we speak."

"And you'll drop everything here to go and play loving wife?" Daphne tilted her head and raised her eyebrows in a bemused expression.

"Of course not." Annie was vaguely annoyed, though she knew Daphne was teasing. "I'm sure I can manage to do the poems. Besides, I don't have to follow right away."

"You use the word follow. I'm not sure I see you that way."

"Just how do you see me?"

"I see you as a lot more than a dutiful, obliging wife. As a matter of fact, I think I see you more clearly than you see yourself."

"And how is that?"

"Well"—Daphne paused and appeared to consider this thoughtfully—"for one thing, I see you as someone ready to get rid of a lifetime of restraints. I know it's a cliché, but I think you are just about to hit your stride. You've told me how you miss your mother, how you never knew her. Well, I have a feeling you're a lot like her. I think you're going to discover all kinds of things about yourself. Maybe you'll laugh"—and here Daphne did laugh—"but I think I'm the one who came along just in time to help you. I view it as my job to get you there."

Annie found this a bit presumptuous. "I'm glad you're so interested, but—"

"Look. Just think about it." Daphne took another sip of tea and got up. "Listen, have a little rest. I'm going to make a few phone calls. We can talk about it later over a drink."

Annie wasn't sure she wanted to continue this conversation at all, though she was sleepy and decided to stay right there by the fire for a nap.

When she awoke, the room was dark, the only light coming from the glow of the coals dying in the fireplace. Sitting up, she was overcome with a sense of peace, an enveloping stillness. She was aware of her own breathing, the ticking of a clock in the hall, and distant sounds coming from the kitchen. Rather than clicking on a light and getting up to help out, like her usual efficient self, she remained perfectly still and watched the fire in silence.

"Well, you're awake," Daphne said. "I'm going to rev up this fire and pour some drinks."

Annie still didn't say a word. She stretched out her legs, rested her head on the back of the sofa, and watched as Daphne added logs and poked the coals. The fire obediently burst to life.

"You look happy," Daphne said, turning around.

"Oh, I feel so much better. Sometimes there's just nothing like a nap."

"How about a whiskey?"

"I never drink whiskey."

"Remember what we talked about. Just try one." She went over to a shelf in the bookcase where several crystal decanters were lined up with a tray of glasses. She poured the dark, honey-colored liquid into a heavy, short glass without ice. Then she poured a second one and came over and sat on the sofa at Annie's feet. She handed her the drink. Annie reached out and lifted the glass to her lips. The whiskey felt vaguely hot as it went down, but not unpleasant. She quite liked the aftertaste.

Daphne came around to the back of the sofa and picked up Annie's ponytail, giving it a brief tug.

"Have you ever thought of cutting it?" Daphne asked, and came back to the sofa. Annie was too astonished to answer. Her hair, while not a particularly exciting shade of pale brown, was thick and in summer took on golden highlights from the sun. She knew Wesley liked it long, and she'd never bothered to do anything different with it. Daphne was looking fixedly at her. Annie took another sip of whiskey.

"Don't be shocked. You've got lovely thick hair, and I think it could be great cut in layers, boyish but longer." Daphne took a sip of her drink and reached over to Annie, unclipping the barrette. "I could do it, you know. I mean cut your hair. I did it all the time in boarding school. The girls thought I was very good." She drew her fingers through Annie's hair.

This time Annie took a big swallow of the whiskey. Some voice, which did not sound like her own, said, "Fine, do it. I'm totally sick of what I look like."

Daphne laughed. "You mean it?"

"I do."

"Okay, bring your drink. Let's go up to my bathroom. I've got scissors there."

Annie followed Daphne up the stairs, into her room and the bathroom beyond. She thought again of the afternoon when she had brought Daphne her tea in that old-fashioned bathroom, spare and functional with a claw-footed tub and two large porcelain sinks side by side. A huge mirror in a mahogany frame covered most of the wall above the sinks. Daphne pulled a wooden chair out into the center of the bathroom. It scraped loudly across the tile floor.

"That's a gorgeous sweater, but take it off and put this over your shoulders." She handed Annie an enormous white bath towel. Annie, with a surge of excitement, felt like a young girl about to do something that might get her into trouble. She set her drink down on the edge of the sink and pulled her sweater over her head to expose her pale winter skin and small breasts. She shivered. At least she was wearing one of her nicer bras. Daphne got the scissors from a drawer and picked up a heavy clump of hair on the top of Annie's head.

Annie heard the snap of the scissors as Daphne made the first cut. She shut her eyes.

"Okay?"

Annie kept her eyes closed and merely nodded. A sense of abandonment came over her. It was like the time she had gone skinny-dipping with Wesley in the pond behind his parents' house in Connecticut. She remembered the delightful sensation of the water caressing her body and the fear of someone discovering them totally naked in the hot summer sun. Now she imagined her head becoming lighter as Daphne cut hunk after hunk of her hair.

Daphne's fingers were cool and firm on her scalp. Periodically, she pulled both hands through Annie's hair before reaching for another clump. Eventually, she picked up the comb and drew it through, cutting small bits and the ends.

"I'm not opening my eyes until you're done," Annie said. "Would you hand me my drink, please? I think I'm beginning to like whiskey."

Daphne laughed softly and kept cutting. Gradually her work slowed and she pulled the towel off Annie's shoulders, brushing off the lingering remnants of hair. "Done," she said, and stepped back to admire the results.

Annie opened her eyes slowly. She stood and stared into the bathroom mirror. The face looking back amazed her. Annie's thick hair was suited to the many layers and curled gently under. Daphne had tucked the short pieces by her face behind her ears. The final effect was young and French-looking, making her features seem more distinct, her eyes bigger, and her mouth fuller. Annie expected the illusion to disappear, but the vision smiled back at her. Daphne handed her the black sweater. She pulled it over her head and tucked the sides of her hair behind her ears as Daphne had done a few minutes ago.

Daphne stood behind her. "You look beautiful."

"Thanks, Daphne. It's wonderful. I can't believe in all these years I've never thought of changing it." She looked into the wastebasket where Daphne had tossed the hunks of hair. The hair didn't look like her own but like that of a stranger.

"It's really more you, very sexy too."

"I wonder what Wesley will think."

"He'd be crazy not to love it." Daphne gave the towel a final shake. "Now let's go down before the chicken in the oven is all dried up."

ELEVEN

La Surprise

Annie enjoyed waking up alone at God House on these January mornings. She appreciated the stillness, the silence, not having to talk to anyone. She pulled her covers up around her neck. The room was chilly; it would be another cold bright day. She thought of winter mornings in Vermont when she could see her breath in the air as she got out of bed. Aunt Kate always lowered the thermostat for the night. By January, the gray landscape would have been securely blanketed by snow that grew deeper with each winter storm. Between storms, the skies would clear and the sun would sparkle against the bright blue. On clear nights, the moon would illuminate the cold, sleeping world in a kind of primeval light that felt like magic.

Spending this time with Daphne at God House had been an unexpected pleasure. She had let go of her usual worries, and she welcomed the freedom from her normal responsibilities. She had shed her hair along with old habits and the pattern of her life with Wesley. Her writing was going well.

This morning, sunlight washed across the pink walls of her God House bedroom. The color reminded her of the pink shirts Wesley used to wear when she first met him. Made of cotton oxford cloth, softened by repeated launderings, they smelled like him, clean and optimistic. She had found their scent and softness so reassuring the first time that he had drawn her into his arms. He had felt so different from Luke, whose black turtlenecks smelled of smoke and the stale odor of men's dormitories. She had equated Luke's smell with sexiness and the alien territory of the male species. She soon learned that sex and love itself could take on another, altogether different flavor, and one she had grown to love. She tried to remember when Wesley had stopped wearing the pink shirts.

Annie's days at God House took on a pleasant routine, each day melting easily into the next. In the mornings she and Daphne moved about quietly in their separate worlds. Annie, usually the first one up, would come down to the kitchen in her nightgown and robe for coffee. Daphne set up the coffee machine the night before, and Annie would switch it on and go out to the glass room to look for signs of life in the garden. She didn't know much about gardening, but like most Parisians, she tended window boxes and pots of plants on the windowsills of her apartment. But here an entire community of birds made their home among the hibernating plants. She watched them dine on seed pods and berries and dive into the bushes for cover. Soon there would be a few fresh green shoots peeking through the dark earth, the tips of spring bulbs.

When the coffee machine gave up its sputtering with a final wheeze, she'd go back to the kitchen to pour her first cup. On particularly cold mornings she'd carry her coffee back to bed, but today she went out to her favorite wicker chair at the far end of the glass room. She liked to start the day by reading something good, and this usually inspired her to start writing. She picked up a book she'd found yesterday in the library about the French writer Pierre Lotti, who wrote at the end of the nineteenth century about the lure of exotic places and his travels in North Africa. She looked at her white feet and wondered how they would feel on the smooth tiles of a Moroccan palace he described.

After a while, Annie would migrate back up to her room and run a hot bath. She might look in on Daphne briefly. Daphne preferred to spend the morning sitting in the middle of her large bed surrounded by piles of books and papers. She had her coffee on one tray and used another as a writing table. By ten-thirty or eleven Annie would hear her moving about and eventually the sound of her voice on the phone as she checked in with clients and antiques dealers. When Daphne set up a simple business appointment, her low, rich voice made it sound more like she was arranging an illicit rendezvous.

Usually by noon both women would meet in the kitchen hungry and ready for a snack or an early lunch. Today Annie found Daphne in the kitchen making a list.

"It's market day." She raised her bent head and put down her pencil. "Why don't we go into the village for some shopping?"

"I'd love to." Annie ran her fingers through her hair, still surprised at the feel of it. "Can you get fish at your market? I could cook mussels for dinner."

"Lovely idea. They bring in a truck from Brittany." Daphne seemed to be thinking something over and then added, "Let's buy enough for three. I talked to your Valmont this morning. He's bringing out some boxes of china late this afternoon, and we need to discuss what he wants to put in for an upcoming auction. I may invite him to stay on for dinner." She bent to add a few more things to the list. "It's okay with you, isn't it?"

"Of course," Annie said. "Why would I mind?"

"He can't get here until after five. I could hardly send him back to Paris on an empty stomach. And after all, he is your editor now and we have to keep him happy."

"It'll be fun. I don't mind at all." She thought of their last meeting, the pleasure of working with Paul in his office and the friendly dinner that followed. There had been that brief awkward moment of parting when he'd touched her face. What would it be like to see him here at God House, to share him with Daphne? "Your Valmont," she had said.

The sign above the door said CHEZ GABBY. They had finished their shopping in the village, and Daphne suggested the slight detour to Morillon, another sleepy little town of houses with closed graying shutters hiding the private lives that hibernated within. A small pâtisserie on the main street was well lit, and Annie could see several elderly ladies bent over the counter studying an array of fruit tarts and dainty cakes.

Just beyond, they came to the antiques shop where Daphne had wanted to check on some brass lanterns that the proprietor, Gabby, had found for her at a recent auction.

"Gabby hunts for me, keeps an eye out for things I'm trying to find for my clients," Daphne explained. "It's a two-way arrangement." She pushed the door open into the shop. "I send her plenty of business too. You'll like her things."

Annie followed Daphne into the hushed, velvety gloom. She had never seen so many objects crowded into one space. She maneuvered carefully around aging upholstered sofas and chairs and in between elegant marqueterie tables with finely carved legs. Almost every surface was covered with bits and pieces: small bronze sculptures, vases, boxes, Chinese lamps, silver candlesticks, brass ornaments. Annie could imagine a story behind each carefully chosen object: a beloved grandmother's sewing box; an aging spinster's wedding linens; yellowing, lace-edged embroidered pillow slips, never used; a set of studs and cuff links worn by a turn-of-the-century dandy at the Paris Opéra. Annie could see the allure of collecting these items, rich in history, unique, and far more interesting than newly fabricated things.

"Have a look around. Gabby's probably having her coffee and afternoon cigarette in the back. I'll tell her we're here." Daphne disappeared behind a louvered door at the back of the shop. Annie detected the particular scent of a Gauloise, so unlike tame American tobacco.

Left on her own, Annie was drawn to the far wall of the shop, covered entirely in paintings. She immediately noticed a landscape of a wide, sun-washed field dotted with hay bales against a blue sky. Soft, puffy clouds lazed horizontally across the canvas. She could practically smell the newly mown hay and hear the blur of bees humming on a summer afternoon. The picture made her think of Wesley's parents' house in western Connecticut. The fields beyond the barn looked just like this. She remembered visiting there one August. The weather had been hot and dry, and the sound of the mowers came through the windows one morning while they sat at breakfast. Annie had expressed her regret in seeing the swaths of wildflowers cut down along with the hay.

She tried to recall the details of that visit. Was Sophie only seven or eight? It must have been the summer when Wesley made partner at Wilson & James. She remembered how excited he had been to tell his father. Wesley, still in his thirties, was proud of his blossoming career.

They had been so happy then, their lives uncomplicated and sweet. Despite the easy summer days, the pristine country air, and Wesley's admiring parents during that visit, Annie remembered longing to return to Paris. She missed the life they were building there, missed the cafés, the busy streets, their apartment. In Paris she and Wesley were the grown-ups. They were adults creating their future. In Connecticut they remained the grown children, honoring their parents, still caught up in their past.

"You seem far away."

Annie turned. "This is a wonderful painting. It reminds me of Connecticut."

Daphne nodded. "Do you wish you were there?"

"No. Of course not. Not now, anyway."

"It's a lovely painting. Why does it make you look so sad?"

"Sorry. I don't mean to look sad." How could she explain the mood that came over her? "We spent our summers in Connecticut when we were younger, when Sophie was little. Sometimes I wish that I could merely snap my fingers and recapture those days."

"I know what you mean," Daphne murmured nostalgically. She turned away from the painting and surveyed the many objects on a nearby antique desk. She reached for a silver letter opener resting in a satin box.

"Look. It's monogrammed." She pointed to the elaborate swirling A at the base of the handle and handed it to Annie. The blade glinted briefly and Annie felt the smooth handle in her palm.

"It would be perfect on your desk in Paris." She laughed. "It has your name on it."

"It's very handsome."

"Then it's yours."

"Daphne—"

"I want to buy it for you."

"No. Really you mustn't." She handed it back to Daphne. "You gave me a Christmas present, and it's not my birthday."

"Presents are best when you least expect them."

"That's so kind. But—"

"I'll take it back to Gabby. She's wrapping the lanterns."

Before Annie could protest further, Daphne went through the door in the back of the shop. Annie listened to their voices, one melodic in a poetic French cadence, the other in crisp English vowels. Annie was touched by Daphne's generosity, her gesture to cheer her up. It was as if Daphne understood what she barely understood herself. Annie knew that she must seize on all the good things in her life now, her writing and the challenges ahead, but she couldn't stifle an elusive longing, something triggered by the artist's landscape.

Later that afternoon when they returned from their shopping trip, Annie hurried straight to the kitchen to put away the groceries. She set the mussels to soak, and they clattered down into the old stone sink. Annie decided not to work in the library as Daphne had planned to meet there with Paul. Daphne had explained that she needed some time alone with him to discuss the final sale of his wife's furniture. "You know the French—so private, so formal." Annie assured Daphne that she understood and decided to work upstairs in her bedroom for the rest of the afternoon. Rather than write at the desk, she gathered her notebooks and pen and sat in the chaise longue by the windows.

The day had started to cloud over, but there was still plenty of natural light. Annie opened to the page where she'd left off and stared at the words. They looked empty and lifeless to her now. She closed the notebook and turned her attention to the darkening sky, trying to match color names to the imperceptible variations: pearl gray, dove, graphite, charcoal. The words sounded inadequate to her ears. All too soon she became aware of the sounds below—first the arrival of a car, then the jolt of the heavy knocker on the front door, and finally the murmur of voices.

She reached for her leather calendar book and looked at the date. It was already Wednesday. She'd been at God House for almost a week. She thought of the pile of transcripts sitting at home. They were due before the start of the new semester. Mary was counting on her. She had let the days slip by, ignoring all that needed to be done back in Paris. She let out a sigh. For the first time since her arrival at God House, Annie felt the intrusion of her other world.

Knowing that Paul was downstairs made her feel uneasy. Thankfully, she had completed several new poems. She was proud of this work and eager to show it to him. The new poems were stronger than the first ones, and she thought she had been able to keep the voice of the earlier section alive. There needed to be some kind of thread to weave the collection together. Hopefully, he would see it too. He and Daphne had been talking in the library for quite a while. Would he accept Daphne's invitation to dinner? Annie touched her hair. What would he think?

Trying to gather some resolve, she went into the bathroom to wash her face and freshen up. She turned on the light and studied her appearance. This time she didn't feel sexy; her short hair looked harsh and shaggy to her. She planned to have Raoul, her neighborhood hairdresser, give it a touch-up when she got home. She pulled on her nicer black trousers and a red sweater she hadn't worn yet, wanting to make more of an effort and knowing that Paul might stay. Some makeup and a splash of perfume also helped to improve her spirits.

It was time to start dinner, so she headed down to the kitchen. She heard the faint sound of their voices coming from the library. Daphne must have shut the door to keep from disturbing her. Annie turned on the lamp in the hall and passed through the dining room to the kitchen. She saw that Daphne had arranged a bowl of daffodils, the flowers they'd brought back from the market. They glowed in the twilight on the long polished table.

Annie scooped the mussels out of the sink and put them in a pot, covering them with more cold water for another soak. She examined them carefully and pulled off any remaining beards with a sharp knife. The shimmering navy-black shells smelled of the sea, a pungent wet saltiness. She reached into the icy water, grabbed them by handfuls, and tossed them into an ancient enamelware colander, allowing the excess water to drain into the sink. There was something so elemental about food dug right out of the sand, a peaceful coexistence of land and sea.

"How's the chef?" Daphne asked.

Annie jumped. "I didn't hear you come in," she explained. "You scared me." She laughed uncertainly.

"You're just off in your poetic world." She grinned. "Listen, I'm going up to change my clothes before dinner. We just moved some boxes into the carriage house." She pushed her hair back off her face. "Paul will be here in a minute. I put him in charge of fixing drinks. He decided to stay for dinner."

Daphne hurried away, closing the door behind her. Annie reached back into the sink to give the mussels one more soak. Knowing Paul would be dining with them made this evening already feel different from the previous dinners when she and Daphne had been by themselves. They'd eaten in the village a few times, but mostly they'd enjoyed simple suppers in the kitchen or had eaten on trays in front of the fire.

"*Bonsoir.*" Now it was Paul's voice interrupting her reverie. "Daphne promised me a surprise guest if I agreed to stay for dinner." Annie turned. "I am happy it is you," he said. "I see you are not only a writer. You are also a chef." Paul smiled. He wore jeans, a light blue turtleneck, and a tweed sport coat she recognized from a previous meeting.

"Hardly a chef," she said, happy to see him. "A cook is more like it." She extended a cold wet hand and quickly apologized. "Sorry, you caught me wet-handed." God, what a stupid thing to say. She wondered if he understood her unexpected pun. She could feel her cheeks grow warm.

"Do not let me interrupt. Daphne says you are making *moules.*"

"Yes. I'm glad you'll be joining us." She looked around for a tea towel.

He handed her one from a nearby hook and watched as she dried her hands. It felt very strange to have him here in the kitchen. It took away the professional feel that marked their previous encounters.

"Your hair." He lifted his hand as to reach out to touch it and then pulled back. "It is most charming."

Annie was happy with the compliment. She fingered the neckline of her sweater and felt a blush creeping up her throat. Without the weight of her hair, her neck seemed exposed, vulnerable.

He seemed to sense her unease. "May I bring you a drink?"

"I'd love a white wine." She paused. "No, make that a whiskey."

"Shall I bring it in here, or do you want to join us in the library?"

"I'll come and join you in a few minutes," she said. "Thank you," she added self-consciously. She turned back to the sink, relieved to have a few moments to compose herself. Somehow, having Paul here at God House changed everything. Annie drew her fingers through her hair. It still felt like the head of a stranger. She took a large soup pot from the cupboard next to the stove. She poured in half a bottle of white wine and added a handful of chopped shallots. From the fridge she took some greens for a salad as well as the cheeses that they would have for dessert. She put them on a plate near the stove to warm to room temperature. She wanted everything to be right.

"*Bravo!*" Paul exclaimed. "These *moules*, they are excellent." His eyes in the candlelight appeared especially dark and lustrous. Annie smiled and agreed that she was pleased with the results. The enormous dish of mussels disappeared in no time.

Daphne sat between Paul and Annie at the head of the table and she talked with Paul about La Motte and some of the other towns in the hills above Saint-Tropez. "Have you been to Bistro Luna?"

He shook his head.

"They do an extraordinary *soupe au pistou*." Daphne swished a hunk of bread through the remaining broth in her bowl. "Totally divine." She licked her lips.

"Do you know this part of France?" Paul asked Annie. The bowl of discarded mussel shells lay between them.

"Not well. When we didn't go home to Connecticut in the summer, we used to go to Brittany."

"Those beaches are always freezing, even in August," Daphne said. She turned to Paul. "We always went down to the beach at Sainte-Maxime. Less crowded than Saint-Tropez, don't you agree?"

"I suppose you are right, but—"

"Is the peanut lady still there?"

Paul laughed with Daphne as she told Annie about the scantily dressed woman selling sugared peanuts on the beach, teasing the men by tucking a few nuts between her breasts and daring them to take a taste. Daphne lifted her hair onto her head, leaned toward Paul suggestively, and said in a silly high-pitched tone, "*Cacahuètes? Mesdames, messieurs.* Come, come let me offer you a little taste."

When Annie got up to clear the table and bring the salad, Daphne launched into a story about people she knew on the French Riviera and a trip she'd taken one summer with Tim. Annie was growing weary of trying to look interested in Daphne's tales of the south. She'd begun to wonder if it was all true. It seemed liked Daphne was doing everything she could to keep her out of the conversation. She stayed in the kitchen a few moments longer than necessary. She thought again of her apartment and felt she needed to go home.

She carried the freshly tossed greens back to the table. Paul looked glad to see her. "Tell me, how are the poems coming?" He smiled encouragingly.

"Please, have some salad," Daphne said, pushing the bowl in his direction.

"I think I've finished two more," Annie said.

"Which photographs did you choose?"

"Now now, we're not going to talk about work," Daphne said before Annie had time to answer. "Paul and I just spent several hours on business, and he needs to have a little fun this evening."

Annie thought she saw a shadow of annoyance cross his face. "I don't think Paul minds talking about the book." She helped herself to salad and passed the bowl to Daphne.

"He's far too nice to say anything," Daphne said. "You can have your little literary chats another time."

Literary chats? What sort of comment was that? "For heaven's sake, Daphne, I just want to—"

"Annie, dear. You're sounding like a sensitive whining poet. Let poor Paul have a little time off."

"Why don't you send me the poems?" Paul said, looking baffled. "We'll meet soon in Paris. We can talk about them then."

Annie was furious at Daphne. She tried to regain her composure. "Yes," she said. "I'll do that."

"I plan to keep Annie here for a while longer," Daphne said. "She does her best work here at God House."

Paul made no comment but looked quizzically at Annie.

"Excuse me," she said, and stood up. "I forgot to bring out the cheese."

Annie returned to the kitchen. She rearranged the cheeses on the platter, in no hurry to go back to the table. What had gotten into Daphne? It was like she was wound up about something, and she was treating her like some kind of temperamental younger sister. She couldn't imagine what Paul must think. When she returned to the dining room Daphne was regaling Paul with stories about discovering a rare collection of small bronzes.

At last they went into the living room for coffee. Daphne had brewed a dark espresso in a glass plunger pot. She handed Paul a cup and motioned to him to sit beside her on the sofa.

"Will you be bringing other things out here for Daphne to sell?" Annie asked.

"No, this is the last of it," he said. "Most of the furniture was sent to the auction house by lorry a few weeks ago."

"I did persuade Paul to keep a few things," Daphne said. "I don't like my clients to have regrets." She smiled at him.

"I thought I only wanted to keep the books, but I will keep an armoire and chest of drawers. I will have them moved to my new apartment."

"I'm eager to see your new place," Daphne said. "Moving to a new apartment was a good idea."

"Everyone told me not to sell. They say it is better not to make decisions too soon, but staying in the old place was too depressing. I could not stand being there without Marie Laure." He shook his head. "I am always thinking she would walk through a doorway or that I would find her when I returned home."

"It must be so difficult," Annie said, remembering the photograph of his lovely wife.

Paul took a final sip of coffee and went to stand closer to the fire. He put his hands deep in his pockets.

"Come now," Daphne said, going over to join him. "I don't want you looking sad again." She put her arm around him and guided him back to the sofa. "I think a nightcap is in order." She went to the tray of liquours she'd set out earlier in the evening. "Annie won't approve, but a little brandy might do you good." She removed the stopper from a crystal decanter.

"Daphne," Annie said, horrified, "what do you mean I won't approve?"

"Drinking and driving. These Americans do have their rules."

"I never said—"

"I do have to drive back to Paris," Paul said. "And it is late." He looked ill at ease.

"Oh, nonsense." Daphne looked annoyed.

He got to his feet. "I have several appointments tomorrow morning."

Daphne shrugged. "Well then"—she drew one hand back through her hair—"we'll save nightcaps for another time." She put the stopper back into the bottle.

Daphne and Annie walked into the hall with Paul, who now seemed in a hurry to leave. Daphne helped him with his overcoat, and he repeated his thanks for dinner and kissed her on both cheeks. Then he took Annie's hands in his and held them briefly. "I am so happy the work is going well. I will call you in Paris."

"Well, well. Don't we look glum." Daphne poured herself a brandy.

Annie sat on the sofa where Paul had just been. Now what? she thought. She ignored Daphne's comment.

"I hope you know you're making a fool of yourself." Daphne set down her drink and added a log to the fire. She kicked it farther back into the grate. Sparks flew up and a moment later new flames bounced to life.

"What on earth do you mean?"

Daphne stood in front of her and looked down. "Just because you're doing the poems for his book doesn't mean you have to fall at his feet like a lovesick adolescent."

Annie felt like she'd had the air knocked out of her. "Daphne, you're crazy." She could no longer hide her anger. "You were the one falling at his feet. I never got a word in edgewise. I don't know what you're talking about."

"Very simply, my dear, I'm talking about your sipping whiskey, batting your eyes at him, and nearly falling into his lap before we even got to dinner." She went to the far side of the room and turned her back to Annie.

"That's ridiculous. I had one drink, and we talked about French poetry and—"

"You never would have acted like that if Wesley had been here."

"Acted like what?" She thought madly back to the hour before dinner. She had sat beside Paul, she had laughed at a silly story he told. She certainly hadn't done anything inappropriate. "What do you mean 'if Wesley had been here'?"

"I know what you're thinking about Paul." Daphne smiled strangely and came to sit beside her. She raised her eyebrows.

"What?" Annie could hardly speak. "What I'm thinking about him?" She looked away, uncomfortable.

"Wesley wouldn't like you having those thoughts." Her manner was taunting.

"Daphne. Stop it. This is nuts."

"Listen to me. I went out on a limb for you. I called Paul. I sang your praises. It's thanks to me that you have this chance."

"Please. You know I'm grateful to you for that."

"Well then, don't go acting like another lovestruck dithering female." Daphne cupped Annie's chin and drew her face toward her. Annie felt sick. Daphne's eyes had taken on a funny color. "I won't stand for it. Do you hear me?"

Annie pulled away. "This conversation is absurd. I'm going to bed." She left Daphne by the fire, made her way up to her room, and closed the door behind her. She stood looking out the window, barely able to breathe. She didn't turn on the lights. There was a full moon and the night was still; not even a whisper of wind marred the silence.

———

The next morning Annie heard a tap on her door, and Daphne came in carrying a tray with a pot of coffee and two large cups. She wore soft knit lounge pants and a loose gray man's robe tied with a scarlet tasseled sash, the kind of attire Annie imagined an actor wearing in his dressing room.

"Your coffee, madame." She smiled and made a funny little bow. She set the tray down by Annie's feet, crossed the room, and swept open the curtains. The large silk panels slid easily on the rod. She paused at the window to look over the gardens and the river beyond. Annie pulled herself up against the pillows. Daphne no longer seemed angry. For a moment Annie wondered if she had dreamed the entire thing: Daphne's domineering behavior at dinner, her ridiculous assumptions about her own behavior with Paul, the unpleasant conversation before bed. In the clarity of morning, it seemed hard to believe.

"I like the garden best in winter," Daphne said. "All the plant life is silently dreaming down in the frozen earth." Daphne shivered and pulled the collar of her robe around her neck. "It's also a lot less work." She laughed. A few rays of weak winter sun fell across the carpet. Annie sat up further, taking care not to knock the coffee tray by her feet. Daphne picked up an extra pillow from the floor, propped it behind Annie's back, then collected the tray at the foot of the bed and carried it to the other side. She set it down in the middle.

"I just turned up the heat. This room is freezing. Do you mind if I join you?"

"Not at all."

Daphne got up onto the bed and sat cross-legged next to Annie. She lay the duvet across her lap and pulled the tray closer.

"Antoinette and Mummy always started the day with coffee in bed. When I was little, I sat at their feet." She poured the coffee and hot milk into the cups and handed one to Annie.

Annie took a big sip from her cup. It tasted much better than the coffee she made at home.

"You look tired," Daphne said. "Didn't you sleep well last night?"

"I was awake for several hours, I'm afraid. Some of the things you said upset me. I hate arguments. I always have."

"We're going to forget about all that." She drank from her cup and set it back on the tray. "I forgive you. Today's a new day."

"Forgive me?" Annie shook her head. "I felt that you—"

"I know you're going through a lot. Haven't you had a good time here?"

"Of course, but—"

"And you've gotten lots of writing done?"

"Yes. Yes, it's been wonderful."

"That's all that matters then. You, me, this beautiful place. You can't argue with that." She lifted the covers and straightened her legs beneath the sheets.

"No. Of course not."

"I want you to see the garden this spring." Daphne leaned back into the pillows. "It's amazing. You can practically smell the earth when the ground warms up. The tiny silent microbes bursting with life and ready to color the fields with new green. You've got to be in the country to really appreciate spring."

"It sounds wonderful."

"See. You are happy here." She reached across the covers and patted Annie's hand. Her touch was cool.

Annie was relieved by Daphne's change of mood, though she still felt wary. She didn't want to talk about Paul. "Of course I'm happy. I've had the best time." She looked toward the window and wondered if this winter world would ever turn green. "It's just that I have to go home. I never finished the transcripts for Mary, and I have so much to do before classes begin. Also, pretty soon Sophie and Wesley will be getting back."

"You're thinking of leaving? Already?"

"Daphne, you've got things to do too." She watched her face. "I heard you make appointments. You have clients to see."

"It can all wait. I don't want you to leave yet. This time together has made us so much closer. I'm sure you feel it too."

The word us rang in Annie's ears. "I'm not sure what you mean."

"For God's sake, certainly you feel the attraction." Daphne pulled her mouth into an unattractive pout and turned toward Annie. Her eyes, gray today, the color of her robe, had delicate violet circles under them. They were smudged from last night's mascara. She reached over and smoothed Annie's forehead. "Don't look so worried. Just stay a few more days." She ran her fingers through Annie's tousled short hair. Her touch was soothing but unsettling as well. "I know you're drawn to me. It started the first time you saw me. You watched me in the Métro."

"Daphne, I—"

"Quite a coincidence when we both turned up at the Verniers'." She laughed softly.

All this time and Daphne had said nothing. "I didn't know that you'd noticed me." Annie took another sip of coffee. It was growing cold. She set her cup on her nightstand. "Daphne, I did watch you. I'm always observing people. You were different. But it's not like that. You must understand, Wesley and I—"

"You are so naïve. Sweet girl, I sometimes like men too." She smiled coyly. "With women, though, it's different."

Annie shook her head. She had come to understand that Nora and Antoinette were lovers. Should she have seen this coming? There had been glances, touches, a lingering hand from time to time. Annie had told herself it was Daphne's tactile nature, her sensuous side, the more relaxed attitude of Europeans toward their bodies. None of this had bothered her. "Daphne, I don't have those kind of feelings."

"You're sure?" Daphne raised her eyebrows and grinned.

"I never have before and—" Daphne put her finger on Annie's mouth as if to silence her.

"Don't say anything. You're an artist, a poet. You feel things deeply. I know you do. Just wait and see. I think you'll surprise yourself." She withdrew her hand from Annie's lips and pulled gently at the sleeve of Annie's nightgown. It slipped down off her shoulder, exposing her bare skin. Very gently, Daphne caressed her. Annie, stunned and confused, didn't move. She sat perfectly still, unable to imagine what would happen next. "Close your eyes. Just let yourself go."

Annie did as she was told. Was she capable of this? The boundaries of love had always blurred across the lines of poetry. She took a deep breath and tried to ignore her doubts.

Daphne touched Annie's face. Her hand was warm. She drew her fingers down along her neck, tracing the line of her collarbone back to her bare shoulder. A moment later Annie felt Daphne's lips pressed to her skin. The kisses, warm and soft, could have been those of a man, just kisses after all. Then she remembered seeing Daphne in the bath.

Annie pulled away. "No, Daphne. I'm sorry. This doesn't feel right." She threw back the covers and got out of bed. She put on her robe with trembling hands and tied the sash firmly around her waist. "I'm sorry. I think you've misunderstood. I want to be your friend. I do feel very close to you, but—"

"I know you feel something. Annie, you just need to let it happen. You shouldn't deny what you're feeling." She shook her head and reluctantly got to her feet.

Shaking and bewildered, Annie drew her arms across her chest and looked out the window at the dormant garden below. "I'm going back to Paris. I need to get home."

"Look, my sweet," Annie could hear Daphne putting the cups on the tray, "just think about it. There's so much you have yet to discover about yourself. Perhaps in time." Daphne walked soundlessly from the room.

TWELVE

La Rentrée

"Dépoussierant meubles," the can read. "Nettoie et fait briller." This is exactly what she wanted to accomplish: clean and shine. Annie had arrived home a few days before to stale air, dust, and the hush of an empty apartment, barely an echo of life. All that soon would change. Wesley and Sophie were arriving the next morning, and she wanted to restore some semblance of the way things used to be on the rue des Archives. While at God House, she'd become almost a different person: a woman with short hair, a woman who drank whiskey, a poet who couldn't stop thinking about her work. She'd also become involved in a complicated friendship, a friendship that had taken on unexpected dimensions. The thought still amazed her.

She pressed the top of the spray can. A cloying mix of floral fragrance and chemicals wafted up. She pushed the soft flannel cloth loaded with gray residue across the top of her desk. The sprigs of ivy that she kept by her mother's picture hung limply in the vase. The water had dried up completely during her absence, leaving the fine web of roots brittle and dry, impossible to save.

Feeling the need for air, she pushed open the tall windows and stood for a moment holding the railing on the narrow balcony. The ornate black wrought-iron grill sent a stream of cold from her hands to her elbows. Daphne, she thought. Would there be more surprises? Looking back on the days at God House, she realized that Daphne had the ability to yank her from one feeling to another; one moment Daphne bolstered her and gave her confidence, and the next she told her she had been a fool. Annie couldn't forget the way she had mysteriously turned on her the night Paul had come to dinner. Tim's warning had begun to haunt her. Daphne offered so much. But what kind of strings were attached? Annie drew her arms across her chest and looked up.

The buff-colored sky was velvety and still, the air damp. François Naudin had captured this same light in one of the photographs. Was it the one of the booksellers along the Seine? She wanted to work on her poems this afternoon. One last quiet afternoon before her family came back. Taking in a final deep breath of winter air, she watched pedestrians hurry along the sidewalk below. Sophie's voice, her laughter, her youthful enthusiasm, would soon fill the apartment. Annie could hardly wait to see her, to hold her in her arms. She smiled, glad to be home in Paris, and stepped back inside, closing the doors tightly behind her.

Once every surface gleamed, she dragged the vacuum cleaner out of the hall closet and tackled the floors. She threw herself gladly into all her neglected chores, enjoying the simple physical work. The sturdy hum of the motor helped to drown the voices in her head. She didn't want to think about Daphne. How incredible it all seemed now.

When the apartment was clean, she made up the daybed in Wesley's study, changing it back to Sophie's bedroom. She pulled the pale blue sheet taut over the mattress, removed the duvet from the closet, shook it, and put on the freshly pressed cover. Next she found the pillows and slipped on the white ruffled shams. Last of all, she set Olly Ours, Sophie's childhood bear, in the center of the bed. Missing one button eye and having a limp ear, he looked like the adored childhood toy that he was. Annie kept him in her bottom dresser drawer and brought him out each time her daughter returned.

Despite Wesley's desk and computer table in the corner, the room began to look more like her daughter's old bedroom. She had polished Sophie's silver baby cup and filled it with pink roses that were already opening in the indoor warmth. She set it on top of the chest of drawers and picked up the framed picture of baby Sophie held securely in the crook of Aunt Kate's arm. Aunt Kate, with the wisps of white hair escaping the bun at the back of her head, stared down with such loving acceptance at the baby, a little girl she would never know as she was now, all grown up, an adult. Annie was struck by the importance of continuity in a family, one generation looking to the next.

Aunt Kate had always given Annie that kind of love, generous and unquestioning. She had provided the cozy warmth of childhood cuddles, attention to her school-age games and imaginary play, a patient ear during the fragmented moods of adolescence. Annie hoped that Sophie felt that way about her own upbringing. Right now she focused on making Sophie's homecoming just right. She would cook her favorite dinners and they would go out to the places she loved. Most of all she wanted to re-create the atmosphere they used to have, all three of them, tucked safely into their home on the rue des Archives. Indeed, maybe Sophie's visit would restore balance to their lives.

"À la famille." Wesley raised his glass and toasted his family in the clatter and smoke of the Bistro Miravile. Lunch at Miravile was an important part of the Reed family routine to conquer jet lag. After they stumbled off the plane from the United States, groggy and disoriented, Monsieur Vartin, the taxi driver they had used for years, would maneuver them home through the morning rush hour. First a hot shower and some time to unpack, then a visit to their favorite neighborhood bistro for lunch to get them on "tummy time," and finally the reward of a big nap.

Today they'd walked together through a mild drizzle the few blocks to the restaurant and were seated at their regular table along the wall, Annie and Sophie on the banquette. "At last I get my two girls back," Wesley said. He looked weary this afternoon, showing all of his fifty-one years, but there was something endearing and familiar in his dimpled smile. His hair was longer than he usually wore it. Annie found it attractive. She ran her tongue over her lips while reading the menu and thought back to the way he'd kissed her when he got home, awkward and uncertain. He'd looked at her almost as if he no longer recognized her.

"I know you don't like my hair," she'd said.

"It's just a surprise. That's all. It doesn't seem like you. I'll get used to it." And he stood back and studied her as if trying to decide.

"Moms, I think it's absolutely beautiful. Really hip, and it makes you look so young." Sophie had flashed her sweet lopsided grin and then hugged her mother again. Annie loved the feel of Sophie's arms around her. It made her feel like her old self.

Now, in the crowded bistro, they listened to Sophie chatter on about her time in California.

"It was so great to get out of New York for a bit. It's always sunny in L.A. I bought new sunglasses." She reached into her bag and pulled them out. "What do you think?"

"Very glamorous. You look great." Annie couldn't remember the last time she had worn sunglasses, could barely remember a time when it wasn't winter. The last time she saw Sophie it had been the beginning of summer, but also the onset of Wesley's troubles—what she thought of now as the big chill that had made its way into their marriage.

Sophie looked so fresh and pretty beside her. While jet-lagged and tired from too much work, she had the moist bloom of youth and the optimism of so much life ahead of her. Her hair was the same pale blond as Wesley's before his had grayed, but her features looked like Annie's, the wide eyes and narrow nose, the long slender neck, a face still free of lines.

"You certainly seem to love your job," Annie leaned closer to her daughter and studied her face. "Did you have time for some fun too?"

"We had fun working, if you can believe that. Two of the guys in the office are very cute. I really like one."

"Aha. I thought there might be someone special."

"Mom." Sophie grinned. "It's not that big a deal."

"What's his name?" Annie asked.

"Daniel. But I'm not really seeing him." She cocked her head. "Not yet anyway."

"Any young man would be lucky to go out with you," Wesley said. "I can imagine them lining up to try to get a date."

"Daddy, you're sweet, but it doesn't work that way." She grinned at her father. "Let's talk about your news. Have you told Mom yet?"

Before Wesley could speak, the waiter arrived with lunch: two steaming plates of *poulet frites*, and *steak au poivre* for Wesley. "Eh, *voilà*," he announced. "*Bon appétit*." He told them how pleased he was to see the whole family together and left them to enjoy their meal.

"Tell her, Dad." Sophie cut into her chicken, her favorite dish at the Miravile, and Annie held her fork and knife poised above her own plate, waiting for Wesley's inevitable announcement.

"Well, it's official. I've been offered the job at Duncan Payne. They'll take me on as a full partner, and they want me to start right away." He looked confident and relieved. It was settled.

"And you accepted?"

"Of course I did."

"There's no way you could do the work for them and still live here?"

"Annie, the firm is there. You'll love Washington. Parts of it even feel kind of French. The Potomac River has wonderful big bridges leading to Virginia, and there are wide avenues planted with trees." He began to eat his steak and became more animated. "I rented a little studio apartment near the office for now. I thought you could come back with me and help look for a house."

"Well, I guess that's that," Annie said. She noticed the red juices from his steak running across the plate.

"Mother, can't you be happy for Dad?" Sophie looked at Annie with an accusatory expression.

"Of course I'm pleased for him." She regarded Wesley thoughtfully. "You deserve it, Wesley. That firm is lucky to have you."

Wesley took this as encouragement and told them more about the partners and the work he'd be doing. Annie listened politely. His plans were evolving without her. He'd accepted the job, made arrangements for a place to live, and assumed she'd willingly follow along and help pick out a house. It was like watching a movie on fast-forward. The question was, did she want to be in it?

"Moms, New York is only three hours away on the train. Dad's right. If you find a house now, you could move in the spring when the cherry blossoms are in bloom."

"It sounds very exciting." Annie didn't want to argue with either of them. She didn't want to spoil their time with Sophie and hoped they could hang on to their old world a little bit longer. "There's lots to talk about." She cut into her chicken, determined not to dwell on all that was ahead.

When they got home from the restaurant, Sophie went into her room for a nap. Wesley decided to have a look at the basket of mail that Annie had sorted for him.

"Don't you want to get a little rest too?" she asked.

"Maybe later. I've got a lot of catching up to do." He carried the mail to the sofa in the living room. "Annie, we really need to talk about this."

"What do we need to talk about? You seem to have planned everything." She went into the living room with him but did not sit down. "What about my job here? What about my book?" She heard the rising pitch of her own voice. "You and Sophie are so caught up in your own important jobs that we haven't talked about that."

"Of course we care about your book." He got up from the sofa and came over to where she stood. He took her by the shoulders. "Annie, the winter is a quiet time for you at work. You can come back to the States with me. I know Mary can manage without you for a few weeks, and she can find a replacement for you later this spring. You can work on the book anywhere. Fax the poems back and forth."

She pulled away from him. "It's not as simple as that," she said.

"Annie, you're making this more complicated than it needs to be."

She shook her head. "Look, I need to go out for a bit." She went to her desk and got her notebook. "When I get back, we'll all have a nice dinner together. Sophie's only here for a week. Let's make our plans after she goes back to New York."

"Annie, my flight to Washington is the day after hers. That doesn't leave us any time. I want to get you a seat on the same plane as mine."

"I can't leave then."

"Can't or won't?"

"Wesley, I want to have one nice week while Sophie is here. I don't want to have to think about moving, or any of this yet." She clutched her notebook to her chest. "You're asking an awful lot. I just need a little time."

He threw up his hands and turned away from her. "Whatever you say."

Annie heard the chill in his voice. She had gained a little time. It was at best a small victory.

The Cimetière de Passy was on a raised embankment above the place du Trocadéro. Annie decided to take the bus. It had become colder when she went out again, but she was heartened by a few rays of winter sun that emerged after the earlier drizzle. She loved riding the bus, so much less crowded than the Métro, and it was nicer to be above ground to enjoy the passing sights. The bus took much longer than the Métro, but the passengers were more likely to be older people, housewives, and those not in a hurry, a more courteous crowd.

It was a relief to get out of the house. Wesley's arrival had added a new kind of pressure to her life. The imminent move weighed on her. He expected so much, and now that he was home she wondered if she would be able to write; she felt her creative energy starting to seep away.

Sophie would be asleep all afternoon, and she had a feeling that Wesley would succumb to a nap as well; so she had made her escape. She had never visited the Passy cemetery before. François's photograph of it was mysterious, otherworldly. Annie hoped that visiting the place itself would unlock the imagery that eluded her.

The bus passed the elegant shops along the Fauberg Saint-Honoré, where wealthy women in furs lined up at the counters of Hermès to buy silk scarves, leather goods, and perfume. Then onto the vast open place de la Concorde punctuated with the Egyptian obelisk in the center and the wide avenue of the Champs-Élysées with the monumental Arc de Triomphe that spoke of the spirited conquering heroes, the glorious past. Eventually, the bus eased into the Sixteenth Arrondissement with its quieter residential neighborhoods of wide, tree-lined avenues. Hélène Rocher lived in the Sixteenth, and Annie thought wistfully for a moment of her peaceful, ordered life. She hoped they could meet again soon. For now, the poems would have to come first.

She pressed the buzzer and the red *arrêt demande* sign lit up on the panel above the driver. The bus drew to a halt, and she got off at the place du Trocadéro with its breathtaking vista of the Eiffel Tower and the surrounding park. She took a small side street in the opposite direction and entered the Cimetière de Passy. A fraction the size of the famous Père Lachaise cemetery, which suffered from continual bouts of vandalism, the monuments scarred and spoiled by graffiti, this was an enchanting place and she understood what had led François here with his camera. This cemetery was like a village of tombs and mausoleums nestled closely together along pebbled paths.

The mausoleums seemed to Annie like miniature cathedrals, the size of phone booths. She stopped in front of one whose elaborate iron gates sat ajar. Inside was an altarlike structure with a statue of the virgin. Below it, a pot of chrysanthemums all withered and brown, about to turn to dust. Whoever had brought them might be in the grave as well. Reading the stones, most from the nineteenth century, Annie got a feeling not of sadness but of community. The remains of these people were together in a beautiful, quiet spot exactly where they were supposed to be, a community of souls with a view of the Eiffel Tower.

And where did she belong? It made her sad to think about leaving Paris. If she were to stay behind forever, it could only lead to divorce. She tried to imagine herself living in some small apartment, something she could afford, where she would write, do her job, and manage on her own. She turned and pushed this thought aside.

Annie's feet crunched on the gravel path. She sat on a bench in the sunshine and began to write. It felt good to start a new poem. Soon she was able to play with the images and let the powerful mystery of language take over.

> Sleeping souls blanketed in winter sun
> share their stories, while those wandering above in waning light
> search in vain for answers, hearing not the sound
> of murmured truths, nor melodies of wisdom
> cradled in the frozen ground.

Annie let the words flow freely, knowing that the real work, the real satisfaction, came with the endless moving of phrases, the combinations of sounds that shaped the poem and brought it to life. As her pen glided over the page, she trusted that some part of what appeared

there would be right, and that it would capture what François's images were telling her. It was astonishing really, the way her writing
made her feel better. After an hour or so she could feel the cold creeping in from her seat, so she stood and gathered her things. The poem
had begun to take form, and she was ready to go home.

"So, Moms, what's going on between you and Dad?"

Annie and Sophie sat on the sofa in their living room drinking tea.
Sophie was leaving in the morning. It was late afternoon, and they'd
come back earlier from the monthly lunch at the Verniers'. Wesley,
wanting some exercise, had gone out for a walk.

"What do you mean?" Annie couldn't bring herself to look into Sophie's eyes. They were the same color as Wesley's, that clear, honest blue.

"What I mean is, you were both happy and cheerful talking with
the Verniers about moving to Washington, but you never talk about it
at home. It's like it's some kind of forbidden topic."

"Haven't you had a good week? We've loved having you at home."

"Mother, I've had a wonderful week. What's not to love? We've
done everything, all my favorite things."

Sophie's short week at home had flown by. With Wesley, they'd
gone to restaurants, seen a Molière play at the Comédie-Française, and
braved the long lines for the Gauguin show at the Grand Palais. Annie
had taken Sophie shopping, and she'd found a new handbag, blue
denim with BEAU SAC written in sequins across the front.

Sophie reached over and put her hand on Annie's arm. "You're not
answering my question. You don't seem the same anymore, and you
hardly talk to Dad." She stared at her mother with her lucid, intelligent gaze.

"Sophie, sweetie, it's complicated. I'm not sure I understand it myself." Annie kicked off her shoes and drew her feet up under her on
the cushion.

"Understand what?" Sophie tilted her head. She wore an unaccus-
tomed worried expression.

"It's been a difficult year. It was hard for Dad when Wilson & James
closed. He tried working at home, but that didn't work out."

"So? He's got a job now. I don't see what the problem is."

"Well, I wanted him to look for a job here," Annie said. "I'm not sure that moving is the best thing for us." She wouldn't tell Sophie how cold and self-absorbed Wesley had been all those months, or how he'd shut her out and acted as if she didn't exist when it came to determining their future. "You know I've gotten very involved working on this book, and it's thanks to Daphne that my own career is finally taking off."

"Just what is the deal with that woman?" Sophie now sounded angry.

"What do you mean?" Annie asked.

"Dad thinks you're spending too much time with her."

"He said that?"

"Yes, and I don't get it. She's supposed to be your friend, and she spent the entire lunch today flirting with Dad, laughing and flipping that mop of hair out of her eyes."

Annie cringed. Sophie was right. She thought back to the lunch. In the beginning everything had gone well. Céleste and Georges had made a fuss over Wesley and were thrilled to celebrate his new job. Céleste had admired her new haircut, "Oh, mais ça fait jeune," as if looking young was what mattered most.

Annie had been pleased to see Sophie talking animatedly with Céleste's two nieces, whom Sophie had known from childhood, and Wesley had their parents and the other guests listening to his opinions on what was going on in Washington, as if actually living there and breathing the air gave you more insight than tuning in to CNN.

Céleste had invited Daphne to join them, and Annie wondered if she would become a regular Sunday-lunch guest. She'd arrived in the blue velvet cape, a poignant reminder of that first lunch, when she'd breezed so unexpectedly into their lives. Annie was initially uncomfortable seeing Daphne at the Verniers', and the memories of their awkward morning in bed reared up in her mind. She thought of the kisses, Daphne's touch. Daphne acted as if nothing had happened between them as she talked to all the guests with her usual charm.

After lunch, when they'd settled in the *salon* for coffee, Annie slipped out to get more sugar, and Daphne followed her to the kitchen. She closed the door behind them. "I wondered if you'd disappeared from my life completely," she said. "I thought you'd at least call."

Annie breathed in the faint scent of lilacs. Daphne's mouth was drawn into a hard line. She looked less pretty, less the dramatic stranger now that Annie knew her well.

"It's been a crazy week." Annie's explanation sounded hollow in her own ears. "I've been so busy with Wesley and Sophie. She's only here a week." Annie knew she should have called Daphne to thank her for her visit, but getting through the last few days had consumed all her energy. A leaden sense of guilt weighed on her, yet she'd done nothing terribly wrong.

"So, you're moving to Washington?"

"I don't know what I'm doing. You know I don't want to leave. There's my book and working with Paul. It's still a long way from being finished."

"It sounds like you're going to give it all up."

"I'm not giving up anything."

"I wonder now why I bothered encouraging you, why I ever took your poems to Paul." She sounded bitter.

"Daphne, don't say that. You know I appreciate all you've done." Annie held the sugar bowl like a weight in her hand. "I'm so grateful to you, and I've been writing every day in spite of everything." She set the bowl down on the table. She hated this feeling of indebtedness. Where would she be without Daphne? She felt close to tears.

"You've been so wonderful to me, so encouraging about my work and letting me stay, but—"

"You mustn't be afraid of your feelings for me." Daphne's tone was cajoling. She stepped closer and gently ruffled Annie's hair.

"Daphne, I have thought about you. I really don't have those kinds of feelings." She didn't know what else she could say. She felt a rush of heat coming to her face and turned away.

"My instincts are rarely wrong," Daphne said.

"I don't want it to be like that." Annie bowed her head.

"It doesn't have to be like anything. We just need to stay friends."

Annie felt the weight of Daphne's arm around her shoulders and the pressure of her body pressing gently into hers. Then the soft breath on her cheek as Daphne whispered, "Sweet friend, you spend far too much time thinking."

"What's this, a party in the kitchen, *dans la cuisine?*" Georges's voice boomed behind them. "Come back to the *salon.* We're having a little Cognac. Best thing on a winter afternoon."

"You're a darling, Georges," Daphne said brightly, withdrawing her arm and stepping away. "You know just what a girl needs." Daphne took his arm and they made their way back to join the others. After that Daphne had ignored Annie and turned her attentions to Wesley.

Now, sitting beside Sophie, Annie found it impossible to explain any of this.

"You know, Moms, she called Dad twice this week, and he took her to lunch when we went shopping on Friday."

"I know that. He's helping her get a shipment of antique quilts from Madeleine. He told me about that." Annie smiled at Sophie and took her chin in her hand. What would she ever do without this precious daughter? Loving a child, she thought, is so pure and simple, the kind of love that never wavers. "You don't need to worry about us, sweetie." She wrapped her arms around her daughter and gave her a hug. Her most precious antique quilt hung on the wall behind them. Annie glanced up at it and wondered what Daphne and Wesley had talked about besides the quilts.

"Aren't you coming to bed?"

Annie looked up at Wesley from her chair in the alcove off the living room. She'd pulled the afghan over her legs, and her poetry notebook sat on her lap. Sophie was already in bed, her clothes packed for her trip to New York the next day. Wesley's flight was booked for the day after that. Annie knew they needed to talk. He sat down by her feet, and she moved them over, giving him more room.

"Annie?" His hair was mussed. His blue button-down shirt was open at the neck. He looked vulnerable and sweet. She didn't want to hurt him.

"Wesley, not now. I'm working."

"I love you." He put his hand on her bent knee and rubbed gently. "I've missed you. You know that, don't you?" He took off his glasses and rubbed his eyes. He looked tired and defeated. She could see the purple veins in his pale hands. He put the glasses back on as if needing to bring her into focus. "I want you with me, Annie."

"I know that. We'll talk tomorrow." She looked down at her notebook. She was trying to bring back the image of the carved stonework from the mausoleum in the Passy cemetery.

He stood up, bent down, and kissed her forehead. He drew his hand across the top of her head. "Tomorrow, then." He stood and lingered a few moments longer.

She kept her eyes on the page and wrote. When she said nothing more, he left her alone.

She didn't want to write anymore, but she didn't want to go to bed.

THIRTEEN

Le Doute

Wesley's last day. *"All's well that ends well,"* Annie thought to herself. She remembered seeing a student production of that play with Wesley, one of their first dates in Cambridge. She doubted that this day would end well. It was already beginning badly. The sky was an unpleasant pewter shade, like before a summer thunderstorm; a stiff wind rattled the shutters. Sophie had left the day before, and her absence was palpable.

Mary called first thing that morning. She was at the office, having returned from visiting her parents in the States during the Christmas holidays. "What happened to the transcripts?" she asked. "They should have been sent out a week ago. I already have messages from several universities asking why they're late." She was furious.

"Mary, I'm so sorry." All her excuses—the poems, Wesley and Sophie being home, busy days—sounded weak and selfish.

"You can't imagine what my life is like now," Mary said. "I can't have things falling apart at work too."

Annie could hear the pain in her voice. She immediately remembered Tom and the day that she and Wesley had seen him outside the hotel with another woman. What could she say? She couldn't imagine how her friend was coping with this. She promised Mary that the transcripts would be finished and ready to send out by the end of the afternoon.

Annie rushed to the office and immersed herself in the task. She didn't stop until the papers were complete and neatly stacked on Mary's desk. She'd never neglected her job before, and she promised herself she'd find a way to make it up to Mary. Perhaps she could take her out for lunch, to some especially nice place, a quiet restaurant where they could have a good talk.

Relieved that the tedious job was finally done, she put on her coat and set off for home. She pulled her scarf more tightly around her neck. The sky looked ominous, and the same unsettled wind continued to whip through the streets. Annie hated wind. It made her feel discombobulated and fragile, the vulnerable feeling you have when you're about to get sick.

She hadn't intended to be gone for Wesley's last day. That morning he was taking cartons of files to a shipper on the outskirts of Paris. Sophie had helped him pack the boxes before she left, and Annie had had to rush off to the office, leaving him with the tedious task of getting the boxes downstairs and loading them into the car. They had not yet had their discussion about the future.

Annie was in no rush to return home. What would she say? She didn't want to go to Washington. She tried to picture herself there, writing, a blank notebook before her. What would it be like to see Paris from a distance? What would she remember? Perhaps the dark, winding cobbled streets, the wide boulevards, the grand vistas, and the monuments would come to mind. Maybe she would recall the Luxembourg Gardens, once her private paradise, flower-filled and lush with trees, its benches set in dappled shade. She might picture the small shops, the hand of the cheese vendor reaching for the perfect chèvre, selecting the one ready to eat that day. How soon would the memory of ordinary days in this extraordinary place fade and blur with time?

No, she couldn't imagine leaving Paris. Certainly not yet. The city, her poems, her life here, were so completely intertwined, she couldn't conceive of pulling them apart. It was as if the book project had cast a spell on her and she wanted to write her best poems ever. She needed to be in Paris for that. Maybe she'd be finished by the summer.

She had enjoyed her time alone. Taking a break from her marriage might not be such a bad thing. Wesley could get settled into his new job; she could finish her book. Once or twice, she allowed herself to think of what it would be like never to join him, to end the marriage entirely, and when she did, the word *divorce* had always felt like a lump of ice caught in her throat. She loved Wesley, despite his insistence on moving away. Part of her didn't want to hurt him.

But Daphne was right; something in her had changed. As a child, she remembered learning how snakes shed their skins at a certain stage in life. After the few quiet weeks when she was in Paris by herself working on her poems, she had been able to shed the skin of wife and mother.

Rather than descend into the Métro or take a bus home, Annie decided to walk for a while. She turned off the rue de Rennes onto the wide boulevard Saint-Germain. The shop windows didn't interest her that day, and after a few blocks she wandered into the quieter streets in the heart of the Latin Quarter. This was Paul Valmont's neighborhood. She'd sent Paul the poems she'd written at God House, but he hadn't called. Suddenly, she had to know what he thought.

His office, tucked back on the rue Clément, was not far away. She knew she was avoiding Wesley, but she wasn't ready to go home yet. She passed the Café de Flore and recalled her first lunch with Daphne. It now seemed so long ago. She turned onto the narrow side street, trying to avoid a cluster of pigeons waddling aimlessly in the gutter. It was a quiet street. The only shop was a bookstore specializing in medical texts. There was a lifelike poster of the internal organs, the heart with its ventricles and chambers colored in liverish shades of red and purple. She looked away. She arrived at number 20, pushed open the finely carved oak door, stepped in off the street, and took the stairs up to his office on the second floor. The walls were cracked and could have used a coat of fresh paint, but the brass nameplate by his door shone warmly in the dim light.

"I was in the *quartier* and thought I'd stop," Annie, still out of breath, explained to his assistant who was typing on a computer. "I know I don't have an appointment." The assistant shrugged and said she'd see if Monsieur Valmont was available. She was a tiny woman, more a girl really, in a black leather skirt and fuchsia sweater. She pushed a lock of dyed red hair behind a pale ear and, after one swift knock, stepped through the door behind her.

She didn't come out right away. Annie felt ridiculous and wished she hadn't acted so impulsively. She heard their voices through the closed door. She was considering slipping out when the girl reappeared carrying a stack of folders.

"Take a little time off and you pay the price," she said in the fast-paced French of a Parisian, referring to the documents that she plunked down on her desk.

Annie, still in her coat and wishing she'd made her escape, got up.

"He said to go in." The assistant gestured to the door behind her. Annie wondered if she ever smiled.

Paul sat bent over at his desk, reading glasses she hadn't seen before resting on the tip of his nose. He smoothed his hair back and came around the desk to greet her. "Annie, what a surprise." Today he spoke to her in English. His dark hair looked like it needed a wash; there were circles under his eyes. He greeted her with the customary kisses on both cheeks, like an old friend, but he looked distracted.

"I enjoyed the dinner at God House," he said, returning to his chair. "Please sit down." He nodded toward the chair where she had sat the last time. "I am afraid I have been very busy. I am trying to finish a book on Napoleon. The writer, he is a renowned biographer but a difficult man—slow with revisions. We are coming soon to the deadline."

"I'm so sorry to bother you." She felt her heart sinking. She knew he worked with many other writers, and it was presumptuous on her part to show up unannounced in the middle of a busy day. "I'm sure you haven't had time to look at the last poems, but I thought I'd—"

"It is never a bother to see you," he said.

She wished he would smile. He removed his glasses and rubbed his eyes. Then he reached for an envelope on the side of his desk. She recognized her own writing. He pulled out the pages and skimmed over the first one.

"Yes, I had a few thoughts on this." He looked at the next page. He frowned. "I have not had time to look at the others."

"That's all right. I was silly to have come."

"No, no." He looked concerned. "I wanted to get this off my desk first." He patted a fat unruly pile of papers. "I am quite busy now, that's all. Coping with this book has put me in a bad temper. But how are you? You said the work was going well."

"Not quite as well this week," Annie said. "My husband and daughter have been home. I haven't had much time to myself. I'm finding it hard to get going again."

"We all have slow days." He waved his hands again across the papers on his desk. "I would not be concerned." He looked at his watch and furrowed his brow. "I am sorry, but this is not a good day for me."

"Of course. I'm sorry to have interrupted you. I need to get home anyway."

"Please," he said, starting to rise from his desk, "I do want to talk about this work, and we will find the time soon. We also need to meet to discuss the order of the photographs."

"Certainly. Anytime. But please, don't get up. I can show myself out."

"*Alors, à bientôt.*"

Annie said a quick good-bye and closed the door to his office. She had obviously made a mistake to stop in without an appointment. How could she have forgotten that the French were more formal? His pouting young assistant barely looked up as she made her way out. Now, thoroughly embarrassed that she had come, she hurried out to the street. She felt too tired to walk home and decided to wait for the next bus.

"So what's it going to be?"

They sat at the kitchen table that evening, the casserole of beef stew steaming on a trivet between them. Annie spooned a large serving onto the plate of noodles and passed it to Wesley. She filled her own plate, wondering if she would be able to swallow, if she would be able to eat anything at all.

"I'm not sure what you mean?"

"Annie, you've been avoiding me all week. We haven't had one decent conversation since I've been home."

She could tell he was trying to be patient. "Sophie's been here. I didn't want to upset her."

"Well, she's gone now."

Annie put down her fork. She'd been pushing a piece of meat around the edge of her plate.

"I don't know what to talk about. What's for me to say? You've gone and accepted this job. You never really discussed it with me. You never once asked how I would feel about moving." She held her napkin tightly and began to twist it into a knot.

"Fine. Okay, fine. I've gone ahead with this. But I'm back, and we have to figure out the logistics. If you came over during your midwinter break, we could look for a house then."

"That's next month. My poems for the book won't be finished by then."

"For God's sake, just bring your computer."

"I told you that won't work." She tossed her wrinkled napkin onto the table. "Look, Wesley, my priorities have changed. The most important thing for me is finishing this book, writing my best poems ever. I've made a commitment to that. I'm not going to drop everything and jump on the next plane for Washington."

"You know I never expected that. Take a little more time here if you need it, and then bring the photographs with you. You can write anywhere." He set down his fork. "Did it ever get through your head that I can't do what I like to do just anywhere? I'm over fifty. Getting another job, another decent job that is, isn't easy. It's almost impossible, and I'm damn lucky to have this one." His voice grew louder. "The thought might have occurred to you if you weren't so self-absorbed."

"Self-absorbed." Annie felt a surge of indignation sweep through her. "If anyone is self-absorbed, it's you. Since last spring, almost a year now, you've been totally consumed with the firm closing, not having enough work, not paying any attention to anything in my life." She tried to keep her voice level. She knew that blaming him wouldn't help. "I tried to be understanding. I know it was hard, but you've been cold and impossible for months."

"You're being unfair," he said. "I've tried to spare you. I didn't want to dump all my troubles on you." His face was white with anger.

"You spared me all right; you shut me out completely. You barely allowed me to touch you. We stopped making love. How do you think that made me feel?"

"I'm sorry, but I had other things on my mind."

"So much so that you couldn't love your wife? You couldn't bring yourself to have sex with me?" *Sex.* The word exploded in her mouth, and the image of Tom leaving the hotel with another woman came back to her. "Maybe there's someone else. Maybe you just didn't want to have sex with me?"

"Jesus, Annie. Now you're being ridiculous." He pushed his chair back from the table and staggered to his feet. "There's never been any-one else. You know I love you. Things have changed. I have a job and I feel better—about everything. It will be different now."

"I see. And you can just pick up where you left off and start loving me again."

"I've always loved you." He sat again and faced her across the table. The stew had grown cold on their plates, a brown, gelatinous pool. "Have you forgotten God House? New Year's Eve?"

"Wesley, that was sex, plain sex, after too much wine. I don't seem to remember any love involved." She turned away from him. "You were just jealous of Tim that night. It was like you wanted to prove something."

"Now you're the one totally off base. Your poetic imagination has carried you away and blown this all out of proportion." He went over to the kitchen counter and picked up the bottle of wine. He poured himself another glass and put the bottle down with a bang on the counter. "Look, let's just get on with it. We need to make our plans."

"That's the problem."

"Now what problem?"

"I'm not sure about how we're going to 'get on with it,' as you call it," she said.

He stood across from her, gripping the edge of the table. "I don't think it's that complicated. I leave tomorrow. I can manage on my own for a while, and you can come over in another month or so. Maybe during your spring break." He took a swallow of wine. "I just want to know when you're coming. I need you with me as soon as possible. I'm going to be really busy. I don't have time to figure out where we'll live. Besides, you'd want to look for yourself."

"Wesley, I don't believe this. We're not even on the same wave-length."

"What's that supposed to mean?"

"I mean it's not the simple logistics of moving. We're talking about leaving Paris. We're spent most of our married life here. You automatically assume that we can leave all this."

"Annie, listen. We are leaving all this. We're moving to Washington. You've got plenty of time to settle things here, to finish your book."

"I accept the fact that you're moving to Washington. I've come to grips with that. I just don't know if I can leave this place." There. She'd said it, but telling him didn't make her feel any better.

"What do you mean? You won't come with me?" He shook his head. He leaned toward her, his elbows on the table, his hands clasped. "Okay. I know things have been rough. Maybe I haven't been considerate of you, of your feelings, but you must know I love you." He reached across and took her hands in his. "Please, Annie. I love you. I want you with me."

She pulled her hands away. She didn't know how to put into words what she didn't really understand herself. "Well," she said softly, as if trying to find her voice, "I'm not sure what I want, except right now I want to stay here. I need to immerse myself in my writing. I need to be in Paris. This is the city that brought my poetry alive. You know that. This is where I'm supposed to be. Once I've finished the book, I'll think about Washington."

"Annie, you haven't lived many places. Naturally Paris feels like where you're supposed to be after Sudbury, Vermont, or even Boston. Give me a break." His words were clipped and cold. "Are you saying that Paris wins out over our marriage?"

"It's not just Paris. When you were away, I got so much done. I think I just need some time alone right now. While I was at God House—"

"God House. Maybe that's it? I bet it's Daphne who's putting these ideas into your head?"

"No one is putting ideas into my head." She glared at him.

"Look, maybe this problem you seem to be creating is not about me but about you. Yeah, maybe it's you, Annie. It seems like you're the one who's pulling away. You're the one who's no longer interested in me."

"Of course I'm interested in you. I want you to be happy, and this job may be the right thing. I see that now. It's just that I've never had time on my own, and a few months away from each other might be good for us." As she spoke these words, Annie knew that that was exactly what she needed. She wanted to see what it would be like to live without Wesley. Some part of her wanted to take this risk. "Daphne said—"

"Daphne said . . . See? She's talked you into this. You've been dazzled by her and her appealing life."

"It's not Daphne." How wrong he was about her. If he only knew what Daphne really wanted. "I have not been dazzled by Daphne," she insisted. "For heaven's sake, you've been spending more time with her lately than I have. You met her for lunch; she called you almost every day this week."

"Now, wait a minute. I've been helping her arrange a shipment of quilts. I brought her the pictures and all the information from Madeleine."

"Well, she was sure happy to see you again. Sophie thought she was flirting with you at Céleste and Georges's lunch." She looked at him defiantly and pushed away her plate. She could no longer stand the sight of her food.

"You're being ridiculous," he said. "I can't believe you're even thinking like that. It's like you've become a different person. He pressed his hands to his temples.

"I'm not a different person. Maybe you just need to try to understand me for a change. Maybe I'm not always the good little Annie, the person who always cooperates, goes along with what everyone else wants." She could hardly breathe. "I need to find out what's right for me and not just follow along doing what I'm told." This sounded more harsh than she intended. Her last bit of energy drained away.

Wesley stood and carried his plate to the sink. His longer hair now looked unkempt, and his shoulders sagged in disappointment. He looked physically wrung out, defeated. He turned to face her, leaning against the counter for support. "Annie, I will not tell you what to do. Please give me more credit than that. I will tell you that I love you and that I want you with me. I will also tell you one last time that I want us to be together, and for now that means coming to Washington. I would guess it means a good ten years there, if it works out as I hope."

He spoke deliberately, evenly, as if each word had been carefully thought out.

"I appreciate what you're saying. I just need time. That's all. I'm sorry." She could no longer stop the tears that trickled down her face. She wiped them away with the back of her hand.

"I'll give you time," he said. "I'm going to finish getting ready for my trip. I have more files to pack up in the office, and I'm going to sleep in there tonight. We can start getting used to living apart."

His words stung her but she didn't argue, didn't go after him, try to smooth things over. Annie drew herself to her feet and carried the rest of the dishes to the sink. She hoped she hadn't gone too far.

FOURTEEN

L'Orage

Annie returned to her apartment chilled to the bone. A bilious black sky had released a torrent of water that turned into an ice storm as the temperature dropped. Ice storms and snowstorms were almost unheard of in Paris. There had been two winters, at the end of the nineteenth century, when Paris was blanketed by snow. The Impressionists had painted scenes of the city and the surrounding countryside, capturing that astonishing winter light. It was rare for Paris to get more than a dusting of snow.

She pulled off her coat and wet shoes. She never should have worn her best Italian loafers in this storm. Just walking the six blocks from her subway stop had ruined them. This horrible weather was like a final affront after her argument with Wesley the night before.

Annie assumed Wesley's plane had taken off, though she had not heard from him. It was dreadful weather for flying. She had left him earlier that morning to go to her office at Liberal Arts Abroad. Mary was counting on her to prepare the schedules for the second semester, and she didn't want to disappoint her. Wesley had not spoken to her when he got up, and he had remained in Sophie's room, ostensibly to pack the last of his files. She decided it would be easier to be out when he left. Nothing had been solved by their argument. It was as if she had put her future up in the air like a question mark inside a balloon.

She needed to get back to her work on the poems. In a matter of weeks all the students would have returned and she would have few long stretches of time to write. Now she thought only of submerging herself in a hot bath. She went to the bedroom to undress, her teeth chattering the way they used to on the way home from an afternoon of sledding in Vermont. Her snow pants would have been heavy and wet with melted snow, her woolen mittens riddled with small chunks of ice. Only now there was no Aunt Kate to fix her a big cup of cocoa. She was alone.

Annie lowered herself into the steaming tub. A steady stream cascaded against the window, high above the cracked white tiles. Hopefully a hot bath would make her feel better. "Nothing like a good soak in the tub," Aunt Kate used to say, "to wash away your troubles and give you a clean start."

Easing farther down into the water, she propped her head against a rolled washcloth and braced her feet against the far end. Her knees broke the surface of the water, her legs too long for the tub. When bathing in the generous bathtub at God House, she could fully extend her legs, allowing them to float freely in the deep water. She thought again of taking tea to Daphne in her bathroom at God House and the uneasy sensation of seeing her without her clothes.

Her own body was nothing like Daphne's. Wesley used to tell her she had fine bones, delicate for a person of her height. Lying here on her back, she saw her hip bones protrude. Her belly was pale and concave. She ran her hand across the flesh. It was soft and pliant and no longer as firm as it used to be, gone with the tautness of youth. She brought her hand up to her breasts and cradled one, pushing it up and out, the way it used to be before gravity started to take its toll.

Annie felt bruised and battered, as if the harsh words that she and Wesley had exchanged last night had been actual physical blows. It felt like the air had been sucked out of their relationship and their marriage was literally struggling for breath. The hot soak was not making her feel any better. Part of her wished that Wesley would return immediately and say that he understood, that he would take her in his arms, comfort her, repair the damage. She worried about him flying in this weather. She let go of her breast. It sank below the surface and floated uselessly.

Bending her knees more, she slid down below the surface of the water to soak her hair and face. She would pull herself together; she would go on. She sat up, poured a large helping of shampoo onto her hand, and massaged her hair into a thick lather. The floral soapy scent rose and mingled with the steamy bathroom air.

The weekend alone in the empty apartment loomed before her. The storm had not let up. Annie decided to take a cup of tea into the living room and start working on the poems. The slate-colored sky had darkened further, and she turned on lights as she made her way to the kitchen. She would not want to be flying on a day like today. Poor Wesley. She was overcome with a sense of emptiness, as if she had spent every last emotion during their argument. It had been a relief, though, finally to speak about their feelings, to tell him the truth.

Once she was settled again in her chair, she opened one of her notebooks. This one was a teal spiral, with cream-colored pages. Annie loved paper and pens. The physical act of moving a pen across the blank page was part of the magic of poetry, the ink bringing her words into the world for the first time. She wrote and rewrote poems over and over on her pages, and only at the very end did she put down her pen and transcribe the finished work on the computer.

Sophie and Wesley indulged her interest in fine papers and pens. She had quite a collection of fountain pens and a few special favorites that she used frequently and kept filled with the ink she preferred, Waterman's South Sea Blue, *bleu des mers du sud*. Perhaps it was a silly affectation, but she saw no reason to give it up. Besides, it was part of her routine. A British poet who gave a reading at the American Church in Paris years ago had given her advice on the importance of routine. "Go to it every day. Be with it fully. Practice your craft even when you do not feel called to it." Annie could still see that elderly lady poet with her deep-set eyes and beaklike nose. She'd worn a black dress and a purple shawl. She had stressed the importance of ritual, going to the same place, having the quiet, opening the notebook, uncapping the pen.

However, sitting now in her corner in the apartment sheltered from the storm, Annie felt blank. The paper, her pens, none of her rituals were working. Leafing through copies of the latest photographs left her uninspired. Unable to work, she pulled one of her art books down from the shelf and opened to Courbet's painting of the young girl reading. She hadn't looked at that picture or the poem based on it since she'd started to work on the book project.

This time, seeing the bare shoulder of the young woman in a forest reminded her of her own bare shoulder that last morning at God House. She hadn't forgotten the strange moment of tenderness, and how surprising Daphne's touch had been. She had tried hard since that moment to imagine returning some kind of intimacy. The idea of actually kissing or caressing Daphne overwhelmed her. She admired Daphne's physical beauty, her sensuality; it heightened her own feelings and made her come more alive. And yet she knew that she was sexually attracted to men. There had always been Wesley, and she had not forgotten the spark she felt the first time she met Paul Valmont. Poor Paul. What a tragedy to lose a wife so young.

Heavy rain still beat on the windows. Annie tucked a shawl around her legs. Daphne also was alone in this storm. She had called Annie the day before yesterday, the day of Sophie's departure, urging her to come again to God House.

"I'm helping Sophie pack," Annie explained. "I don't really have time to talk tonight." Sophie had given her a dark look and shoved another sweater into her bag.

"You have time for everyone but me," Daphne said, sounding peevish, "or so it seems."

"Daphne, that's not fair." She carried the phone into the hall.

"You're letting them consume you. You're being swallowed up."

Them, Annie thought; but it's my family. Daphne's tone implied some sort of prehistoric beast devouring her limb by limb. "Please try to understand. Sophie's leaving in the morning, Wesley the day after. They need me right now."

"I might need you too," Daphne said. Her voice grew softer, plaintive.

"We'll talk soon," Annie said. Daphne seemed to be incapable of understanding the reality of family life.

"You think it's easy for me. You're like all the rest. 'Daphne can manage. She's a good sort. She never minds.' "

"Please don't say that."

"Why shouldn't I? You've got what you want." Daphne's words lashed out. "You've got a husband, a daughter, a dishy French editor up your sleeve."

Annie pictured Daphne alone in the library at God House with a tumbler of whiskey in her hand. "No," she said. "It's not like that."

"I see it all clearly," Daphne went on. "You're going to push off and leave me behind. And I was the person who made it happen. Or have you forgotten?"

In a hushed voice Annie tried to soothe her friend. She told Daphne not to worry. She was not leaving with Wesley, and she intended to stay in Paris as long as necessary to finish the book. "I would never waste this chance," she promised. Gradually, Daphne became calmer and Annie assured her that she would return to God House soon.

Annie studied Courbet's softly curved woman. Why not go to God House now? Wesley was gone, truly gone, for months ahead, and she had the entire weekend free. Her writing was stalled. Daphne needed company and Annie knew that time spent cheering her up would take her mind off her own problems. They could eat good meals by the fire, take walks along the river, and she would have time to write. The white page of her blank notebook glared up at her. A few days at God House would be good for her too.

She reached for the phone. The line to God House was busy. During the next hour she packed a bag and dressed warmly, wearing boots and taking out a waterproof coat. She knew the train left on the hour late in the afternoons, and she hurried to make the earliest one possible. She tried several times to reach Daphne on the phone, but the line remained busy. She pictured the old house, the ivy dripping with rain. Perhaps one of the telephone wires had blown down.

"You will come? You promise?" Well, why not surprise her? She would simply catch the next train and appear unannounced. She smiled. Daphne had teased her repeatedly, telling her to loosen up, to live in the moment, to let life carry her where it would. Now she could.

On rue des Archives, Annie closed the door behind her. Despite the terrible storm and the driving rain, she felt her spirits lift.

The empty commuter train rattled along through the dark landscape. Annie had left Paris well after the crowded evening rush. It had been a struggle to get to the train station. The sleet had changed back to rain, and Paris was plagued with flooded streets, canceled Métro trains, and a taxi shortage. Glancing at her reflection in the train window, Annie drew her fingers through her hair, matted down from her hat, and removed her long paisley scarf. It was damp from the rain. She'd dressed for the weather, and the overheated train made her neck itch in her heavy cabled turtleneck sweater. She knew she'd be glad to be wearing it once she got off the train. She supposed it was cold enough for the rain to change to snow.

She wondered if she was doing the right thing. What if Daphne had left for the weekend? The possibility of wandering down the lonely country road only to find the house empty and dark was chilling. She would call Daphne again as soon she got off the train. She tried to relax on the uncomfortable seat. Her mind refused to stop churning. Ten minutes later the train pulled into the Villandry station. In her rush to leave her apartment, she'd forgotten her cell phone. She stepped onto the platform and looked for a phone booth to call Daphne.

"*Non, madame! Ne marche pas!*" A craggy-faced old man in a blue smock stepped out of the railway station to tell her the phones in the village were out. He spoke sharply and scowled at Annie as if she might have caused the problem, as if the failed lines or even this storm were her fault. No wonder she had been unable to reach Daphne earlier that afternoon. On the one hand it was a relief to know why she hadn't gotten through, but it meant she'd have to walk the final kilometer in the dark.

There was nothing to fear, she told herself. She needed to get used to doing things on her own. She knew the way, and if for any reason Daphne wasn't there, perhaps Berthe could let her into the house. At the very worst, it meant walking back to the station for a return train to Paris.

When she first got off the train, the cold night air felt good. Her feet were warm and her canvas coat kept out the rain. Gradually the rain intensified. She left the village streets and headed down the narrow country road. Her hat blew off in a gust of wind, and the rain immediately soaked her head. She searched for her hat, but between the water streaming into her eyes and the darkness, it was impossible to see. The road dropped off to a steep embankment covered with rocks. A gully of rushing water surged below. She walked back and forth but couldn't find the hat anywhere. She worried about slipping and falling down the bank.

Finally, giving up and putting one foot in front of the other, she focused on God House and concentrated on her imminent arrival. It helped to picture a fire crackling in the deep hearth in the library and Daphne bringing her a towel for her hair along with a snifter of brandy to help her recover. Daphne would sit on the sofa opposite Annie with her feet propped up on the table between them.

Annie would explain what had happened, how things had been with Wesley, how she'd tried to explain to him her need to stay in Paris. Perhaps talking it over would help her to make sense of it, of what she had said. Daphne would offer her encouragement. She might even congratulate her for having had the courage, at least temporarily, to shed the constraints of married life.

Annie stepped in a few puddles, difficult to miss in the dark, and water seeped into her boots. She felt the sodden wet wool of her scarf against her skin. She'd tried to pull it up to protect her head, but to no avail. She must look like some kind of refugee, clutching her bag and tromping through the muck. At last the drive to God House came into sight. She quickened her steps, barely hearing the crunch of her feet on the gravel in the howling wind. She rounded the bend, and there, thankfully, God House sat solidly against the night sky, the lamplight peeking out behind the draperies drawn against the cold and the dark. Annie smelled smoke from the chimney and was relieved that her imaginings were coming true. Daphne was at home; her little car had been pulled up close to the carriage-house doors.

With a great sense of relief Annie climbed the front steps and knocked. After a few moments, her knock unanswered, she tried the handle; it yielded, and she stepped inside. Relieved to escape the lashing rain, she savored the sudden calm in the large silent hall illuminated only by the lamp on the table. Petals from a vase of white roses past their prime lay scattered on the softly polished wood.

Daphne must not have heard her in the roar of the storm. Strains of music came from somewhere in the back of the house. She quickly shed her wet coat and decided to carry it to the kitchen so it wouldn't drip and leave puddles on the marble floor. She passed through the dark dining room on the way. It was hushed and still, no hint of the sparkling New Year's Eve almost a month ago.

"Daphne!" she called, pushing the door open to the kitchen. Finally, signs of life. There were pots piled up on the drain board, and several plates sat soaking in the sink. Small clumps of grease had coagulated in the murky suds. Annie sat at the table and pulled off her boots, noticing the empty wine bottles and two glasses stained with purple sediment. Further evidence of a cozy dinner by the fire—a dinner for two. Annie felt a wave of disappointment. Daphne was not alone. Perhaps Tim had returned from one of his yacht deals in the south of France. Maybe he was trying to wend his way back into her heart.

She set her boots by the back door and went into the hall in search of her friend. She moved silently in her sock feet and this time heard voices from the library along with the sounds of a soprano at full volume coming from the CD player. She passed through the living room where the portrait of Daphne's mother looked down at her, the eyes following her across the room. Annie could feel her haunting stare even in the semidark. She heard the muffled tones of Daphne's voice through the door. Annie couldn't make out the words and couldn't hear the unknown guest's reply over the music.

She tried to fluff up her wet hair, and she smoothed down her sweater. Gathering her dwindling courage, she knocked as she pushed the door open. The scene was almost exactly as Annie expected. A huge fire crackled in the hearth, and shadows from the firelight played across the walls and floor. The aria drew to a close as if on cue. Daphne sat low on the sofa, her wavy hair resting languidly against the velvet upholstery. A man was with her, his feet extended beyond the end of the sofa, his head still in the shadows, presumably resting in her lap. Daphne lowered the glass of amber liquid from her mouth and set it on the end table.

"This has been quite a day for unexpected arrivals," she said. Her voice was tinged with amusement and clouded with too much wine. "Not the kind of weather you'd think would bring visitors to this part of the world."

The man sat up and reached for the lamp switch by his head, nearly knocking over Daphne's glass. Wesley's face emerged from the gloom. His hair was mussed, his skin creased as if from sleep. He grabbed his glasses and struggled to get up. Daphne remained on the sofa. Annie gasped.

"Annie, what are you doing here?" He came toward her, but she stepped aside, grabbing the back of the other sofa for support. She didn't think her legs would hold her. He put his hand on her shoulder.

"Don't touch me. What you're doing here is the more appropriate question?" Feeling her knees giving way, she sat down. "You're supposed to be on a plane to Washington." Her voice came out in a wail. She could barely move her mouth to form words. Tears ran down her face.

"Annie, it's not what it looks like." He squatted down in front of her. He put his hand on her knee and she jerked it away. He got unsteadily to his feet. "I went to the airport and the flights were postponed. I waited all afternoon. Eventually the flight was canceled." His words blurred. He'd been drinking. "It's been rescheduled for tomorrow."

"Wesley came to God House to talk things over with me." Daphne alone remained unperturbed by the situation. "Nothing but a little fireside chat." She wore the gray robe tied loosely, it appeared, over nothing underneath.

"She's right," Wesley said. "I came to ask for her help. I thought she could talk to you and make you understand . . ." He thrust his arms up as if frantically trying to find the right words, the words that would soothe her and make it all right.

"What I understand is that I've found you curled up on the sofa with my friend, your head in her lap." Her anger was making it easier to talk.

Daphne spoke up. "Oh, come on. We had a little wine. We—"

Annie didn't wait for Daphne to finish her sentence. "It seems like more than a little wine is at work here. I find you curled up on the sofa together. What's next? What was the plan before I blundered in?" Annie was breathless with fury. She looked at Daphne's long white fingers, the fingers that had been stroking Wesley's hair, the same fingers that had touched her own bare shoulder. She felt physically sick. The awful truth began to dawn on her. They had already had sex. "Oh God—you . . ."

"Listen, Annie," Daphne spoke more forcefully. "Don't be a provincial idiot. We've been talking. That's all. Wesley came out here when his flight was canceled. He called me from the airport, terribly upset because of some kind of row you'd had. I told him to come. He wanted me to persuade you to go back to America. As you can see, we had got a bit into the sauce . . ." She shrugged.

"Don't lie to me." Annie held her head in her hands.

Daphne stood up and took her drink. "Look, I don't know what's best for you two, but it's not up to me to decide. I'm going up to bed." Daphne's hair was in disarray and her lipstick smeared.

Annie listened to the thud of the door closing behind her and then to the sound of Daphne's receding footsteps. Wesley, looking ashen, poured a Cognac for Annie and set it on the table in front of her. His shirt was only partially buttoned, no longer tucked into his trousers.

"I don't want a drink." She stared into the fire.

He nodded and sat down across from her, leaving her alone, perhaps fearful that being near her only made it worse. "Annie, you shouldn't make too much of this."

"Of course not. It's perfectly fine to discover your husband out in the country in the middle of the night with another woman."

"It's not like that." He enunciated each word, as if knowing full well he'd had too much to drink.

"When your plane was canceled, why didn't you come home?" she asked. "Why did you come here, to her?" Annie spat out the last two words.

"Why on earth would I go home?" He sounded angry, more clearheaded. "You made it pretty plain you didn't want anything to do with me. The last thing you wanted was to see me come back in the door. Remember, you said you wanted time to think, a little time off from our marriage." His tone was sarcastic now. He rested his head on the back of the sofa as if suddenly depleted. "Look, I was tired and upset. I hoped Daphne could help me. She told me to come."

"Upset? And how was our dear friend going to help you? A nice supper by the fire, cozy little drinks on the sofa? You'd have to be a fool not to see what was coming."

"I didn't think like that."

"Right." Annie stood up and stared down at him. "What makes me really sick is you don't touch me for months and months, you ignore me when I turn to you for love, and then you come here. Here, to nice consoling Daphne. Sexy Daphne."

"Annie, you're being ridiculous."

"You wanted to make love to her."

"For God's sake. No. No, I did not."

"Well, what did you think was going to happen? Lovely young woman all alone in a big house. Did you plan to spend the evening in quiet conversation?"

"Annie, no." His words sounded like a sob.

"Don't tell me you didn't think of it, that you didn't want her."

"Annie, stop it. I told you. I thought Daphne could make you understand that I need you, that I want you with me. She talked you into writing that book; I thought she could convince you to come with me."

"She doesn't talk me into anything. It was my decision to stay in Paris and write. I don't want to follow you to the States just because you need me there. Did it ever occur to you that I'm a little sick of always being needed?"

"You made it pretty damn clear."

"Ah yes. The darling wife doesn't cooperate. How do we solve that problem? Maybe a little comfort, a little sex? Wouldn't that feel good? Sex with her dear friend. Yes, there's a solution." She couldn't stop. "How long before you took Daphne up to bed?"

Wesley looked away. "Look, we had a lot to drink. I never meant for anything to happen."

"Oh God." Annie rocked forward and back, overtaken with sobs. "Wesley, how could you?"

"Annie, this never should have happened. What's important is that I love you. I want you to be with me. I don't want our life together to end. That's why I came here when the plane was canceled. I thought Daphne could persuade you to come with me. I want you to believe that."

"I don't know what I believe." She thought of Daphne upstairs in her bed. Was she crazy? She remembered Daphne's meeting with Wesley for lunch, presumably to discuss the quilts. But Daphne was attracted to her. Why would she want to seduce Wesley?

Wesley swallowed the last of his drink. "I'm going to bed. I'm taking an early train to the airport. I want to forget that this ever happened. All I'm asking you to do is to think carefully about us, about all we've shared and the future we could have together. I love you, Annie. Nothing will change that." He left her. She heard the click of the door closing behind him.

Alone again by the fire, Annie pulled up the cashmere throw and covered herself. She had never felt such utter despair. The wind had calmed and she no longer heard the raindrops pounding against the glass. How would she ever be able to sleep? She listened to the sounds of faucets turning on and off, the fire hissing softly. Finally, utter quiet blanketed God House.

FIFTEEN

La Solitude

The storm had ended. Annie stood in the glass room overlooking the garden.
The day had dawned eerily calm. The branches of the trees and shrubs
were still, and the river, far below, looked flat and dull, the color of
stone. It was as if the earth were heavy, weighed down from all the
rains. She held a mug of coffee, her fingers wrapped around the
steaming warmth. Her head ached. She had watched the fire for hours
and finally drifted off to sleep around dawn. The ashes were cold in
the hearth when she awoke, and she knew that Wesley had gone. She
was shocked by the intensity of her jealousy when she'd found him
with Daphne the night before. It remained with her, like the aftertaste
of a bitter medicine. This morning she felt numb, her body a mere
shell, void of any sensation.

"You found the coffee, I see." Daphne spoke quietly.

Annie hadn't heard her come out from the kitchen. She kept her
eyes fixed on the river.

"I gather you didn't sleep very well," Daphne said.

"No. I did not."

"We need to talk." Daphne carried a mug of coffee and sat in one of
the wicker chairs at the table. Annie remained at the window.

"Come on," she coaxed. "Everything looks better in the morning."

"My aunt Kate used to say that," Annie said coldly. "Some mornings, things actually look worse."

"Look, Annie dear, your husband came out here seeking my help."

"I don't want to hear this again."

"Okay." She laughed lightly. "We had way too much to drink.
Things got a little out of control."

"Indeed. I'd say seducing your friend's husband is a bit out of control."

"I didn't seduce him."

"What would you call it? You had sex with him. I think that's the bottom line." Annie didn't want to start crying again. Her anger was clear, understandable, whereas the loss of her marriage was more than she could bear. She hated being exposed, vulnerable like this, in front of Daphne.

"He was miserable. We were drunk." Daphne threw Annie a petulant look, as if she were a fool to take the matter so seriously.

"Well, perhaps you might explain a few things." Annie took a seat opposite Daphne and folded her hands across her chest. "I thought you were interested in me. I thought that was pretty clear the last time I was here. When did you decide to go after my husband? Or was that part of the plan all along?"

"I didn't plan anything." Daphne laughed softly. "Wesley—well, he sort of fell in my lap—so to speak."

"God. How can you be so cruel?" Annie thought she had cried every tear, but now her face was wet again. Laying her arms on the table, she lowered her head, no longer able to prevent herself from weeping. "You betrayed me."

"Annie, Annie. It didn't matter. It had nothing to do with you." Daphne spoke softly. "Look, you knew your marriage was finished. Wesley's more interested in his bloody job than anything else, and you—well, you've moved on too. I can see that in your poems." Daphne stood and moved behind Annie's chair. She placed her hands on the back of her neck and massaged gently. She rubbed her shoulders and slowly drew one hand down her back. "Come on, love." She whispered into Annie's ear, "You don't need him anymore. It's over."

Annie felt the kiss on the back of her head. "Stop it." She pulled away. "Stop it." She stood and walked back to the windows. "Don't ever touch me again." She couldn't believe what a fool she'd been. "You're right. It is probably over. But you're not the answer. Someone who would betray a friend like that is not worth anything."

"I think you're making far too much of this," Daphne said. "You led me to believe that you and Wesley were finished." Her voice grew gentler, more coddling. "It's you I care about. You know I'm not a big fan of marriage. Too much sacrifice. Anyway, I can't see how it's made you very happy."

"No, not now. But there was a time when being with Wesley made me very happy, happier than I ever thought I could be." She paused and rested her forehead against the cool pane of the window. "I wanted it to be that way again. I wanted to recapture what we had." She wiped her face with the back of her sleeve. "Now it's too late."

"Oh, come on—not all is lost."

Annie looked directly at Daphne for the first time that morning. Her hair was pulled back smoothly in a clip; her face was freshly washed and free of makeup. She looked younger again, almost sweet. It was difficult to believe what had happened. Annie realized with sudden clarity that they were worlds apart. "You're right, all is not lost. I'm going back to Paris." She would go see Sophie as soon as she could. In the meantime, there were the poems and her job.

"Oh, please stay at least another night." There was pleading woven into Daphne's words. "Last night shouldn't have happened. I want to make it up to you."

"No. That's impossible."

"Please, Annie." Now Daphne looked about to cry.

"I'm going home," Annie said. She left Daphne alone in the glass room at God House. She couldn't get to Paris soon enough.

"Mom, we haven't heard from you in so long. Is everything all right?" Sophie's clear, youthful voice sounded distressed. It was almost the end of February, and in truth Annie couldn't remember the last time she'd spoken to her daughter. They'd left messages on each other's answering machines but hadn't managed to connect. Annie had been busy at the office and consumed with writing until late in the evening. The poems were going well, and she had just sent another envelope to Paul Valmont.

She'd returned from God House determined to forget that dreadful night. Some days a gnawing anger burned just below the surface, and on other days she managed to forget completely as she rushed from home to work and then back again to write. It was ironic, really, how well the poems were going. Paul's comments were favorable and often enthusiastic. Wesley used to tease her, saying that the best poets were the most miserable poets and that only by truly suffering were they able to do their greatest work. He may have been right.

"Mom, are you there?"

"Sorry, sweetie." Annie was chagrined. She held the receiver tightly. "We've just had a busy stretch at the office. I'm sorry I haven't called much lately. I was just heading out to meet Mary for a drink."

"I didn't think you and Mary were such buddies."

"I've seen more of her lately," Annie said. "Tom's left her and she's lonely. It helps her to talk."

"Well, speaking of lonely, you should at least call Dad more often. He sounds unhappy. We both wish you'd finish your work and come over here. Can't Mary find anyone to replace you?"

Annie wondered what Wesley had told her. "I've been distracted lately, and you know what a nuisance the time difference can be."

"I think he's upset because you haven't decided when you're coming."

"I'll talk to him, sweetie. I haven't had time to make any plans yet."

"Look, Mother, Dad needs you." Sophie's voice was accusing. "This is a big change for him."

And what about me? Annie thought. There was so much to explain to Sophie, and she didn't want to do it over the phone. She looked at her watch. She was late to meet Mary. "How are you doing, Soph? Are you still seeing Daniel?"

"He's been busy. So have I. We haven't had much time together lately."

Annie knew these were the kinds of things that would be so much easier to talk about in person. It was hard having her daughter so far away. "I see. Well, what's going on at work?"

"I've got a good client, right in New York. Not as complicated as our last one. It's funny, I'm not working as hard now, but I'm really tired."

"You mustn't let yourself get run-down."

"There you go. Nagging again."

"Come on, sweetie. I just care about you. Your health is my concern." Annie carried the phone to the kitchen table and sat down. She felt suddenly weary herself.

"All you care about is your stupid book," she said, annoyed. "It's like you've forgotten us."

"Sophie, that's not true."

"And I'm supposed to believe that? Look, Mom. I've got to go."

"Sophie, please." Annie was shaken.

"Just promise me you'll call Dad. That's all I'm asking." Sophie's voice became cold and aloof.

Annie sensed that Sophie knew that there was something wrong. She wasn't a fool. "Yes," she said. "Yes. I'll call."

"Promise?"

Annie nodded, unable to reply.

Later that night she thought of her promise to call Wesley. He'd called her repeatedly after leaving God House, and each time she'd dissolved into tears, unable to speak. He'd written several letters begging her forgiveness. Eventually she'd answered, telling him that she needed to be in Paris and that she assumed their marriage was over; she didn't see how it could change. After that they exchanged short e-mails, having to do with the apartment, bills, taxes, and the like. There was no point in calling him now. There was nothing more to say. Annie accepted her solitude, inevitable like winter—a price she had to pay.

Annie had become accustomed once again to the empty apartment. Her routine shifted. She read late into the night, skipping meals altogether or eating small take-out dinners from the local shops. She left manuscript pages spread out across the big table in the living room, took over Wesley's shelf in the medicine cabinet, and slept with the window opened wide when she finally went to bed. She shifted her work hours at Liberal Arts Abroad to afternoons. Mary didn't mind; it was the advantage of having a part-time position. Mornings were for her poems. Some days she set the alarm early, her notebooks and pens at the ready, next to her on the bed. After particularly late nights, she'd sleep late and lie in bed thinking of the photograph she planned to work on next.

There were days when she was almost happy, when her independent life felt good, when she was productive and consumed with her writing. Then she'd see some reminder, like the biography of Benjamin Franklin on Wesley's bedside table, the bookmark at the place where he'd been reading the story of that other American in Paris from a much earlier time.

Once, while dusting, she discovered an old scratched pair of glasses he'd left near the computer. It was as if he'd come back to haunt her, except the memories were often sweet. One day she found a pale blue oxford shirt pushed back into the far reaches of the closet. She brought it to her face and breathed in the faint scent of him. Seeing these poignant reminders of Wesley made her feel a pinch in her heart, and she found it hard to swallow. On days like that, she couldn't bear to look at his side of the bed or at his favorite chair in the living room. Everything in the apartment would remind her of him, of their shared life, of what they once had.

Paris came to her rescue when sadness threatened to overcome her. She would wander the streets, letting the beguiling beauty of the city ease her pain. It was impossible to be lonely when engulfed in the powerful elixir of Paris. If the weather was bad, as it often was that winter, she'd make a table in a café her living room. There she'd read, write, and sit for hours watching the people until the bad patch eased and she felt brave enough to go home.

Before she knew it, February became March. The bitter weather that had gripped Paris since early December began to loosen its hold. On the milder days the Parisians piled into the sidewalk cafés to sit outside, sip drinks, and enjoy the passing crowds. They loosened their scarves and tilted their heads into the sun, like early spring bulbs coveting the fragile warmth. Everyone was out, it seemed. Everyone was hungry for this change in the weather. The city hummed with a new rhythm. Today on her way to the office, Annie had seen large flats of primroses being unloaded at the Luxembourg Gardens—pink, purple, and yellow blossoms ready to douse the winter parks with color.

Paris grew lighter with each successive day. At five in the evening the city was enveloped in a softer light, reflecting the shimmering pastel shades of sunsets on the elegant buildings, the wide avenues and squares. The evenings rolled in more slowly, gently, with no imminent weight of darkness. Dusk blurred quietly to night.

Now and then she'd remember her promise to Sophie and feel guilty. There was so much to explain, but she knew it had to be in person. She planned to visit her daughter during her spring vacation. Perhaps they could take a short trip together. By then, she hoped, the poems would be finished.

Daphne, after an initial flurry of phone calls, was silent. Looking back, Annie could hardly believe they'd ever been friends. In some ways, it was like having been caught in a spell, pulled into another life temporarily, like being a ship sailing off course. Maybe one day, after the pain had lessened, she'd think of it as her bohemian phase, the winter of God House, the winter when Wesley went away. However, now it was a mixture of anger and shame that overwhelmed her when she allowed Daphne back into her thoughts. Still, she couldn't forget that Daphne had taken her work seriously, seriously enough to introduce her to Paul.

Annie began to look forward to her weekly appointments with Paul Valmont. At first they had sent work back and forth. She enjoyed receiving his flat gray envelopes in the afternoon post. He made comments and queries in the margins. His handwriting was bold but legible. Eventually his schedule cleared and he suggested they discuss the poems at his office and choose the next photographs from which she would work. Each meeting, he seemed a little less sad, almost as if his grief was fading away like the winter weather.

Today Annie left her office early and decided to stop in Le Bon Marché department store to buy a lipstick. The store was close to his office, and she had plenty of time before her appointment. She hadn't been shopping since before Christmas, and she thought a brighter color for her lips would be a nice change for spring.

The *vendeuses* bustled behind the glimmering cosmetic counters, each representing a different brand. A young mother with two small girls trailing behind her stopped in front of the Chanel counter and pointed to a display of moisturizing creams. Attired in black, like all sales personnel in the store, she explained in detail the attributes of each product. The mother listened attentively, and the two daughters followed every word, their eyes riveted on this exchange. Frenchwomen took their grooming seriously, and the two little girls looked like young beauties in training, studying to take their turn when they reached the appropriate age.

"*Et madame, vous désirez?*" the young woman in black asked. Her skin was as smooth and even as a porcelain doll's.

"*Un rouge à lèvres.*" Annie asked for her lipstick at the Lancôme counter, where she'd bought makeup before. This turned out to be more complicated than she had anticipated.

"Here is a lovely one, madame, very fresh. It will bring your color alive." And then, "Madame is looking a little pale, may I suggest a new *fond de teint*, a makeup to give you more light, more radiance? Here, let me do your *maquillage.*"

Annie had started to protest, then decided it might be fun to freshen up her look. She'd gone to her hairdresser every month, and Raoul insisted her shorter hair had been his idea all along. She asked the saleswoman, Gabrielle, to keep the makeup natural.

A few minutes later she admired her reflection in the handheld mirror offered by Gabrielle and vowed to make more of an effort. Her face did indeed look brighter, her expression less worried. She felt pretty for the first time in weeks. She left the store with the distinctive Bon Marché orange bag filled with the new makeup, blush, eye shadow, and lipstick. This small ritualistic artifice made Annie feel in sync with the throngs of late-afternoon shoppers, true Parisians, who considered it their duty to make the most of their feminine attributes.

Annie climbed the stairs to Paul's office, quite pleased with herself for making the stop at Le Bon Marché. She drew her shoulders back and entered, feeling more confident than the time she had stopped to see him without an appointment earlier that winter. His assistant, whom she now knew as Danielle, was wrapping a scarf around her neck, biting her lip in concentration, this activity as important as any other she'd performed that day. She'd already buttoned her coat, a cheap leather one with some kind of fur trim at the cuffs and hem that made Annie think of an animal she couldn't quite picture, a yak or a llama.

"Monsieur had to step out for a few minutes. He asks you to go in." Danielle smiled. She had gradually warmed to Annie and liked having a chance to practice her English. "He leaves you the photos to study. They are on the desk. He be back very soon."

Annie stepped into Paul's office and picked up the final envelope of photographs. They were nearing the end of the project. She took off her coat and left it on the sofa with her briefcase and shopping bag. She wore her black sweater, not new anymore but still capable of making her feel good, along with her skinniest black pants.

She'd thought carefully about her outfit that day, trying to find the right balance between literary and fashionable, feeling somewhat like an imposter in either category. She had embarrassed herself with her thoughtful preparations, but she told herself it was all right. She had no intention of flirting with Paul. She thought of her efforts more as trying on a new persona, part of getting used to living as a single person.

The envelope contained the last six pictures in the collection. Leafing through, Annie remembered her first meeting with Paul, months ago, when she'd seen the photographs of the nude torsos. That recollection, along with the sensual feeling it had provoked, was still vivid in her mind, and she wondered again if it had been Paul's wife. It was the kind of thing she thought a Frenchman might do, have photographs of his wife to look at when they were apart. She had never seen the pictures again.

François was a master at capturing Parisian life. There wasn't a photograph Annie didn't like. The gradations of light, the subtlety of the subjects, and the careful compositions were brilliant. She studied the final photograph in this series, entitled "Le Souvenir." It portrayed a young couple kissing in the place de Furstenberg, a charming square not far from Paul's office. The woman's face reflected the pearly light, her cheek turned up to face her lover. The man's dark hair, his arms tight around her waist, his complete infatuation, made Annie long for that kind of intensity. She knew that lovely square, surrounded by tall, elegant houses, and the four pawlonia empress trees that blossomed each spring.

Annie envied the couple's private embrace a few steps from the bustling Paris streets. "Le Souvenir." She reflected on the meaning of that French word, understanding that François was referring not to the actual thing that you might take away to remember a place but to the elusive, intangible memory itself.

"I like that one too." Paul's voice surprised her. He had a way of catching her unawares. He was wearing a dark suit, as if he had come from an appointment.

Annie felt color coming to her face and placed the photograph back with the others in the envelope. She smiled. "I hope I'm up to a poem that will capture that."

He didn't comment, but raised his eyebrows before smiling back at her. "These are the final pictures. François and I are very pleased with your last poems. I ask myself if it is now the poems that carry the book even more than the pictures."

"I'm glad you think that, but the photographs speak for themselves. It's the images that make the poems come alive."

"You are too modest." He paused and looked at her more carefully. "You are looking very well. Please forgive me for keeping you waiting this evening. I had a meeting with my lawyer. Tedious matters of my wife's estate."

"That must be very difficult," she said, pleased with his subtle compliment.

"It is becoming easier," he said. "Life is change, n'est-ce pas?" He gave a quick Gallic shrug.

"Some changes are more difficult than others."

"You are right, of course." His voice sounded crisp and businesslike again. "How long will you need to write the last poems?"

"A month, maybe six weeks," she said. "I have more time now. My husband has moved back to the States, so I'm on my own. I have more time for writing." Annie felt the words gushing out. This was the first time she'd told him anything about Wesley's absence.

Paul didn't say anything right away, as if trying to comprehend what she said. "Does that mean you will be going there too? Are you leaving Paris?"

"I'm not sure. It's complicated. I'm not sure I can leave Paris."

"How can he think of leaving you behind?"

"Well, he has. It's been a difficult time for me." She looked away, immediately wishing she hadn't said all this. It felt ridiculous to be complaining when Paul had certainly suffered far more. Wesley had been unfaithful. That was nothing compared with having someone die. She turned and picked up her coat. "I'm sorry. I shouldn't have said anything. I'll take the photographs and be on my way."

"Please." A look of concern crossed his face. "Please, there is no hurry to go away. Perhaps a drink? Are you free for the evening?"

Now that he knew she was alone, Annie felt strangely exposed. He seemed to be studying her closely. "No, not tonight. But thank you. I really must be going."

"We need to meet soon to talk about the final form of the book."

"Don't you and François work that out?" she asked.

"The writing, the poems, are what bring the photographs together," he explained, "and I wish to have you decide this with me."

"Of course. I'd be happy to help."

Annie felt shy and suddenly foolish in her newly made-up face. Paul appeared alarmingly handsome in the unfamiliar suit. She wished she hadn't told him about Wesley. She stood to put on her coat.

"Please. Let me help you." Paul took her coat and she reached back and fumbled trying to put her hand in one sleeve. He stepped closer and her hand slid in easily on the second try. He smelled vaguely of eau de cologne and the hint of smoke from some earlier visit to a restaurant or café—the scent of a man not her husband.

Annie turned up her collar and pulled on her scarf, aware of his proximity, the fixity of his gaze. His eyes looked especially dark that day, almost navy, like his suit. "Another time, though, I would like it," she said. "I mean a drink or something."

What would she like? A drink with him, his hands lingering on her shoulders, his hands around her waist pulling her to him with the urgency in that final photograph? She liked imagining all of those things. She couldn't deny it.

"I will call you," he said. Annie left the office and stepped into quiet rue Clément before joining the crush of pedestrians flowing along the rue Saint-Germain.

Annie picked up the telephone. It wasn't Paul.

"Do you have a moment?" Wesley asked.

She shouldn't have answered. She'd started the poem on the romantic photograph late that afternoon when she arrived home from work. Wesley's voice broke the spell. She hadn't noticed it was getting dark.

"I saw Sophie this weekend," he said. "I thought you'd want to know."

"Of course," Annie said. "How is she?" She put down her pen, truly eager for news of her daughter. Sophie hadn't returned Annie's calls lately, and she feared that they were growing farther and farther apart.

"She looked great," Wesley said. "You know that grin. In a split second she looks like she's seven again. I can't believe in May she'll be twenty-three."

Annie pictured Sophie's endearing smile, and her face softened.

"You should see her, Annie. God, I keep forgetting how grown-up she is. So sweet, but sophisticated too." His voice was loving, filled with pride. "She got a huge raise. They love her at work."

"Were you in New York?"

"I met her there and we went to Madeleine's for the weekend."

Annie pictured Wesley's sister's lovely house in Connecticut. It was in a beautiful spot nestled in the hills, a peaceful retreat. She could see the three of them gathered around the fire. Whenever Sophie came to visit, Madeleine made hot cider and her favorite ginger cookies, rich with molasses and raisins. For a moment, Annie felt like she was homesick, but Connecticut was not even her home.

"Did you talk at all about us?" For a moment there was silence. The vast Atlantic hung between them. "I know Sophie's worried. She's—"

"I tried to be honest," he said. "I told her we'd had some unhappy times"—his voice faltered—"but I hoped we'd work it out soon. You know I want that, Annie."

Her heart hardened. Of course he wouldn't tell her about Daphne, about what he'd done, how it had torn her apart. "So she thinks I'm the ogre. I'm the selfish one, the terrible mother who won't move back, who doesn't care—"

"No. God no. It's not like that. She misses you. I miss you."

"Wesley. This isn't fair." Anger, outrage, grief, all the feelings deep within her bones rose to the surface. The events of the stormy night at God House came into focus once again. If she could only forget, if the memory could only fade.

"I know you're suffering," he said. "I know you don't believe it, but I'm suffering too. More than you can imagine."

For a moment she believed him.

"Annie, there's something else."

She waited.

"The office manager gave me the name of a terrific Realtor. I've set up some appointments at the end of the month, and I was hoping—"

"Wesley—"

"Annie, please."

"It's over. I told you that."

"Won't you ever forgive me?"

"Tell Sophie I'm coming over for spring break. Tell her I'll see her soon." Her voice broke and she could no longer speak. She hung up the phone.

The living room had grown dark. Annie went from room to room turning on the lights and closing the shutters against the night.

SIXTEEN

Les Amies

The following morning Annie sat at the table in the living room looking at several drafts of her poem to accompany the photograph of the two lovers embracing in the place de Furstenberg. The photograph had a compelling quality. She'd propped it up against two books, but she no longer needed to study it. Every detail was engraved in her memory: the pressure of the man's hands on the back of the woman, the plane of her face, the curve of her neck as she tipped her head up to meet her lover's lips, the angle of his jaw. She closed her eyes and could still see the façades of the elegant stone buildings gently blurred in the background, along with the baroque curls of the iron balconies above the street. The entire image was veiled in lambent moonlight.

Now, as she read through the drafts of her poem, the words glared back at her. The results were trite and flat, and each attempt looked more amateurish than the last. Paul wanted to meet with her that afternoon to work on ordering the photographs and poems. Annie worried that she wouldn't be ready. She felt it important to finish this poem. It brought closure to the collection.

Annie closed her notebook and went over to the sofa, stretched out and dangled her legs over the arm at the far end. Her legs felt leaden, as if they were pulling her down. Perhaps she was pushing too hard. She knew better than to force a poem. She had written more in the past four months than she usually wrote in two years. Many of the scenes in Paris had come, if not easily, at least willingly, as if they had been in her, part of her, for a long time. They were based more on images of place. Now she was trying to infuse a level of complexity that had more to do with people, in this case the passionate relationships they make.

She drew her hand across her eyes. She had not slept well and had awakened abruptly from a dream about Wesley. It was so vivid. He was young in the dream, the same age as when she first knew him. She still remembered that night, a long-ago New England spring, during her junior year in college. Meeting Wesley had been like turning a corner, turning a corner onto new scenery, new people, new light. It must have been a month or more after her boyfriend Luke's departure for New York. She had been crushed when they broke up, and she had thrown herself into her studies, choosing to do a senior honors thesis in art history. She chose to write about Gustave Caillebotte, an accomplished painter, represented in few museum collections but held privately by collectors abroad. Her thesis adviser had recommended her for a research fellowship in Paris that summer.

Her friends accused her of working too hard. "Come on, Annie," Lucy had said. She was a lively, redheaded senior who lived down the hall. "It's just a party. You need to get out more. You can't spend another weekend holed up in the library."

"But over at the law school?" Annie was dubious. The undergraduate artsy crowd was a long way from those serious law students, several years older.

"Look, just come for an hour," Lucy had said. "If you're miserable, you can leave. It's no big deal."

It was a beautiful evening, a rare night in an otherwise rainy spring. The trees had the just green freshness of new leaves, the setting sun still warmed the air, and the streets were filled with students eager to have a good time. Annie walked to the party with a group from her dorm. As they got closer, she began to have second thoughts. What would she have in common with a bunch of young aspiring lawyers on the fast track to success?

The sounds of Bob Dylan poured from the open windows and grew louder, mixing with the roar of voices as Annie and her friends climbed the steps to the suite of rooms on the third floor where the party was. The first room was crowded and colored with the blue haze of smoke.

"Beer and May wine in the other room!" a voice called out.

Annie, caught in the throng of her group, was propelled forward and handed a plastic cup of pink liquid that smelled of sweet fruit juice and grain alcohol.

"This isn't May wine at all."

Annie turned to see a tall young man in a pink shirt looking down at her. He lifted his glass and smiled.

"May wine is flavored with sweet woodruff, a shade-loving herb that blooms in the spring," he said. "It's a German tradition to drink it on the first of May."

He had to be well over six feet tall, with longish blond hair that fell across his face, regular features, and dimples that gave him a boyish handsomeness. "Another jackass prep" is how Luke would have described him. Maybe the prep-school types were what had sent Luke running to New York City in search of what he called "authenticity." This fellow wore glasses, light tortoiseshell frames, that gave him an intelligent appearance. And, from the very beginning, he was kind.

"You'll have to forgive me. That's the kind of trivial bit of information I picked up while an undergraduate here." He smiled at her. "I was a history major," he said apologetically. He must have sensed her uneasiness. She was used to hanging out with poets and artists and wary of anyone aspiring to something as sensible and ordinary as law.

She wore a long flowing red skirt made in India, with tiny mirrored disks embroidered into the hem, and a sleeveless black T-shirt. That night she had pulled her hair into a braid that hung down her back, accentuating her large gold hoop earrings. She had them still, in a box in the back of her top dresser drawer.

He stood next to her drinking the "May wine," and they proceeded with the typical preliminary topics: where she was from, what she was studying, what she thought of her professors. It was hard to hear over the alcohol-infused voices and the music that would grow louder as the evening progressed. After a few minutes of yelling back and forth, he asked her if she would like to take a walk.

In many ways he was exactly as she expected, a product of a tame, prosperous Connecticut family: private schools, hiking in the East, skiing in the West, tennis his favorite sport. But there was something in the way he held his head and looked down at her with interest, the kinds of questions he asked, the knowing look in his blue eyes, and a genuine optimism that captivated her that first evening. Unlike cynical Luke, he looked at the world and his future with hope. He talked about places he wanted to travel, books he wanted to read, things he planned to accomplish. He was the sort of man whose hopes would come true. And his name was Wesley, Wesley Reed. She liked his name.

Much to Annie's surprise, he asked her out often that spring. He was interested in her work, and he told her she wrote beautifully about art. He talked more about history than his law studies. He was fascinated by the founders of the country and the first Americans who shaped the nation. He would rather sit for hours in the tiny ethnic restaurants in Cambridge than go to the big weekend parties at the law school.

That summer he came to see Annie in Paris when she had the grant for her thesis research. She was never sure who she fell in love with first: Paris or Wesley. It all happened at the same time. When she wasn't working on her thesis, she wrote poems, the first poems she was proud of, poems she shared with Wesley.

Annie pulled herself up off the sofa and went back to the table. She was living another life now. She thought back to the girl in the Indian skirt and dangling earrings talking to the young man in the pink shirt. Was there anything left of that girl? Had she changed so completely? She looked at the photograph once more and picked up her pen.

She met Paul at his office at five that afternoon. He seemed businesslike again and eager to begin work. She watched while he placed three different scenes of parks in a row, followed by two churches and the picture of the cemetery in Passy. He spread the rest of the photographs out across his desk and onto the floor. The poems, printed out on heavy white paper, were clipped to the back of each photograph. Only a few were missing.

Annie watched him work. He was a man comfortable in his body. She detected only a trace of the limp caused by the car accident. His spirit seemed to be healing as well. Annie knew that it had been almost a year since Marie Laure's death. Time does make a difference, she thought, and now there was the promise of spring.

"What do you think?" he asked, stepping away and gesturing toward the pictures.

"It looks good," she said. But, I was thinking . . ."

"Please, you must feel free to tell me." He turned in her direction. "You wrote the poems. You must advise me."

She thought a moment. "What if we arranged them by gradations of light? We could start with the early-morning shots and finish with evening scenes."

He didn't answer immediately but bent down and moved the first outdoor scenes so that the one done earliest in the morning came first. He stood up and looked at her inquiringly.

Annie shook her head. "No, I mean the entire series. You see, this one of the children on the merry-go-round is a park scene, but the light is brighter, more the middle of the afternoon. The lady on the bench would stay first, but after her I would put the Maubert market picture." She felt herself gaining confidence. "More like this." She rearranged the images. "We don't know for sure what time of day each one was shot, but I think we can get a sense of it from the light and from the action in the picture."

"*Mais oui.* Yes, yes, I see." He reached down and moved the picture of Notre-Dame toward the middle. "Like that?"

"Exactly. By arranging the photographs in order, spanning a day, it will make readers think they are living in Paris throughout the course of an entire day." She moved Saint-Eustache toward the end of the row. The architectural elements appeared bathed in fog. "Though, it's not always easy to determine." She frowned. "Some of the cloudlike ones could be any time of day."

"But it is right. It is the right way to start."

They both bent down and began to move the images around. The pictures covered almost the entire floor. Annie almost stepped on one, so she took off her shoes. He reminded her that they were only copies, but he took off his shoes as well. His feet, in dark socks, were much smaller than Wesley's.

It was a slow process. He would move a picture, then reconsider. Sometimes he asked her to read a poem aloud, followed by another. He wanted the words and the mood of each poem to flow into the next. They agreed often on the chronology, and when she raised an objection, he listened and considered her point of view.

When he picked up the photograph of the Eiffel Tower from the end of the sequence, he backed into Annie, sending her sprawling onto the rug. They both laughed and he pulled her to her feet. His hands felt warm and comfortable.

He pointed to the photograph. "You see, this is first light. It is morning, do you not think?" He was excited and found it hard to stop laughing. "So you see, your plan does work. If we begin here, we start with the symbol . . ."

"The icon of Paris." She touched his arm. His sleeve felt smooth and crisp. "Yes, of course. It's the anchor of the book, the right place to begin." She withdrew her hand. Placing the photographs into sequence made the book come alive.

"The last poem should be the place de Furstenberg. It is the finale, how do you say it, the climax?" He gave her his now-familiar Gallic shrug.

Annie looked again at the picture of the couple in their passionate embrace and murmured her appreciation. "It's the light, of course— moonlight. How did François ever achieve that? I mean, capturing the couple in that way, in that place." She smiled at Paul. "It's pure magic."

"And your poem will be magic as well."

"Oh no." She leaned back against the desk. "I hate to tell you, but I've had an awful time with that poem." She shook her head, feeling inadequate again. "It's my very favorite photograph, and all my attempts so far have been terrible."

"Please. I will not hear this." He took one of her hands and then the other. His touch was gentle but firm.

Annie imagined some kind of energy flowing from him directly into her. She didn't want him to let go. His eyes met hers.

"Annie, I want to see your smile again, *ton beau sourire*." He touched the corner of her mouth. "I know you can write this poem."

Annie released his hands and stepped away, overwhelmed by his touch. It didn't feel like a familiar friendly gesture, like one of Georges's hugs. He wanted to see her smile, she thought. She needed to get hold of herself. This was her editor. They had work to do. She was responsible for finishing the final poem.

"Perhaps dinner," he said. "Are you free? We mustn't work all of the time."

"I wish I could," she said. She looked at her watch. "I'm meeting some old friends tonight. I'm afraid I must go." She smiled and looked around for her briefcase. She was having dinner at the Verniers'. She had accepted Céleste's invitation that morning and now regretted having to say no to Paul.

"Ah—too bad. Another time then?"

Annie nodded and he helped her with her coat.

"*Alors*, you two friends, I will leave you here to have your *tisane*. There's a great film, a detective one, on the *télé*, that I don't want to miss." Georges bowed at Céleste and Annie in a mock solemn gesture. "I will let you have your girl talk, now." He retreated to the tiny study off the kitchen where the Verniers kept the television.

They had finished dinner, a lovely chicken dish with mushrooms and cream, and Céleste carried the tray with the herbal tea into the *salon*. Annie followed her, carrying a small plate of cookies.

"These look delicious," Annie said, "but I don't know if I can eat another thing."

"You are looking too thin," Céleste remarked. "Perhaps you are not eating enough with Wesley away." She poured the pale tea into fine white china cups. The tea was chamomile, made from loose leaves that she bought in the open-air market. Céleste preferred fresh herbs and never bought simple tea bags from the grocery.

"I'm eating well enough, but you're right. I'm not as inspired cooking just for myself." Annie reached for a cookie, hoping to placate Céleste.

"How much longer before you go to join Wesley?"

"I'm going to go visit Sophie in New York in a few weeks."

"And Wesley? When are you going to go and find a new home?"

Annie knew Céleste would ask her this. She sipped her tea, wondering how to answer. She could feel her friend watching her, lines of concern across her face.

"Annie. I can see something is wrong. You can speak to me freely. Georges has his program. We won't see him for a while."

"I'm not planning on seeing Wesley this trip." She set her cup down and clasped her hands, bringing them to her lap. "Wesley and I are not very happy right now. I'm not making plans to join him in the States."

"But, Annie, non, non. Ce n'est pas possible."

"Sadly, it is possible. In fact, it's possible that our marriage may be over."

Céleste put her cup down and joined Annie on the satin love seat, the same place where Daphne had sat next to Wesley during that long-ago November lunch when they met for the first time. "You love Wesley," she said. "You and Wesley are like me and Georges. You are made to be together."

"Not now, I'm afraid."

"How has this happened?"

"Oh, goodness." She sighed. How to explain the months and months of unhappiness? "I think it started when Wesley wanted to move to Washington. I wasn't sure if it was the best thing for us, for me anyway. I've been so happy here. I was afraid of leaving, but he was insistent. I just wanted more time here, until—" She might as well tell Céleste. Why should she protect Daphne? "Wesley and I had a terrible argument. Shortly after that, he had an affair with Daphne. I found them one night—"

"Oh, mon amie, I am so sorry."

"Wesley was supposed to have been on the plane. You remember the big storm at the end of January? He went to God House because he was angry with me. They were together there."

"Just that once?"

"I think only once, but why does that matter?" Annie brought her hands to her temples. Her head ached. Telling Céleste that her marriage was over made it horribly real. There was no going back.

"Annie, you must come to your senses." Céleste almost scolded. "Look at me."

Annie let go of her head and leaned back against the cushions.

"Are you listening?"

"I am," Annie said, resigned.

"You must not throw everything away over one indiscretion."

"Indiscretion? I think you might feel differently if it were Georges."

"Annie, it is our duty to make the family, the home. Wesley had a long struggle to find the job. You told me he had not been himself. Men are sometimes, how do you say? Fragile. Yes, fragile. It is partly his age too."

"Céleste, what are you saying? I'm to make allowances for his age?"

"Not only his age. You can change this. As women, it is up to us—"

"No, Céleste. It is not always up to us." She was outraged by Céleste's reaction. "I'm sorry. It's hard to talk about this. It's upset me deeply." She felt tears again and brought her hands to her face.

Céleste put her arms around her. "Annie, chérie, do not be foolish; at least think about what I said."

The place Saint-Sulpice was one of Annie's favorite squares in Paris. It was indeed square, with the church on one side, perfectly balanced with the surrounding buildings. Sitting in the Café de la Mairie while waiting for Hélène late one Saturday afternoon, she listened to the rush of water from the large fountain, an anchor in the center of the square. Place Saint-Sulpice was so quintessentially Paris: stylish, elegant, urbane. The activity around her was essentially Parisian as well. A dark-haired young man ruffled the hair of the girl beside him and bestowed kisses regularly on her full lips. Mothers and fathers pushed baby carriages bearing stylishly dressed offspring out for a weekend stroll. The couple next to her paid their bill and took off on Rollerblades, joking and teasing as they glided in and out of traffic, unconcerned about their safety. An older woman hobbled by on perilously high-heeled shoes the same shade as her dove-colored suit. She looked determined not to reveal the discomfort caused by her shoes or tightly fitted skirt.

Annie tried to imagine how François would photograph this late-afternoon scene. He might capture the gentle opalescent light on the lushly budding trees that lined the rue Saint-Sulpice. Or perhaps he would take a close-up of their trunks, *les platanes*, with their mottled bark that reminded her of sycamore trees. She recalled sitting at this same café with Wesley one summer evening when the leaves were fully open, large, fresh, and green, creating a rooflike canopy overhead.

Now, on this spring afternoon, Annie was one of the few people sitting by herself. Weekend afternoons were a particularly lonely time for her, and she liked having an excuse to escape the apartment. Céleste's advice had bothered her. Perhaps she shouldn't have told her as much as she had. She had confided in Mary but only in the vaguest of terms, having kept Wesley's affair to herself. How do you explain that you miss your husband and are angry with him at the same time? This winter she'd found herself questioning everything she'd once believed in: her marriage, her creative life, the meaning of friendship.

"*Bonsoir, mon amie!*" Hélène slipped into the seat next to Annie. "How can you look so serious on this beautiful spring evening?"

Annie leaned over and kissed Hélène on both cheeks. "Just thinking. Sometimes I wish I could pull a switch and turn off all the thoughts in my head." She smiled.

"*Ça va mieux!* Yes, that is better. One should smile on an evening such as this." Hélène untied the apple-green silk scarf from around her neck and unbuttoned her raincoat.

The waiter swooped in and they each ordered a kir. The city around them seemed to hum with pleasure. Free from schools and offices, the Parisians filling the sidewalks were in a celebratory mood, their faces hinting at a smug happiness in being alive in this magical place. Annie felt more relaxed, even secure, now that Hélène was by her side.

"And what are these thoughts you wish to turn off?" Hélène raised one eyebrow and tilted her head. She looked serene, beautifully groomed as usual, unflappable.

"I don't mean to be gloomy. Some of them are happy thoughts."

"Such as?" Hélène asked.

"I've been having a wonderful time working on the book. I spent yesterday afternoon with Paul. It was so exciting to see it all come together. We figured out the order of the photographs. I loved being part of that." She thought again of the pleasure she'd experienced working by his side. "He listened to what I had to say, and he really loves the poems." She leaned back in her chair and looked up at the powder-blue sky. "It was exhilarating, really."

"So it's completed then?"

The waiter set down their drinks. Hélène raised her glass of wine, pink from the cassis, and offered a toast, "À la fin!"

"We can't toast the end just yet," Annie said, her glass raised. "I still have one more poem to write."

"That's not much. Now you can plan your trip to America."

"I'm afraid those are the thoughts I'd like to turn off," Annie said ruefully.

"What do you mean?" Hélène took another sip of her kir.

"Did you ever think of leaving Bertrand?" Annie asked. Though Hélène had been widowed for many years, she spoke of her husband often.

"Ah, I see." Hélène looked out across the square. She said nothing for a while. She seemed far away, no longer in the place Saint-Sulpice. "Well, ma chère, forty-five years is a long marriage, and yes, I must admit there was one time." The line between her neatly arched brows deepened.

"I don't mean to pry. I know you miss him now. My question must seem unfair."

"I don't mind."

"Why did you stay with him?"

"There is no simple answer. We were apart for some time after living in Argentina. I had come back to find a home for us in France." She turned toward Annie and gently shook her head. "You know, I have not thought of this in years."

"I don't mean to upset you." Annie wished she hadn't asked, but there was something in Hélène that inspired confidences.

"It no longer upsets me. Bertrand stayed behind to complete his assignment. He became involved with a woman who worked at the embassy. I found out quite by accident. That part is not important."

The church bells of Saint-Sulpice rang six times. Hélène waited patiently until the last ring fell silent. "It was a strange time," she continued. "Bertrand did not act like himself then. He was very distant. He no longer seemed like the man I had married."

"You never confronted him?"

"It was odd how it resolved itself. Bertrand's mother died and he came back to France. We were together then. First the funeral, then a few weeks in the country with his family. Somehow, I knew that he'd decided to break it off."

Annie listened carefully, trying to imagine what it must have been like for her friend. She pictured Hélène as a younger woman, her lovely face quietly masking the inevitable pain. She reached over and rested her hand on Hélène's arm, giving her an affectionate pat.

"Gradually, we grew closer." She lowered her head. "I suppose, at the time, I asked myself if I truly wanted to give up all we had, the years together, our life with our son. Alexis was a teenager. I felt he needed his father. That's when we had the first student from the program come to live with us." She looked up, her face clouded. "I think I must have considered our future and how it would be to grow old without Bertrand. And now, of course, here I am." She smiled but her eyes were sad.

"I'm sorry, Hélène."

"C'est la vie, hein?" She took in a big breath of air and lifted her glass one last time. "That is my story. I'm not sure it makes sense. Other women might not have made the same choice. In a way, starting over can be much the easier thing. It takes work to make the repair."

"An awful lot of work for us, I fear."

"Ah, ma chérie, often the things you work for have the greatest value."

Annie wasn't sure this was advice she was ready to take. She finished her glass of wine and looked out at the square. The sun had gone down and the air had cooled. She pulled her coat around her knowing soon she would have to return to her empty apartment.

SEVENTEEN

L'Amant

Annie was relieved to hear Paul's voice when the phone rang late the next afternoon. She'd spent the entire day writing. She'd been tempted to go out, to join the thousands of Parisians walking in the parks or sprawled in cafés with their shirt collars unbuttoned and scarves and gloves cast aside, excited by the extraordinary burst of tropical air, but her poems had consumed all her attention. The place de Furstenberg poem remained unfinished. Instead, she'd focused on some new work. It was strange how the poems on Paris seemed to inspire her to take off in other directions. These first drafts were like sketches that might eventually work their way into full poems.

She'd opened the tall living room windows, and the warm air lifted her spirits. It was time to replant her window boxes, have the curtains cleaned, and trade her winter coat for her trench coat, all the rituals that marked the change of season. She'd been enjoying her freedom, writing until late at night, not bothering to cook, and leaving her bed unmade. It had become easier and easier to let things go, though now and then she spent a frenzied day paying bills, cleaning, and shopping to make up for it.

"I'm on your side of the river," he had said. "I am glad you are at home, but you are working too much. Will you meet me for a drink on the terrace at Georges? *Il faut profiter*, the day is so beautiful, *non?*" He sounded lighthearted, like a younger Paul Valmont, one she had not met before.

Now she hurried to meet him. She normally avoided the Pompidou Center, named for the former French president, with its crowds of tourists and the often controversial exhibits. Annie had never liked the enormous modern building that looked inside out to her, with its strange colorful ductwork and elaborate pipes that made her think of the anatomical workings of some machine. She was not drawn to the French attempts at modernism, but the restaurant on the top of the building had spectacular views of the city, and the sea of white tables set up outside, each decorated with a single rose, allowed the panorama to take precedence.

The evening was almost unbearably beautiful, and she was glad she didn't have to spend it alone. She glided through the streets, not bothered by the jostling crowds, absorbing the intoxicating air. She felt like she was swept up in a current, and she didn't mind the sensation of being carried away.

He had said he was in the neighborhood. She had turned down his previous invitations. Her thoughts tumbled out in a jumble. Would they talk about the book? Or was this purely a social occasion, a date? She was a married woman meeting a man. It was only for a drink. She'd been alone. When would another day like this come along? "Il faut profiter." There was no exact equivalent in English for what he had said. Maybe "take advantage of," or the overused expression "seize the day."

She rode the escalator, a glass-enclosed tube that looked like a caterpillar on the outside of the building, to the rooftop terrace. With every level, her anxiety increased. Would something happen between them? She remembered the feeling of his hands clasping hers, his finger lightly brushing her cheek. Did she want more than that? The moving stairs hummed, carrying her higher and higher. She clutched the handrail and the city drew farther away at her feet. She looked over her shoulder at the Sacré-Coeur basilica, a white mirage floating in Montmartre. The pale blue evening sky was tinged with a pink blush.

She stepped off the escalator at the top of the Pompidou Center. The days were longer now, and though it was close to six in the evening, the sun still held its warmth. A soft breeze, perfumed with spring, gently lifted her hair. The vast view, diffused in a golden light, made her think of some idyllic warmer city like Marseilles or Nice, but she looked out on the glimmering monuments and tree-lined avenues of Paris. Days like this were rare in early April.

Annie saw Paul before he saw her. He stood silhouetted against the view of Notre-Dame and the majestic dome of the Panthéon above it on the hill. It was the perfect place to be, one of the finest views in the city. He wore dark pants, a blazer, no overcoat. He'd draped a scarf around his neck, that sure mark of a Frenchman.

She joined him at the rail, where he gazed out at the view. She wished that she could slow every gesture, to feel the brush of his lips on her face, his hands touching the sleeves of her coat, his fingers on her elbow guiding her to the table, perhaps a premonition that it would pass too quickly, perhaps fearful of what lay ahead.

"*Une coupe de champagne?*" he suggested when they sat at their table.

She nodded and he ordered the champagne along with a plate of smoked salmon.

"*C'est un peu touristique*, but I cannot think of a better place to watch the sun go down," he said.

He seemed different today, here on the crowded roof terrace, but no less engaging or attractive. She liked observing him. She was still not accustomed to his looks. Each time she saw him, there seemed to be more to discover. Annie could imagine him with a cigarette dangling between his parted lips, the typical guise of a Left Bank intellectual, but she knew that he didn't smoke. "You are very quiet," he said.

"Sorry. Just busy watching everything. It feels wonderful to be out. I don't think I've ever experienced such a beautiful evening in Paris." She hoped she wasn't gushing like an idiot. "I feel like I'm falling in love with this city all over again."

"So, it was love at first sight when you came to Paris?"

She was glad they were speaking English. In her state of excitement she didn't want a layer of language between them. "Completely." She decided not to tell him about her first summer there with Wesley. "My first winter here it did nothing but rain. You know, that cold, continual drizzle that chills you to the bone. Sophie was a toddler then, and sick all the time. She did nothing but cry." She met his gaze. "I still thought I was in heaven."

Their champagne arrived. Annie wondered if he felt the same energy, a sexual pull, that had been there all along. He gave no sign of it. He told her more about his childhood summers in the south of France in the little village of La Motte. He adored his grandmother, and he talked about her garden, the fields of lavender, the buttery peach tarts she made for Sunday lunch. He didn't discuss the book. It was like they were on holiday, and any talk of business was off limits.

The champagne worked its magic, and the salmon was a perfect balance of salty and sweet; it melted on her tongue. She reached for the butter, a plate of pale yellow pats shaped into leaves. He handed her the basket of rolls, plump crusty rounds that felt warm in her hand. The formality they'd clung to on previous meetings faded completely.

"I've always adored French butter," she said. "The butter in the States is flavorless in comparison." She slathered her roll with a daringly large amount.

"I must take you to Normandy. Mon oncle, he has a farm. He doesn't work it any longer, but there, wait until you taste the cheese, and le cidre." He brought his clustered fingers to his lips in an appreciative culinary gesture. "You have never tasted anything like the cider from his place."

They continued to talk about food, their favorite dishes, where they liked to eat. Later a comfortable silence fell between them. They had a second glass of champagne, the air cooled, and bit by bit, as the sun disappeared, a sea of lights twinkled below them.

"I'm afraid I still haven't finished the final poem." She didn't want to spoil their lovely evening. Though he hadn't asked, she felt like she needed to offer some explanation.

"I am not worried about that. You should take your time."

"I want it to be just right. Perfect."

"Oh, but you must not. In art, perfection is a bad thing."

"What do you mean?"

He leaned in toward her. "Think of a poem like a garden. No, a flower." He motioned to the rose on their table. "One must pick the flower before it comes to full bloom, before it is perfect. A poem is the same. It is the reader who takes it home and makes it his own. The reader brings his own life to it. It is he who makes it fini."

"You make me feel better." Annie smiled, relieved.

"For this I am glad." He hailed their waiter and paid the bill.

He suggested a walk and she agreed. She followed him down the escalator. The entire evening now seemed predestined to her—wherever they went, whatever they did, was bound to happen. There was nothing to do to stop it, even if she had wanted to. By the time they reached the quay along the Seine, she had taken Paul's arm and fallen comfortably into step beside him.

They crossed the river to the Île Saint-Louis and walked the entire length of the island, down the narrow center street, peering in the windows of bookshops, antique-print stores, and tiny restaurants. Voices and laughter rose and echoed between the buildings, along with the buzz of motorbikes. She leaned into him when they stepped onto the narrow sidewalk to avoid a passing car brave enough to maneuver the tiny street.

They crossed to the Left Bank and at place Saint-Michele began to wander in the warren of tiny streets between the boulevard Saint-Germain and the river. Annie loved the feeling of village life in this part of Paris. The darkened streets bustled with activity as people went off to dinner and filled the cozy restaurants, two or three to a block. Annie felt she could walk like this for hours, but she sensed by now that something was about to happen. Paul became more quiet and acted as though he had a specific destination in mind by the way he chose each particular street, turning left and then right with intent. She wondered if they would stop somewhere soon.

They reached the place de Furstenberg, the beautiful square that François had photographed and the site of her unfinished poem. That photograph and her poem were to be the final page in the book. Annie knew that he had brought her here on purpose. They stood together in the intimate space, at the center of the smallest square in the city of Paris. It was quiet here, and the only light came from gas lamps and the glimmer of a few lighted windows several stories above. The tall, elegant houses surrounded them, sheltering them from the real world, that other world that for the moment they didn't inhabit.

Neither spoke. Paul took her face in his hands, as she knew he would, and kissed her. She could feel the photograph come to life. He put his arms around her and she pressed against him, feeling her blood pulse through her veins like the Seine flowing through Paris.

"You will come to my apartment?"

She stepped away and nodded. She gave no thought to right or wrong. She was powerless to stop. He didn't need her, she thought; she didn't need him. It was the pure, simple, uncomplicated thing called desire that was bringing them together. Only that.

He took her hand, and they walked to his apartment building on a narrow street not far from where they'd stood. He kissed her again in the tiny elevator inside the building. Whether it was months of being alone, the champagne, or the magic of a Paris night that had gone to her head, she no longer cared. The elevator came to a stop and he fumbled for the keys to his door. The hall light clicked off just as the door yielded, and they stepped into the foyer of his apartment. She followed him into the living room, their feet soundless on the heavy carpeting.

He did not turn on the lights, but a wall of windows flooded the room with an aqueous glow. He pulled off his scarf and took her coat, tossing it onto a chair. Annie was more aware of the play of shadows on the rug than any furnishings or domestic details. He kissed her again, more emphatically. There was nothing to decide. She followed him into the bedroom.

Later she barely remembered the shedding of clothing, the first sensation of his skin against hers, the weight of his body, the softness of the bed that held them.

The next morning he brought her coffee and they made love again. This time more slowly, in the light, their eyes open. She allowed her fingers the luxury of lingering in his hair. She stroked the muscles down his back, his legs, his chest. She didn't want to forget his body, how he felt, the texture and shape of him. This time it was Paul who seemed to lose himself while Annie noticed every nuance of pleasure. She was the poet savoring the details, cataloging each sensual touch, observing and storing the memories.

The sex was of course different from married sex. There was a certain degree of fear, fear of the unknown, fear of disappointing. But the power, the sense of excitement, could have swallowed her whole; the very newness brought her senses to the edge. That morning they took their time and prolonged the pleasure. He whispered endearments, he whispered words she didn't understand, he whispered in French. Once, she heard him say "Marie Laure." He said it clearly, like the tinkling of a bell, and his wife's name hung momentarily between them.

Afterward, he pulled her tightly in his arms, her back to him, like one shell tucked into another. "I am sorry," he said.

"No, it's fine." She did understand. He still thought about his wife, just as she couldn't help but think of Wesley.

"I have not been with another woman since the accident."

She rolled over to face him and put her fingers to his lips. There were tears in his eyes and she kissed him there and on his forehead. She traced her fingers down his nose, across his lips, and across the firm line of his chin. She kissed him lightly behind one ear and tried to inhale all of him one last time before slipping out of bed.

Annie walked home along the quays, taking the bridge at the foot of Notre-Dame. Paul had wanted to come with her, but she insisted that she wanted to be by herself. She kept her coat open despite the cold air. A damp wind whipped across the Seine, and Annie stopped on the bridge and watched the stiff current passing below, barely feeling the change in the weather. The river was high, and people had started grumbling about the possibility of closing some of the roads close to the riverbanks.

This didn't matter to her; nothing mattered to her that morning except the exquisite sense of freedom she felt, like some cloud had lifted in her life. She felt energetic and infused with a new awareness, a kind of clarity that would carry her in the days ahead. She had done it. She had allowed herself that one selfish act, and for now it was all that mattered. The old Annie would never have slept with a man not her husband. She had committed adultery. She smiled down at the churning water. A flat barge passed under the bridge. The laundry of the captain's family flapped on the line on the rear deck. Would his wife, presumably the woman who had clipped the laundry to the line, have ever slept with another man?

She looked up at the sky, the pallid gray she was accustomed to. She buttoned her coat, turned up the collar, and continued across the bridge. She wanted to get home and finish the place de Furstenberg poem. The words were busily taking shape in her head.

Annie was standing at the windows in her living room when the doorbell rang late the following afternoon. The last poem was complete. She had printed it out and set it aside for one more review in the morning, but she knew she had it right. It spoke of love, of disappointment, the bittersweet taste of desire. When she read the poem aloud it sounded like music to her, the proper melody to accompany François's photograph.

Annie went to the door. Maybe it was Céleste or Hélène stopping by for a cup of tea. Instead, Daphne stood in the entranceway. She looked pale, tired, like a transparency of her former self. "I know you didn't expect me."

"It's been quite a while." Annie realized she hadn't thought about Daphne for a long time.

"I decided to take a chance—that you might be home."

"Come in." Annie took the cape from her shoulders and led Daphne into the living room. "I have some white wine chilled. Would you like a glass?" Annie felt no animosity. Daphne's unexpected arrival seemed like another predestined moment whose script had already been written.

"That would be lovely," she said. "You look well. I gather single life still suits you?"

"Some of it does."

Daphne studied her as if trying to assess what else had changed in her friend. "Tell me, how's the book coming?"

"Very well. I may have finished the final poem today."

"I remember what you told me about writing them over and over, always trying to find a better word, the perfect metaphor," Daphne reminisced, her voice melancholy.

They sat in Annie's big living room. She poured the wine, a pale Sancerre, into two short-stemmed glasses. The fading light fell on the buttery walls, the quilts, the soft cushions that made it feel like home. Annie loved the leisurely approach of spring evenings.

Daphne nodded toward the long farm table at the other end of the room. "I remember your wonderful solstice party and sitting at that table."

"So much has happened since then," Annie said. She could still see Daphne in the burgundy dress, all the men drawn in by her sultry charm as they sat in the pool of candlelight. Annie remembered feeling sick and at odds during the party. That night, Daphne had quietly taken control of her life. First introducing her work to Paul, encouraging her to make her poetry a priority, and then allowing her to become a part of her world at God House.

In hindsight, it was easy to see that meeting Daphne and becoming her friend had started something, had brought about a shift, a change of outlook in Annie's life. Though he had not sought it, Wesley had undergone a similar change. Both of their lives had spun off in different directions that winter.

"Yes," Daphne said. "Indeed, much has happened." She paused as if she didn't know what to say next. "I came to ask your forgiveness."

Annie stiffened. She had worked hard to forget the awful night when she found Wesley and Daphne together. She swirled the wine in her glass. What could she say now, months later? The damage seemed irreparable.

"Wesley told you the truth. On the night of the storm he did come to God House to ask me to persuade you to go with him to the States. He didn't come running to me to start some kind of affair. I want you to believe that."

"None of that matters anymore."

"But it does matter. It's you I care about. I still do."

"Daphne, that wasn't going to work, not in the way you'd hoped."

"I know that now. I suppose I was asking too much. I wanted us to be like Antoinette and Mother. We'd become such good friends, so quickly, and I hoped you felt the same way."

"I did feel very close." Annie sipped her wine. Maybe it would numb the pain. "You came into my life when I truly needed someone. You were such a help." Annie struggled to keep her old anger at bay. "Why didn't you send him home that night? I mean, if you cared about me, why did you let Wesley stay?"

"I'd like to blame it on the weather," she said, not quite smiling. "But seriously, he was so upset that my first thought was to give him a drink. That led to another. I thought that if I slept with Wesley, he'd realize that your marriage was over."

Daphne looked down at her feet. She didn't act like the bold friend that Annie remembered. She sat holding her wine, her shoulders rounded, and looked hesitant, almost afraid. "Neither of you seemed very happy," she continued. "I wanted Wesley to leave you. I wanted you to turn to me. I was thinking selfishly. I know there's no excuse." She sipped her wine. "If it makes you feel any better, you should know he tried to refuse me at first—"

"I don't want to hear any more," Annie said. She put down her wine and crossed her arms.

"Please, listen," Daphne pleaded. "I truly felt you'd be better off without Wesley. He was holding you back. I could see that. You were happier with me at God House."

"I was happy there, I don't deny that, but Wesley wasn't holding me back." Annie looked at Daphne and shook her head. "He was going through a bad time then, his job and everything. He was under a lot of pressure."

"You didn't see it that way then," Daphne said defensively.

"You may be right." Annie fingered the sofa cushion next to her, drawing her hand across the smooth velvet. She remembered again the texture of Paul's skin, the feeling of his back. She had betrayed Wesley, the one person she'd loved the longest.

"Can you forgive me?" Daphne asked.

Forgiveness. The word fell before her, vast and encompassing. Could she forgive Daphne, who had manipulated her and Wesley and tried to break up their marriage? Could she forgive Wesley for shutting her out, his coldness, his unwillingness to consider her feelings? And for having sex with Daphne? Was his betrayal any different from hers? Could she forgive herself?

"Annie?"

"I'm sorry," she said distractedly. "Of course. I forgive you."

"You'll come back to God House?"

"One day I will," she said. "Just not for a while."

"I see."

"There's one other thing. Something I've wondered about." For the first time in their relationship Annie knew that she was in control, that she had the upper hand. "What happened the summer that Tim met you, the summer in England when you were sixteen?"

Daphne set her glass on the table and leaned back in her chair. "Thinking of that makes me feel old. We were different people then." Her eyes looked colorless and dull. She stared down at a swath of late-afternoon sun pouring across the living room rug. "It was the most heavenly summer." She offered a wistful smile. "My brother, Roger, was home, and Mummy let me go everywhere with him. There were parties, so many parties, pretty wild even by today's standards. Mummy loved to have the house full of people. Everything was perfect, except for this girl."

"A friend of Roger's?"

"More than a friend." Daphne looked directly at Annie. "She was a little fool. Even at sixteen I knew that."

"Roger felt otherwise I guess."

"Oh God. He was mad about her. Tessa this, Tessa that, the darling Tessa Hardwick. She was trying to talk him into taking a year to travel with her. She had pots of money, no interest in finishing school. She wanted him. Only him."

"Why was that so terrible?"

"You wouldn't understand. You'd have to have known her. This little sweet snip of a thing. Roger thought he loved her."

Annie waited. She knew from Daphne's expression that it didn't end well.

"We had a terrible argument one night. We'd come back from a party. It was late. Roger and Tim had gone out to the barn. It was more than a barn really. Mummy had put a billiard table out there, and they wanted to play. We were all drinking a lot, and Tessa had planned to spend the night. I knew what that meant. Mummy did too, but she didn't care. Roger was twenty-one, not a boy. I told Tessa that she should go on this trip without Roger. That he wanted to go back to university and not waste his time traipsing after her. I told her that he had no intention of going with her. I'll spare you all the details. She got terribly upset and decided to go home. She only lived a few towns away. Ten, maybe fifteen miles at the most." Daphne had started to cry. Quiet tears streaked her cheeks.

"They found Tessa early the next morning. Her car had gone off the road into a tree. She died immediately."

"How terrible," Annie said.

"Yes. It was terrible." Daphne wiped her face with the back of her hands. "Roger said it was my fault. He said I shouldn't have let her drive, that I should have stopped her. He accused me of wanting to break them up. He said that I killed her." She looked imploringly at Annie. "I'd had a lot to drink too. I wasn't thinking clearly. Tessa was nearly twenty. She wouldn't have listened to me."

"You were only sixteen," Annie said softly.

"Yes. I was a girl. All the same, Roger hated me then. He went up to London. He refused to speak to me. I kind of went to pieces and refused to go back to school. Mummy took me to God House. So there it was. No father, then no brother, and Mummy got sick just a few years later. Not a happy time."

"I'm sorry," Annie said.

Daphne stood. "Well, now you know. You see, it's hard for me to be with Tim. It's hard for both of us."

"I understand."

After Daphne left, Annie went back to her chair in the corner of the living room and read the place de Furstenberg poem one last time. It was finished. She slipped it into an envelope and wrote "Paul" on the face. The color of the Waterman's South Sea Blue stood out vividly on the paper. It wasn't yet dark. She decided to walk to his office and slip it under the door.

EIGHTEEN

La Crise

"Annie, you need to come to New York," Wesley said.

"I'm coming next week—"

"It's Sophie," he interrupted. "An emergency. She's in the hospital."
He sounded terrible. "She may not make it. She—" His voice broke.
Annie had never heard him in such despair.

"Wesley, what's the matter?" Annie was flooded with alarm. It was
after five. She'd been about to call Mary to see if she was free for dinner when the telephone rang. Instead, Wesley's news shattered the
peaceful lull at the end of the afternoon. She felt like she had plunged
into a pool of deep, cold water, shocking her to attention. "Please,
please," she pleaded. "Tell me. Tell me what happened." Images of car
accidents, planes crashing, fire—all her worst fears grew vivid in her
mind.

"You've got to come." She could tell he was trying to regain control. He began to explain. At first his words were disjointed, his voice
raspy, broken, difficult to understand. "A rare disease. Sudden. Thank
God, this doctor recognized it. Fatal case in the Midwest last month."

Annie tried to wrap her mind around this news. It was too much to
take in. She imagined Sophie pale, deathly ill with some horrific illness she'd never heard of. She couldn't speak.

Wesley gradually grew calmer and hurried to explain. His words
came flying at her now, with such speed and intensity that she
couldn't absorb them. Meningococcal meningitis, bacterial, flulike
symptoms, rashes, loss of limbs, alive one day, dead the next.

Dead. The word pierced her consciousness like a bullet. Annie
couldn't believe what she was hearing. She brought her hand to her

throat. "Wesley, our baby. This can't be true." Now she was the one dissolving in despair. She felt like she couldn't breathe. She opened her mouth to cry out, to beg for . . . what? Mercy, courage, forgiveness. Save my daughter, she thought. My Sophie has to live. Oh, Lord, please don't let her die.

Wesley was talking, and Annie had to force herself to focus. Sophie's life depended on it. "Call Air France," he said. "See if you can get a seat tomorrow on the morning flight. You can pick up your ticket at the airport."

"Wesley, I . . ." Her ears pounded.

"Look, sweetie. I've got to hurry. I'm on my way to her now. We'll talk when you get to New York."

"But, where? And—"

"I'll send you an e-mail with a hotel and the name of the hospital." The phone went dead.

Sophie—her poor Sophie. She hadn't thought about her in days. She couldn't remember when they had last spoken. How could she have forgotten her own daughter? Annie got to her feet and went to the windows, amazed that she could gather the strength to walk. She stared numbly out onto the rue des Archives. It was twilight. *La crépuscule*. The sky, now a cold, smoky blue, edged into evening.

For a few moments she stood very still, unable to move, trying to take in everything Wesley had said. She felt gripped by a bleak emptiness, the kind of feeling that sometimes comes in the middle of the night, when you lie awake, powerless, haunted with regret, when the entire world seems hinged on doubt. She staggered over to her desk and turned on the light.

She picked up the photograph of her mother and dusted the glass with her forearm. She held the frame under the lamplight and studied the face of that young woman, closer to Sophie's age than to her own. She noticed again how her mother's smile tilted up to the right in the exact same way that Sophie's did. This time the sobs came from deep inside her. She felt the weight of her want, the hunger for her mother, blurring into the longing she felt for her own daughter.

As much as she wished to be comforted and loved, she wanted to take Sophie into her arms. She wanted to hold the pale blond sprite of a child, the ungainly, wobbly girl of twelve, and the lovely, mature young woman who was now leading a life of her own. Lowering herself into her chair, she let herself cry. She allowed her tears to pour out, moaning aloud and rocking from side to side. She drew her hands together, clasping them under her chin in a maternal unconscious prayer. Gradually, she felt her strength come back. It seemed that in some way her mother was with her, as if her mother's spirit had eased into her own. Annie wiped her face with the back of her hands, smearing the hot, wet tears. Enough. She needed to call for her ticket. It was time to pack.

Later that evening she called Hélène. She could no longer bear the weight of this worry by herself. "I wish I'd gone to see her sooner," Annie cried. "It's all my fault. Sophie shouldn't have to be in a hospital alone."

Hélène listened to every word. "But you will be with her," she said reassuringly, "and Wesley is with her by now."

"Hélène," Annie said, "I've done everything wrong. I should have paid more attention to her. She wanted me to move back."

"Nonsense. You must not think like that. When you arrive, it will make all the difference. Life is about going forward. It is not living to look back. Annie, ma chérie, what you do now, that is what is important."

"But—"

"Annie, you must pack. Tell Mary if she needs help at the office, I am happy to do what I can."

Annie thanked her, and though still sick with worry, she felt like she had more resolve and the strength to prepare to leave. Once she got started, it was amazingly uncomplicated to put her life in Paris on hold.

She telephoned Céleste, sparing her the true gravity of the situation, and explained her hasty departure to New York. Céleste immediately expressed her concern, and agreed to come and check on the apartment in Annie's absence. She would collect the mail and water the plants. She requested the name of the hospital, and Annie knew she would be sending flowers and a card.

"Stay as long as you need," Céleste said in a maternal voice. "Give Sophie a hug and take care of Wesley too." Céleste had never said anything more about Annie and Wesley's marriage troubles, but Annie knew she was relieved that Annie was finally going to be with her family. Although Céleste had never understood Annie's commitment to her writing, she remained a loyal friend. Her support was comforting.

Annie called Mary next, sharing only the minimum of details. She too was sympathetic and told her not to worry.

"Don't hurry back," Mary said. "Take time for what's important."

Annie hoped she wasn't too late. No, she thought. She would not allow those thoughts. She forced herself to be hopeful, requiring every ounce of energy to fight her fear. She flew around the apartment, gathering her things, packing, not wanting to pause for a minute to allow dread to creep in. Sophie will get well. She will live. She said it over and over, like a mantra, pushing all other possibilities aside.

Annie waited until just before going to bed to call Paul. She had to let him know she'd be away. They had spoken several times since their night together. He had had a publishers' conference in Berlin and had invited her to come with him. She had declined, saying there was too much going on at Liberal Arts Abroad.

"When will I see you?" he'd asked.

"I'm not sure," she'd answered. "Not just yet."

"Do you regret? Are you wishing it had not happened?"

He'd sounded kind. She knew her answer mattered to him. "I'm just not sure what I think," she'd told him. "Nothing like this has ever happened to me before." She wasn't ready to see him again. It would be all too easy to fall into the habit of meeting him and continuing their affair. She thought about him constantly—the shape of his hands, the way he looked at her as if a question were about to form on his lips, the slope of his shoulders before he stood to get out of bed. Would making love over and over change anything between them? Would it ever be more than that, an affair? How long would it be until his skin, his scent, his touch, felt familiar, no longer charged with the thrill of newness?

Tonight he picked up on the first ring. "Annie, I am so happy it is you. I can't stop thinking about us and—"

"Paul." She knew her voice would convey the seriousness of her message. "I'm flying to New York in the morning. Sophie is sick in the hospital." Annie felt tears coming and didn't try to hold them back.

"*Ma chérie,*" he began, "let me come to you. You must tell me everything."

She wanted to shut him out and put an end to everything between them, but she couldn't deny the wave of tenderness that crept in. "No, no, I need to go to sleep. I'm leaving early. I just wanted you to know that I was going away." A lump in her throat was making it hard to continue. "Sophie is seriously ill. I have no idea how long I'll be gone."

"Of course. But if I can help you, you must tell me."

"There's nothing. I'll let you know." Annie couldn't begin to explain her fear for her child, her feelings of helplessness, and what is was like to be a parent. He was incapable of understanding, despite his well-meaning attempt to help her. She promised she would call when she got back. "I will miss you," she said.

Would she miss him? She certainly wouldn't forget him. She couldn't change what had happened, and she wasn't sure, even now, filled with guilt, that she wished it had happened differently. Like Hélène had said, she must look forward.

Annie had a difficult time falling asleep. The city had quieted, but a heavy rain started to fall, and she listened as the cold drops plummeted down on the bathroom skylight. The sound of the rain reminded her of the line from Verlaine, "*Quelle est cette languéur qui pénètre mon coeur?*" He must have listened to a similar sound on another Parisian rooftop long ago. The sadness penetrating her own heart was almost too great to ponder. The words of his poem weighed on her as she lay in the dark, trying to shut out her worries and regrets.

Under different circumstances Annie might have enjoyed the taxi ride from Kennedy Airport into Manhattan and watching the magnificent skyline come into view. New York had its own pulse, so different from Paris, and even in her worried state she could feel the energy and excitement of the city. The taxi, the same kind of beat-up yellow car that

she remembered from previous trips, rumbled along through the traffic, avoiding potholes in the roadway left behind by the hard New
York winter. She was unable to relax against the slick black vinyl seat.
The taxi had an old-car smell despite the pine-tree-shaped deodorizer
that swung from the rearview mirror. She was tired, dehydrated
from the long flight, and had slept little on her final night in Paris.
Everything about her felt creased and stale. Fortunately the driver,
barricaded behind a cloudy plastic divider, made no conversation.

The traffic on the Triborough Bridge was heavy and slowed to
a crawl when three lanes merged into one. Annie could see no signs of
construction other than some stalled machinery and a series of orange
cones. She was desperate to reach the hospital. The taxi inched forward. It was like being caught in quicksand, and the driver was powerless to get them out. Annie held her clenched fists to her mouth.

Despite the gray day, she found herself squinting in the glare. She
still knew so little. Sophie had fallen ill at work, and her boss, Marla,
had insisted that she go immediately to her doctor. Because of a rash
and a high fever, she went directly to the emergency room instead.
Fortunately, a doctor had recognized this kind of bacterial meningitis.
The only treatment was massive amounts of antibiotics, and the key to
being cured was treating it in time. Had it been too late? There was the
chance of brain damage if the infection went unchecked, also the possible loss of limbs.

Now off the bridge, the taxi picked up speed. Annie clasped her
hands together in a kind of prayer, putting all her attention on willing
her daughter to get better. She tried to picture the drugs, some kind of
powerful liquid, traveling through her daughter's veins, fighting to
overcome the hated disease.

Her Protestant upbringing and a pervasive sense of maternal guilt
threatened to overtake her. "What goes around comes around," "Time
to pay the piper," and other tired maxims ran through her mind. What
if she hadn't given in, what if she hadn't had sex with Paul? Would Sophie have been so sick today? Annie was getting what she deserved.
This is nonsense, she thought. She must stop thinking like a child.

Annie cracked her window open, trying to cleanse herself of these
thoughts and ward off the nausea brought on by the cab ride. The

driver had the annoying habit of keeping one foot on the brake and one on the accelerator, lurching the car along Riverside Drive with the speed, but not the finesse, of a Parisian taxi driver. She felt sick to her stomach by the time he slammed on the brakes in front of Saint Vincent's Hospital.

When she stepped out of the taxi, the air was clear and cold and smelled entirely different from that of Paris; it was an edgy metallic smell, the scent of speed and progress. The buildings seemed sharply defined, huge geometric forms that loomed against the late-afternoon sky. A brisk wind whipped down the avenues, typical of New York in late April, when people were totally fed up with the cold and longing for warmer weather that was possibly weeks away. Annie paid the fare and walked shakily into the lobby.

She was greeted by a kind, smiling gray-haired volunteer with a matronly bosom sitting behind the information desk. The woman called her honey, showed her where to check her suitcase, and gave her directions to the Intensive Care Unit. Annie had forgotten the un-failing desire of most Americans to be helpful, and she was relieved to have her questions answered almost before she knew to ask them.

She made her way to the bank of elevators that would carry her to the fourth floor. Annie was unused to the brusque reality of modern American hospital life. She walked down a windowless corridor with highly polished vinyl floors that shone harshly in the overly bright fluorescent lights, the kind of place where there was little difference between night and day. Certainly, it couldn't help the healing process to be cut off from the rhythms of nature.

The hall, smelling of institutional food and the mild odor of anti-septic, made Annie feel uneasy, vulnerable. A heavyset nurse in white jogging shoes appeared at an intersecting hall pushing an empty gur-ney draped in cold white sheets. Annie stepped out of her way and tried to decide which way to turn. At that moment Wesley appeared a few yards ahead of her.

"Annie." He walked toward her, pulled her into his arms, and simply held her. At first he said nothing, just pressed her to him as if feeling her there was all that mattered. She rested her head against him, felt the soft wool of his sweater on her cheek, and breathed in the smell of the cotton shirt that he'd probably put on that morning crisp and fresh from its laundry wrapper. He felt warm and steady. Some of the worry and tension eased from her body. He felt familiar and comfortable, even in these strange surroundings.

"I'm so glad you're here," he said, releasing her. He looked in many ways the same—tall, even-featured, in control—the kind man who had pulled her into his arms countless times. She was struck by how fresh, how innocent, how all-American he looked to her. Even under the trying circumstances and with little sleep, he looked able to cope and deal wisely with any situation.

Annie was overcome with relief and hugged him again. "How is she?"

"The doctors think she'll pull through. There's no sign of brain damage. Thank God, she went straight to the emergency room. If she'd gone home, or even to the doctor's office, it would have been too late." He took her hands and led her to a bench outside the ICU door. "I need to tell you what to expect."

Annie sat like a child, obediently trying to comprehend everything he said. He explained how meningococcal meningitis is an extremely rare disease infecting mostly adolescents and people in their twenties. It's often mistaken for the flu. The bacteria that cause it are found in the nose and throat, and no one knows why they can suddenly invade the bloodstream or spinal fluid. This disease is far more serious than other forms of meningitis.

Sophie was still on life support. The doctors wanted to wait another day before letting her breathe on her own. She was being given huge doses of antibiotics intravenously. Her wrists and ankles were bandaged. The rash had produced terrible sores, like burns, the effect of poison in her blood. They would heal, he explained, and she would probably have some scarring. It could have been far worse.

"I know it's awful," he said. "You'll be shocked when you see her." He squeezed Annie's hand. "But we'll get through this."

Annie looked into kind eyes, ringed with fatigue. The word we sounded sweet in her ears.

She followed Wesley into the Intensive Care Unit. There on a long metal hospital bed lay Sophie, a slender form barely taking up any space.

Her pale, tender arm lay exposed on the sheet, accepting the steady drip from the IV hanging above. Wesley was right. It was a terrible shock to see the unearthly tubes running into her daughter, the machines, the wires, the harsh lights overhead. Annie was filled with renewed terror. Despite the dramatic surroundings, Sophie appeared to be sleeping peacefully. Wesley bent over his daughter, stroked her forehead, and gently picked up her limp hand. He seemed to be transmitting his strength and energy to her, the healing power of touch. Watching the two of them together, Annie felt a sense of hope come over her.

"Sophie," Wesley whispered as he bent in close to her ear. "Your mom is here." At the sound of his voice, she opened her eyes. He took Annie's hand and placed it where his had been.

"I love you, baby," Annie said softly. She felt the flutter of movement, her daughter's hand in hers. She leaned down and kissed Sophie's forehead.

Annie took a sip of coffee from the blue pottery mug. It was warm in her hands, and it felt good to sit on the terrace and watch the day come alive. They had taken Sophie to Madeleine's house in Connecticut to recuperate. And there, bit by bit, Annie imagined the threads of their family life knitting back together.

The lawn was greening up, and a stand of forsythia blazed yellow against the blue sky. A cluster of small brown birds chirped merrily and darted in and out of a feeder just beyond the fence. Aunt Kate had been a bird-watcher and had always kept her binoculars on a peg by the back door of their house in Vermont. As a little girl, Annie loved to watch for birds and always hoped to spot the first robin in the spring. In Paris, at least in the center of the city, there were only pigeons, unremarkable and gray like the streets where they waddled, too lazy for flight.

Sophie was still asleep. She slept hungrily, as if she couldn't get enough of the elixir, but it was a restorative sleep, and each day she stayed out of bed longer and her color improved. She was off the antibiotics, and the sores on her wrists and ankles were healing. The doctor said that rest would continue to cure her.

"I bet you're wishing you were in a sidewalk café in Paris right now." Wesley had emerged from the old stone house to join Annie on the terrace. "You're probably the only person in Connecticut having coffee outside at the end of April."

"I'm not wishing that." She shook her head and stared into the distance. "I do wish I'd see a robin." She smiled up at him. The sun glinted off his glasses, and he wore a green canvas jacket lined with plaid flannel. It was new to Annie, something he'd bought without her. He bent down and kissed her forehead. A sleek gray bird on the wall carried a piece of dried grass in its beak.

"You're not cold?" he said.

"No. The sun's warm. Have a seat." She pulled the chair next to her closer, and he sat down beside her, stretching his legs toward the wall. "I think he's building a nest." They watched the bird sail off toward a tall pine in the field below them. The sun warmed their backs.

"The air is so much cleaner here than in Paris," Annie said. She smiled, thinking of the French who would be outside on a day like today to savor a little sun and watch the world go by. Paris seemed very far away.

"Clean, yes, but a little dull. Not the lively scene you're used to."

"The peace and quiet of the countryside are exactly what we needed," Annie said. "Madeleine has been so dear to take us in." She looked back at the little stone cottage where Madeleine had lived for many years. While the house was small, the big white barn had been just the space she'd been looking for when she moved her business out of New York.

"This place is a little like God House," he said, "only a barn full of folk art instead of French antiques."

"It feels very different."

Wesley shrugged and looked out across the fields. A silence fell between them.

"We need to talk about Daphne," he said finally.

Annie set her mug on the wall. The coffee had cooled. "I haven't been back to God House. I'm sure you understand."

"Annie, I'll never forgive myself for letting it happen."

"You mustn't say that." Guilt swelled in her throat. She too had let things happen, had wanted things to happen. She too had done the unforgivable.

He turned to look at her. The gray bird was back on the wall, hopping intermittently and watching the garden bed at his feet. She could feel Wesley's eyes upon her, a cool, fresh blue like the April morning. She drew her arms across her chest and turned away.

"Please—I want to explain," he said. "This winter has been terrible."

She bent her head, ashamed and sad, knowing how she had betrayed him.

"After the firm closed I sort of fell apart. Everything changed for me. It was like we both became different people. My career was failing. I was failing. Meanwhile your creative life took off. When I got this chance to start over, I wanted it at all costs. I was angry with you when you didn't see it my way. I thought you'd be willing to drop everything and start over too."

Annie didn't dare look at him. She felt like the guilt was all across her face, her affair with Paul there for anyone to read. Telling him would only hurt him. The end of their marriage was her fault as well. She shook her head, wishing he would go back inside, wishing this conversation didn't have to take place. "Wesley, I've been wrong too. I've changed."

"No. Wait. What I'm trying to say is that I want you back. I want whoever you've become. I can see now that writing those poems for the book was the best thing for you."

"But Wesley—"

"Annie, listen. What I really came out here to say was that I want your forgiveness. I'm sorry about what happened at God House. But beyond that, I never should have shut you out. I hate myself for closing down like I did. I'm sorry."

He reached over and took her hand. He held it and covered it warmly with his. "I'm happy in Washington and the job is good, but it's all worth nothing if I can't have you. I don't want to erase all we've had together. I can't." He reached over and cupped her chin in one hand, drawing her face toward him. "Go back to Paris, Annie. I understand what it means to you and how your poetry is part of it. I'm coming back in June, and if you really want to stay, we'll stay. I'll find some way to make it work." He brushed the tears that streaked her cheek. He drew his hand through her hair, patting her gently.

"Wesley, I've changed. If you came back, it wouldn't be like it used to be."

"It doesn't have to be the way it used to be. I know that."

"I don't want you to have to give up your job in Washington." She felt the weight of his gaze. "It wouldn't be fair to ask that."

"But you're not asking. It's my idea. I only want to find a way for us to be together."

"That means a lot." She stood and moved behind his chair, placed her hands on his shoulders, and lowered her face next to his. "Of course, I forgive you, Wesley. You're right. We can't erase the past. I'm not sure about the future. You've given me a lot to think about."

"Annie, please."

She shivered. The sky darkened. Madeleine had told them rain was expected. There were still large patches of blue in the west, and the clouds cast broad shadows on the field beyond the wall. "We'd better go inside." Annie saw no more sign of the gray bird. She turned and Wesley followed her into the house.

NINETEEN

La Paix

Annie stood on the steps of God House and paused before ringing the bell. The sun was out, but small drops of rain lingered in the cupped leaves of the ivy, lush and green, that hugged the house. The budding new-ness of spring was everywhere: the first flush of leaves on the trees, the soft pink-and-white blooms of a mountain laurel, and the sweeps of lilies of the valley along the drive. She had wanted to see God House in spring. She was not disappointed.

Standing in the shadow of the house, she felt protected as well as apart from the rest of the world. This separate peace engaged all her senses. She breathed in the fresh air and listened to the breezes ruf-fling the treetops. The branches, weighted from the earlier rain, dripped onto the gravel drive in a delicate refrain. She thought about the elegant meals they had had at the long table in the dining room, the kitchen suppers, coffee in the glass room at the break of day, walks by the river, reading by the fire, writing hour after hour in the library or seated in her chaise in the pink bedroom. Memories of Wesley, memo-ries of Paul, memories of Daphne. God House held her story along with those of the previous inhabitants. She pictured the pages of the leather photograph albums in the library, replete with all those who had lived and loved there.

Annie felt a kind of solace, a nostalgic pleasure in her return, steeped in the poetry of the place. Now, months later, she'd been able to sift out some of the more painful memories and a curious sense of detachment had crept in as she looked at the pleasing gray house, the curved drive, and the coach house filled with antiques and Berthe's tiny apartment. The winter months in Paris by herself, her trip to the

States, her reunion with Wesley and Sophie, had removed her from this place and given her the requisite distance to see it with new eyes.

"Are you glad to be back?" Daphne stood before her in the open doorway. "I wondered if you ever planned to ring the bell."

Annie stepped into the hall. "I was trying to take it all in." She smiled. "You're right, it's pure heaven in the spring."

"When you see it in summer, the cycle will be complete." Daphne, the hint of a smile at the corners of her mouth, looked quizzically at Annie. She wore her hair shorter now, a tangled halo of curls that softened the wide planes of her face. "Let me take your coat."

Annie slipped out of her raincoat and noticed the bowl of lilacs—Daphne's signature scent—on the front hall table. Annie wondered briefly if she still wore the blue cape. It would be too heavy for spring.

Daphne lingered against the banister at the foot of the stairs. She wore beige trousers and a crisp white linen shirt, the cuffs rolled up at her wrists, revealing a large silver linked bracelet that Annie had never seen her wear before. "I'm glad you came back," she said.

"I said I would." Annie felt the silence of the old house fall around them.

"Sophie's doing well?"

"Better all the time. She's on a leave of absence from her job. Madeleine is letting her help a little with her business." Annie wondered how long they would keep standing in the hall. "She loves doing the accounts."

"I've sold everything that Madeleine shipped over." Daphne laughed abruptly. "Pretty soon everyone in Paris will have quilts draped about their *salons.*"

"So business is good for you right now?"

"Wildly busy. But I have someone to help. A new friend. I found her at Premier, a very posh print shop in the Sixth. She has a degree in European painting, but she's become more interested in furniture."

"She sounds perfect for the job."

"Indeed. I want you to meet her. Come, we've been waiting for you on the terrace. The light is wonderful this afternoon. Caroline brought some gorgeous pâté out from Paris. I planned on the champagne, something to fête your return."

Annie had thought they would be alone. She had envisioned a quiet lunch and time to talk over all that had happened. Daphne had said nothing to her on the phone about this new friend.

Nothing had changed: the row of boots lined up under the hall bench, the coats hanging on pegs under the staircase, the pale peach walls. Perhaps she would paint a room that color one day. Their footsteps tapped crisply on the black-and-white marble floor. They passed through the glass room filled with its old wicker chairs and stepped out onto the flagstone terrace.

The river shimmered in the distance, and the flower beds were patterned with the healthy green mounds of young plants. A perfect May day. A day that felt like freshness itself, sparkling and new.

A woman sat with her back to them, apparently absorbed in the landscape below. At the sound of their steps, she turned and rose from her chair. "You must be Daphne's famous author," she said, no hint of kindness in the crisp elegant vowels of an upper-class Englishwoman. She offered her hand. "I'm Caroline."

Annie laughed uneasily. "I'm hardly famous, and the book hasn't been published yet." She shook Caroline's hand.

"Next spring, isn't it?" Daphne said.

"Yes. It's amazing. You hurry to meet your deadlines and then it takes almost a year after that to have the book in hand." Annie felt herself being appraised by Caroline's intense dark eyes. She was petite, pretty, with small, neat features and the deep red of her lips punctuating her white skin. Her hair looked too black to be natural and was cut close to her head, like a cap. She was a curvy woman and she wore a V-neck black sweater that accentuated the whiteness of her throat. She looked younger than Daphne and had a kind of worldliness that bordered on louche.

"Well, my dears, now that you've met, let's open the bubbly, shall we?"

They followed Daphne to a black wrought-iron table. The champagne sat ready in a silver-bucket filled with ice. Daphne wrapped the bottle in a linen towel and carefully twisted out the cork. The silver bracelet slid down her wrist as she poured the sparkling wine into the flutes. Her hand shook very slightly. "Here's to good friends," she said.

"Here's to new friends," Caroline said, giving Daphne a wry look.

"Cheers," Annie said. She lifted her glass and sipped. "Lovely champagne. Thanks, Daphne."

Caroline passed the platter of pâté, which she had cut into thin slices and placed on diagonal pieces of baguette. Annie accepted one and sat stiffly in one of the iron garden chairs opposite Daphne and Caroline.

"Too bad you missed the daffodils," Caroline said. She waved one hand in the direction of the garden. "Daphne says they were most extraordinary this year. The extremely cold winter was good for them."

"You're interested in gardening, then?" Annie said, holding the cool glass in her hand.

"Oh my, yes. Sadly, my tiny flat in Paris has but two window ledges, both facing north." Caroline drew her lips into a pout.

"I've told you, Caro, you have carte blanche here at God House," Daphne said. "You know I think weeding is a bloody bore. It's neat and tidy now, but it will be a riotous mess in another month." Daphne pushed her hair back from her face, and Annie thought she looked wary, as if expecting something to go wrong.

"I've been enjoying gardens recently," Annie said. "While I was in Connecticut, Madeleine's azaleas were in bloom. She had a lovely scented variety. Pure white with a blush-pink center."

Gardens, like the weather, were always a safe topic of conversation. Eventually the conversation became easier. Daphne talked about the upcoming auctions and two new clients, some American men who had purchased a minor château in the Loire.

"Absolutely pots of money," she explained. "Thank God I have Caroline to help me comb the countryside. The place is empty and they want to fill every room."

"It's such a lark to shop for someone else." Caroline looked approvingly at Daphne. "They trust your eye completely."

"I don't know about that, but it is good fun. Much better than some clients." After a while Daphne swallowed the last of her champagne and stood. "Shall we go in for lunch?"

They rose to follow her. Annie looked back once more at the river and tried to imagine the summer here, when the flowers would be in full bloom. She turned and followed Caroline and Daphne into the house.

Berthe had made a rich creamy vegetable torte and Daphne tossed a salad of bright green frisee lettuce with bits of her favorite streaky bacon.

"Don't you think everything tastes better at God House?" Caroline said, after taking her first bite of the torte.

"Absolutely," Annie said. She looked at Daphne, who now appeared more relaxed, as if she were enjoying her role as hostess. "I love your bracelet, Daphne. Is it new?"

"Caroline brought it to me from London. Very smart, isn't it?"

She extended her arm and Caroline reached over and fingered the silver links. "A school chum has a shop. He's quite a talented designer." Her small hand lingered on Daphne's arm, and Annie thought she saw Daphne color just a bit.

Caroline kept the conversation going during lunch. She was solicitous of Daphne in subtle ways, and she took charge of pouring the wine.

"You don't think this is too dry?" she asked Daphne.

"Not at all, I've been wanting to try this one." Daphne turned to Annie. "Caroline brought me a case of wine from Paris. Unusual bottles the local man wouldn't stock. What do you think of it?" She took another sip.

"It's delicious," Annie said.

Caroline topped Daphne's glass once again. Annie felt herself observing the two women, and she thought of François. She found herself retreating, like he would have behind a camera, quietly bringing the world into focus with his lens. She listened while the two women talked about an upcoming sale in Barbizon and what they hoped to find, but she found it difficult to pay attention and participate in the conversation. She heard herself complimenting Daphne on the dessert, Antoinette's recipe for chocolate mousse, but her mind kept slipping away and carrying her down to the bank of the river.

She wished she were outside. She imagined holding a camera and trying to capture the light on the water. She pictured her very first walk by the river when she and Wesley had come to God House on the last day of the year. She could see the three of them walking back toward the house, the light closing in. Her imaginary camera focused in on the moment Daphne had stepped between them, putting one arm in each of theirs, on that long-ago winter afternoon, perhaps even then tipping the balance of their lives.

Now, sitting at lunch, many afternoons since her first visit to God House, she heard Daphne suggest moving into the drawing room for coffee. Annie waited patiently for the appropriate moment when she could leave.

"I don't know what I want more," Caroline said, "a big walk or a nap." She looked at Daphne as if to gauge her response.

Annie didn't wait for Daphne's answer. "I really must be going," she said, putting her empty cup on the tray.

Neither woman voiced any objection. All afternoon, they had asked nothing about her life or her plans now that the book was finished. She was strangely relieved. She knew she didn't belong at God House any longer. She was relinquishing her place to another, like a French courtesan, giving up her position beside the king. She suppressed a smile.

"May I give you a lift to the train?" Daphne asked.

"No, thanks," Annie said. "I'm looking forward to the walk." She said good-bye to Caroline, who was headed to the kitchen with the tray of coffee cups. Daphne walked Annie out to the top of the drive.

"I'll send you a copy of the book when it comes out."

"Signed, I hope?" Daphne laughed.

"Oh, I almost forgot." Annie reached into her handbag. "I brought you some poems. Only three. New work I did in Connecticut."

Daphne took the folded sheets of paper. "Annie, dear. You really are sweet."

"You know how grateful I am for all you've done," Annie started to explain, "your encouragement, introducing me to Paul—"

"Nonsense. Let's not get caught up in the past again. Let's just say *Pax*, shall we? *Pax* and *au revoir*. *Good-bye* has such finality." Daphne reached out to Annie and kissed her on both cheeks, then held her briefly in a hug. Annie sensed she was impatient to get back into the house.

"I'll never forget this place," Annie said.

"I know you won't." Daphne tilted her head and surveyed Annie one last time, then thrust her hands into her pockets and turned back to the house. She offered a quick wave and closed the door behind her.

Annie proceeded down the drive and looked once more at God House. It was odd, but she felt the same sense of satisfaction now at the end of this spring afternoon that she felt when she finished a poem. There was a definite moment of completion, when she knew that the words were in place, when she realized she should let it rest and do no more.

"I have missed you," Paul said. "You have been gone a very long time." His face was tanned, as if he had spent quite a few sun-filled afternoons outdoors at a café. It suited him. He looked stronger, healthier, than when she first knew him.

"I was gone a long time," she said. They sat at Café des Editeurs just off the boulevard Saint-Germain, not far from his office. She wanted to meet him in a public place, not quite trusting her resolve in the privacy of his office. She hadn't called him immediately on her return to Paris. She had let a few days go by, a few more, then a few weeks. She had been thinking mostly about Wesley, what he had offered, what he had said. She knew he meant it when he told her he would move back to Paris if she wanted it.

She had also thought about Paul. She couldn't deny the allure of resuming a relationship with him and seeing what would happen. It would be, in some ways, so easy to start over, to build something new.

Now, side by side, with a small round table wedged between them, they faced the street and its constant stream of motorbikes, small cars, and pedestrians. Annie reflected on how much of Parisian life took place on the street, on the sidewalks, and in the cafés that filled with people drinking, eating, talking, relieved to be out of their cramped apartments and crowded offices.

"Your daughter is well now?" Behind his solicitude Annie could tell that Paul didn't understand what had kept her away from him for so long.

"She's doing much better. She's staying with her aunt in Connecticut for the summer. She hopes to return to work in the fall. It's a great relief." It was difficult to look at him. Still so handsome, with that touch of neediness. She longed to reach out and smooth his brow or straighten his collar.

The waiter appeared and set down their drinks, a small espresso for Paul, a sparkling water with a lemon wedge for her. He tucked the bill, a small white square of paper, underneath the ashtray and left them to idle away the afternoon.

Paul reached for her hand and drew it to his lips. Annie closed her eyes and for an instant imagined letting it all begin again. He lowered her hand but did not let go. The current was still there; it was unmistakable. Annie gently withdrew her hand and picked up her spoon to press the juice of the lemon into her water. The spoon tinkled against the glass.

"How is François?" François was recovering from a bout of pneumonia. He had been in the hospital while Annie was away.

"Still weak. He's gone to La Motte. He hopes the good air of the south will make him strong."

"He's such a dear man." Annie took a sip of water. She had walked all the way from her apartment, and the afternoon was warm. "Has he seen the proofs?" She loosened the silk scarf around her neck and unbuttoned her raincoat. She leaned forward to take it off, and he helped her pull it up and around her shoulders. He left his arm around her. She didn't move. The weight of his arm on her shoulders was making her uncertain.

"He is very happy. He thinks it is the best of his work, and your poems complemented the pictures exactly as he wished."

"I'm glad to hear that." Annie looked out toward the street. She felt his fingers softly stroking the back of her neck. She fought the temptation to relax to his touch.

"I think it was right," Paul said. His fingers became still. "Our being together was the right thing. Perhaps now it is too late for you?" She felt his eyes on her.

She turned to face him. His brows had furrowed and there was a petulant curl to the corner of his lip. She saw flecks of brown in his blue eyes. He removed his arm from her and touched her cheek, tracing the line of her jaw. She remembered that same gesture, months ago, when he had put her in a taxi.

"You have been with your husband again?"

"Not in the way you mean," she said. The noise of two bikers starting their engines made it difficult to talk. "We spent a lot of time with our daughter, watching over her, and waiting until she began to get better." How could she explain to him that kind of bond, how having a child with a man you had loved was something you would always share? A marriage by itself could end, but never the combined love of parents for a child. The love they gave to Sophie had been woven together, thread by thread, year by year, growing stronger, powerful, and intractable. To think that they had almost lost her, that the sudden terrible illness had nearly taken their daughter away.

Annie blinked back tears. "We stayed with Sophie at Wesley's sister's house, a lovely place in the country. It was nice to be a family again. It's quiet there, and I had time to write." Annie smiled at him. "Surprisingly it came easily. I started several new poems."

"What are they about?"

"Not Paris. I seem to be going off in a new direction. It feels good, but the work is still very new." She shrugged. "I thought I needed Paris. I know it seems silly."

"Annie, I know you have more to say than Paris. Your poems for François's photos are about much more than the place." He shook his head and studied her face again, as if hoping to see some kind of change. "The final poem, 'Place de Furstenberg,' it is about us, isn't it?"

"Yes." She watched his hands, his fingers circling the rim of his coffee cup. "Yes, it is," she said softly.

"You were telling me there is no future for us?" He sipped his coffee. "The poem is ambiguous. *Non?*"

Annie looked into his eyes and saw a flicker of hope. "You have been wonderful to me," she began. "Having the chance to work from the photographs, the opportunity to do the book, it's really changed my life. But——"

"I know. I know what you will say."

"I'm glad you know, because I don't really know. A part of me wants to be with you. Truly, I will never forget you."

"My dear Annie. Please, say no more." He put his arm back across her shoulders. "This is sad for me but no surprise. *Quoi alors, c'est le destin.*"

Fate. She had thought a lot about fate recently. What if she'd never met Daphne? What if Daphne hadn't introduced her to Paul? Would he have found another English poet to do the poems for the book? If that other writer was a woman, would there have been the same kind of attraction? "I'm sorry it has to be this way?"

"That is life. Yes?" He sighed and shook his head in a wordless acceptance. "And what is ahead for you? Do you know?"

"Yes. I think I do."

"I see." They sat for a while longer, both looking out at the parade of Parisians hurrying home at the end of the afternoon. A few minutes later he reached into his pocket and placed the money on the table for the waiter.

"I must go," he said. "But stay a while. I want to look back and see you sitting here in this place. Then, whenever I pass by it, I will think of you."

"I'll stay a little longer then," she said.

He bent down and handed her a package that had been tucked beside his chair.

"What is this?"

"Open it later," he said.

"Paul, how very dear. I—"

He reached across, placed his fingers on her lips, and then kissed her. "*Au revoir, ma chère.*"

He stood and she watched him join the crowd on the sidewalk. He looked back once, and she smiled. He disappeared from view. She wrapped her fingers around the slim package. The motorbikes continued to roar by, men and women hurried to shops and appointments, students shoved and joked as they passed. She wondered how long she would keep this memory of him. After all, she hadn't known him long. What would fade away first? The shock of dark hair, the angles of his face, the full softness of his lips? He was a good man, she thought, a kind man, but a man she didn't love.

Annie leaned back in her chair and felt the last rays of sun on her face. She closed her eyes and let her mind wander back to Connecticut as she had done so often since her return to Paris. She had begun to sort the memories. The color coming slowly back to Sophie's face, Madeleine in the kitchen stirring oatmeal-cookie dough in an old-fashioned earthenware bowl, Wesley seated with them at the kitchen table, making lists, teasing his sister, kissing the top of Sophie's head. Wesley had figured out the complicated logistics of Sophie's absence from New York. He'd arranged for her to have time off from work, figured out her health insurance, and had gone into the city to get what she needed from her apartment. But it wasn't only the practical things. He was able to convince Sophie that she would eventually feel like her old self again. He had her laughing and took her on her first walks out in the garden. Annie loved watching them together.

One evening, shortly before her departure for Paris, Annie discovered them seated in the two wing chairs on either side of the fire. She could see the scene as clearly as when she'd discovered them there. She'd finished helping Madeleine with the dinner dishes and had gone to see if either of them wanted an herbal tea before bed.

"Moms, do you remember the time in Brittany when Dad found a rock in his plate of *moules*?" Sophie giggled. "God, that was the worst restaurant."

"I do remember." Annie had smiled and gone to sit on the arm of Wesley's chair. He had his long legs extended and the firelight flickered across his face.

"If I'm stronger by the end of the summer, Dad said it might be fun to go back to Brittany. Maybe rent a house." Sophie smiled at her father. "I'm not ready yet for a transatlantic flight, but in a few months—"

"Well, if that doesn't work, maybe just a long weekend," Wesley said. "We could try Cape Cod. My parents took us there a few times when I was a boy." Wesley looked up at Annie, his eyes hopeful. "We'll wait and see how everyone is feeling later this summer."

At that moment everything had felt right to Annie. She picked up Wesley's hand. His fingers wrapped around hers, firm and comfortable.

Now, sitting in the café, Annie contemplated the differences in those clasped hands: Paul's hand in hers, her hand in Wesley's. Each a different imprint, each a separate story.

TWENTY

Le Commencement

Annie pulled her robe more securely around her and opened the front door onto Cambridge Place. The old brass handle was cool in her hand, and the door gave way grudgingly, with a few squeaks. The house, a nineteenth-century brick, exhibited its aches and pains in small ways, but for the world outside, it stood straight in the bank of elegant town houses. The bayed fronts made Annie think of tightly corseted bosoms drawn up and in, ready to face the world with propriety. She knew there were stories behind each well-maintained façade, but like proper Victorians, they kept these stories cosseted within, hidden behind the heavy oak doors and lush curtained windows that muffled the outside noise.

Annie bent down to pick up the paper. Her own body spoke to her briefly, a cracking in one knee, a slight ache in her shoulder, probably the one she'd slept on. She slept deeply in this tall, narrow house. These minor early-morning twinges would not speak to her in any significant way for at least a decade, perhaps longer, with luck on her side.

She didn't glance at the newspaper headlines. She preferred to distance herself from the world until later in the day; the newspaper would wait until her cup of tea at the end of the afternoon. Bringing in the paper was part of her morning ritual. She found it necessary to start each day with a breath of fresh air, a glimpse of the outside world. She spent her mornings and often the early afternoons in her study with the door closed. Her work was inside work, inside the house, inside the small room at the back of the house, inside her mind. She didn't allow the newspaper headlines or the mellow-voiced public-radio announcer to muddy the stillness that her work required.

She enjoyed taking a moment to witness the day, not from the window but full on, outside on the top of the steps facing the tree-lined street. The weather served as a touchstone, a launching point for her day. This morning the winter sky hung low, a cloud cover softening the sounds of the morning traffic a few blocks away. The dampness chilled her body, still warm from her bed. She breathed in the air, diesel-drenched, and was carried back to Paris. Yes, Paris on a winter day like this one, tight with wet cold, sad and yet beautiful, the light gentle and shadowless. Annie allowed herself another breath and noticed how the trees were completely bare, sharply outlined against the pearl-gray sky. She stepped back inside and pushed the heavy door closed, turning her back on the cold December morning.

Annie glanced into the living room where the pale peach walls defied the gloomy day, making it look like the sun shone as usual through the front bay windows. Annie was pleased with the effect of the peach paint, and she'd had the two armchairs recovered in a French Provincial print of the same shade. The country pine furniture, shipped over from the apartment on rue des Archives, looked surprisingly at home in this proper Victorian house.

She passed through the dining room and silently admired the huge basket of dried lavender she'd arranged in the fireplace opening. She'd been amazed to find five fireplaces in a six-room house, a small six-room house at that. The lavender reminded her of warm months to come and the garden that Madeleine was helping her plan.

"I can't believe you have so much land in the city and such wonderful old walls," she'd exclaimed on her visit that fall. "People in Connecticut would die for old brick walls like these." Madeleine had given Annie a book on garden design, and the catalogs she'd suggested were already arriving with the afternoon mail.

The scent of coffee led her to the kitchen at the back of the house. Wesley remained bent over the shiny black espresso machine that sputtered on the counter. She crept up behind him and drew her arms around his waist.

"It's cold out," she said. "And it smells like Paris."

"It smells like Washington," he said.

Annie hugged him tighter and burrowed her nose in his collar.

"I hope this time it's strong enough." He reached up and took two mugs down from the shelf. He had been trying to duplicate the perfect cup of French coffee ever since they moved into their house in Georgetown.

"It's not the machine, it's the water," she said. "Anyway, it smells delicious." She kissed the back of his neck. "All I need is you anyway."

He turned and kissed the top of her head. "I'm glad to have a glimpse of you before you vanish into your study." He drew his hands through her hair. It was longer now, and most of the layers had grown out. "I think you work far harder here than you ever did in Paris."

"I break loose from time to time. You're just not here to see me."

Wesley was working hard too, and she'd never seen him happier.

"Sophie called yesterday," she said. "I forgot to tell you. She said she was bringing Daniel when she comes next weekend."

"Umm. This sounds serious." He kissed her on the lips this time and turned back to the machine, purring quietly on the counter. "What time will you be home tonight?" He poured Annie a mug of coffee.

"I just have the seminar this afternoon. No evening classes this week." Annie added milk to her coffee and stirred. She taught poetry at the Writers' Studio, a community-based organization for writers. She loved teaching, and for the first time in her life she had writer friends. "Will you be home in time for dinner?"

They made their plans and Wesley left for the office. Annie carried her coffee up to her study, the tiny third bedroom at the back of the house. She sat in the window seat and looked out at the landscape, silent and still in the pearl-gray light. A pair of doves, the same color as the mottled bark of the crepe myrtle tree on which they sat, reminded her of a poem she'd started last week. She'd begun a series of narrative poems on gardens in different seasons and the creatures who inhabited them. She watched the two birds for a moment and reflected on how they blended in with the colorless winter world, their feathers serving as camouflage.

When they began to sing, early in March, at the first signs of spring, she would plant the new garden. She could picture flowering shrubs and pansies with their velvety smiling faces. No winter solstice party this year. Instead she would celebrate the summer solstice with a party in the garden. She would have roses in bloom by then, New Dawn, Aunt Kate's favorite. Yes, she would have climbing pale pink roses interspersed with Japanese iris and a border of candytuft at their feet. Wesley had promised to build her a trellis.

She wanted her garden to be the perfect combination of symmetrical forms balanced with poetic freedom, neat geometric beds filled with the gentle old-fashioned flowers she remembered from childhood. She thought of the garden at God House and what it looked like on a winter morning such as this: the loosely planted hillside, beautiful and wild, glorious in neglect. She thought often of Daphne and the early days of their friendship. Now and then, she allowed herself to think of Paul. She still felt the burden of guilt, but she was becoming more and more adept at pushing it away. Like Hélène had said, it did no good to look back. She had given up Paris, but she had come to love Wesley in a whole new way.

Annie went to her desk and removed the cover of her fountain pen. The pen, a brilliant peacock blue that matched her favorite South Sea Blue ink, had been a housewarming present from Wesley. He'd found it in a local antiques shop. Annie loved the flat nib and the way the ink flowed lushly across the page. She knew that words came from somewhere beyond a pen, but she liked to think that writing with it made a difference.

To the right of the desk, where she could see it from her chair, she'd hung the photograph of the lovers in place de Furstenberg, Paul's parting gift, a perfect souvenir. Their book was on the bookshelf below. She didn't bother to leaf through it much anymore. Her writing was changing. She could feel a different voice coming in, a voice with new things to say. Now, with her back to the windows, she opened her notebook, lowered her head, and began to write.

1. Why is Annie more inspired now by her work as a poet, and what factors might be contributing to her success at mid-life? Is she selfish to want to put her artistic life first?

2. Throughout the long, dreary Paris winter, what does Annie fear most? What does she want most?

3. Hélène and Céleste, Annie's friends, offer her advice when she is confronted with the apparent failure of her marriage. How does that advice influence Annie's ultimate decision to start a new life in the United States?

4. Is Daphne merely sexually manipulative, selfishly wanting to break up the Reed's marriage? How might her past experiences have contributed to her behavior? Does Daphne bring anything positive to Annie and Wesley's lives?

5. Paul Valmont recognizes Annie's artistic potential and offers her a wonderful opportunity. Would Annie have succumbed to an affair with him if Wesley had remained faithful to her? What keeps her from continuing their affair? Why aren't Valmont and the intoxicating city of Paris enough to keep her in Europe?

6. What makes Annie want to rebuild her marriage? Will her family and career suffer or prosper from her decision?

7. Annie returns to God House at the end of the book. Why is it important for Annie to see Daphne again?

8. François Naudin captures Paris in photographs and Annie captures the city in her poems. In giving up her life in Paris, what has Annie lost? What has she gained? Ultimately, did she compromise too much?

St. Martin's
Griffin